THE
AMBUSH
ARTIST

THE AMBUSH ARTIST
HIS VENGEANCE KNOWS NO LIMITS

A NOVEL
BY
BART AMBROSE

Reach For The Top Publishing, LLC
reachforthetoppublishing@gmail.com

Publisher's Catalog-in-Publication Data
Names: Ambrose, Bart, 1946-
Title: The Ambush Artist / by Bart Ambrose
Description: Reach For The Top Publishing, LLC, 2024 | Summary: A deputy sheriff in Arizona pursues a desert hunter wanted for theft of bearer bonds from a Las Vegas casino and multiple murders in 1945. The hunter is pursued by mob interests trying to recover the bonds. He uses a variety of ambushes to lure and eliminate his pursuers. The deputy's efforts to arrest the murderer lead to a deadly showdown on a remote wilderness hillside between the deputy and the Ambush Artist.
Identifiers:
Library of Congress Control Number 2024904073
ISBN 979-8-9883107-9-2
Subjects: Historic Fiction | Money Laundering – Fiction | Action-Adventure- Fiction | Crime/Murder-Fiction |Arizona- Fiction |
First Printing: February 2024

CHAPTER 1

"Are you ready?" Cutter asked.

"Got a full tank of fuel. Load your stuff, and we'll fire it up," Billy replied.

Cutter looked the aircraft over, rubbing his chin. "You sure you can get us there in this thing?"

"Sure! They don't call it the Stinson Reliant for nothin'!"

Cutter had never flown in an aircraft of any kind. The whole idea made him a little nauseous. He looked the blunt-nosed Stinson over and wondered how it could get off the ground with all the weight of its big rotary engine on the front end. Its broad, straight wings didn't look to him like they could support the aircraft's bulk. The body and wings were painted bright white, with a distinctive lightning bolt emblazoned on its side. Billy had told him it could handle the pilot and two or three passengers with gear.

The Lucky Joker Casino in Las Vegas owned the plane and kept it in a hangar at Alamo Field south of the town. It was mainly used to ferry VIP gamblers from Los Angeles and Phoenix to Las Vegas. The casino owners had managed to keep the plane out of military service and employed a full-time pilot who was on call seven days a week.

Billy took lessons from the casino's pilot and had just completed his first solo flight. His instructor told him he had done well, and Billy puffed up, bragging to all his friends about being a pilot. He was confident he could handle the Stinson to carry out the plan he had made with Cutter a few months earlier.

Cutter said, "Let's load up and get the hell out of here. The bosses are gonna discover I didn't show up with their bonds any minute, and they'll come looking for me. We need all the head start we can get!"

Cutter was a big man with curly brown hair, a craggy face, and a long scar down one side. He looked tough and had proven himself with a gun and his fists, earning the casino owners' respect, starting as a bodyguard and moving up the organization's ranks. One of his current jobs with the casino was serving as a courier when needed. He had, on occasion, moved bearer bonds from a Nevada mining company's office to the casino. The bonds were an easy way for his bosses to launder cash from the casino and conceal the casino profits. Cutter had carried out this duty several times and earned the bosses' trust. His job earlier that morning had been to pick up and deliver one million dollars in bearer bonds from the mine. Another trusted henchman was sent with him for insurance against a hold-up.

He had feigned engine trouble and pulled off to the side of the road before they got into town. Quickly pulling his S&W Police Special.38 from its shoulder holster, he shot his ride-along partner in the head. Blood and brains blew out the open passenger door window and dribbled over the side of the door. He got out and walked around the side of the car, opened the passenger's door, and unceremoniously dumped the inert body out onto the dirt beside the road. Then he headed for the airport.

Cutter and Billy had cooked up a scheme to steal the bonds and fly to southern Arizona in the company's plane, then meet up with one of Cutter's long-time associates with a car. They'd abandon the aircraft at a remote dirt airstrip close to the border and high-tail it into Mexico. The plan was to split the haul three ways and disappear into Mexico or other countries. Cutter doubted the bosses would get wind of where they went before they were long gone.

Billowing thunderheads were forming over the Spring Mountains north of Las Vegas as Billy taxied out to the runway. He had checked the weather forecast for Arizona that morning; scattered thunderstorms were predicted, especially in the southern part of the state. He was unconcerned, confident he could dodge any weather on their route. He had carefully planned the route to avoid the population centers and avoid being spotted. They would follow the Colorado River south after leaving Alamo Field, then turn east into Arizona, skirting the mountains south of Kingman. The plan was to head generally south on a course toward the town of Buckeye. They would stay west of the town, follow the Gila River toward Gila Bend, and land on an isolated dirt airstrip. Cutter's associate would meet them there; it was an easy drive to the border from there through the town of Ajo.

It was late July, and the southwestern monsoon was in full swing. It produced numerous thunderstorms, particularly late in the afternoon. Billy figured they could reach their destination by early afternoon and miss the most active weather. Besides, he was sure of his ability to handle the Stinson despite his limited experience. Bypassing the weather would be a piece of cake.

A tropical disturbance off the Baja coast of northern Mexico was funneling high amounts of moisture into southwestern Arizona. Additional moisture feeding into the state from the Gulf of Mexico collided with the tropical system, creating extremely volatile storm conditions. Great, bruised-bottomed thunderheads were forming, some towering to forty thousand feet or more, and beginning to march across the state. Unknown to Billy, the center of much of the disturbance was directly in their path—the aircraft had no radar to scan ahead for warning of hazardous weather.

Billy could see a line of storms building before them as they traveled south toward the Gila River. The first pangs of unease began to gnaw at the back of his mind. But he lined up on the river, sure he could avoid the storms. At least, that's what he kept telling himself.

The air grew rougher as they passed to the west of the town of Buckeye. Billy briefly considered landing there to wait out the weather, but Cutter was not willing to risk exposure— Billy was afraid to argue with the man. The dry Gila River's course was directly ahead, a simple path for Billy to follow. They were only a few minutes from their destination. The Gila Bend mountains lay between them and their objective, and Billy made sure he had plenty of altitude to cross over them.

They passed between two thunderstorm cells, and the air became rougher. Billy was visibly nervous. Before he could make a case for turning back, the two cells merged into one behind them. They were trapped; the only option was to continue and hope they could pass through the imposing weather. That option was evaporating by the second as the weather rapidly closed in around them. Visibility dropped to zero and Billy was flying blind, relying on his compass. The aircraft began bucking violently as they entered the updrafts of the storms. Cutter became sick and vomited all over his shoes, then grasped his seat and a handle on the side of the cabin, hanging on for dear life. The plane was being violently tossed around in the winds. Billy fought the controls but couldn't maintain his compass heading; he was completely disoriented in the swirling cloud. The altimeter was jumping up and down as the plane was tossed around like a toy. Blinding lightning flashed around them; both men feared the plane would be struck at any moment.

Rain and hail hammered the cockpit as they hit a powerful, violent downdraft. The Stinson felt like it was in freefall, and the altimeter was spinning downward at an alarming rate. Billy struggled vainly for control, but the plane was completely unresponsive. He could do little but try to recover when they were out of the downdraft. Their rapid descent slowed, and Billy fought to get the plane flying level, relying solely on the plane's instruments. He could see nothing through the rain on the windshield.

They passed through a brief break in the cloud, the windshield partially cleared, and Billy saw what first looked like a black cloud face directly ahead of them. He instinctively tried to change course to avoid it but realized it was too late. In an instant, he saw that it was not a cloud at all but a looming mountain face covered in black rock. He jerked back on the yoke and twisted to the left just before the Stinson slammed into the

4

face of Woolsey Peak at one hundred fifty miles per hour. The plane hit at an oblique angle, causing the wing to dig in on the left side and flip the plane onto its back. It skidded across the slope until the front end slammed into a rugged rock outcrop. The cockpit door blew off, and the fuselage crumpled like paper and slid slightly downhill. It finally came to rest against a large black boulder. Both men had been killed instantly. There was no sound except the rain pounding on the aircraft's skin and the almost constant roar of thunder.

CHAPTER 2

Harley Henderson was parked a little west of the crash site on the dirt road north of the mountain. It was little more than a primitive track made by tire tracks of infrequent visitors to the remote area. The track was an offshoot of another road that eventually led to the little development known as Agua Caliente, some miles to the west. It frequently became impassable during the monsoon, crossing numerous washes that could run deep in heavy rains. That didn't worry Harley. He had "the Beast"— a modified 1942 Ford pickup truck with four-wheel drive he had built with his brother. He could always go back to what he called Site One if the weather got too wild. Growing paranoia about the government and a possible apocalypse motivated him to become a survivalist. His father had ranted about the country being destroyed during the Great Depression. He considered it a ploy by evil forces to take over the government and told his sons they needed to be prepared to stop it. A Mormon family lived next door to the Hendersons. Harley had been impressed by the religion's teaching that members should maintain a year's food supply and essentials to prepare for coming catastrophes. The family took the directive to heart and built up a huge supply of home-canned fruits, vegetables, and meats. They even stockpiled large amounts of wheat and rice in water-proof containers. Harley wasn't interested in the religion, but he admired his neighbor's efforts to prepare for whatever might come. He spent years building two bunkers in the mountains and stocking them with supplies similar to what his Mormon neighbors were doing. He could hole up indefinitely in either bunker. He called them Site One and Site Two. The only people who knew about them were his brother and long-time girlfriend, Ruby Reynolds. Each time he made a trip into the desert by himself, he would add to his stash of survival goods in the bunkers along with various weapons and ammunition. He could supplement his food stores with fresh game and live in either of them for months, even years, if he had to.

Harley and his twin brother Harry owned a machine shop in Buckeye called Henderson Machine Works. Their father had started the business before the Depression. He had contracted tuberculosis and died, leaving the business to his sons. Harry did most of the work and took care of the business; Harley helped out on big jobs when he was around. A congenital heart defect had limited Harry's physical abilities. He saved the heavy work for his brother.

The Beast had been modified with a differential acquired from an early Dodge truck to give the rig four-wheel drive capability. A suspension lift raised the body an additional nine inches, allowing the truck to be fitted with oversized tires. Its body was painted gunmetal grey to blend in with the desert landscape. It had running boards on the side, and Harley had built a wooden shell to enclose the bed. They welded brackets on both sides of the bed to carry extra water and gasoline for extended stays on hunting trips. The flathead V-8 engine had plenty of power to cover almost any kind of terrain, and the rig sat high off the ground, giving it the clearance to cross most desert washes, slog through mud, and climb steep grades. It looked like nothing else in the county.

The truck was perfect for Harley's hunting guide business. He was reputed to know the desert and its mountains better than any other man and had a reputation as an expert hunter. His father had taught him to shoot at an early age, and he had become an expert marksman. His father also taught him to hunt before his illness prevented their frequent hunting forays into the desert. The twins' mother died, and their father went off the deep end, leaving them to fend for themselves. Harley became a game poacher after his father's death and developed a reputation for guiding big game hunters for a chance to take an illegal trophy

Arizona bighorn sheep. The game wardens had never been able to catch him in the act. The Arizona territorial legislature had protected the sheep from hunting since 1893, making the rams' heads extremely valuable to trophy collectors all over the world. Those hunters ignored the legality of taking the animals and would pay hefty fees for Harley to guide them to a trophy ram.

He had another money-making deal with a taxidermist. Collectors around the world paid large amounts for mounted Bighorn ram heads. Harley knew where to find the animals and took several of the best trophies from different desert mountain ranges each year. The taxidermist mounted the heads for sale to collectors through extensive contacts, making it a lucrative business with some buyers paying as much as a thousand dollars for a trophy head to mount on the wall in their home or office. The two men split the proceeds. Harley also cleaned and cured the sheep's hides and sold them himself.

He took an occasional job to guide a hunter for a trophy Arizona mule deer when the season was open. It gave him some credibility as a legal guide, even though it was a small part of his activities. He thought it also helped to keep the game wardens off his back.

Harley had been headed for the taxidermist's shop when the storm hit. A prize ram lay in the back of the Beast, but that would have to wait— he knew the washes would run big with the heavy rain. He stopped north of Woolsey Peak and settled in to wait out the storm. Hail pounded the rig, and lightning snapped and crackled around him as strong wind gusts rocked the Beast. He felt safe in the truck and curled up on the seat to nap while the storm raged around him.

Late afternoon sunshine woke him from a fitful sleep. He had been dreaming about his father and how he had become a violent drunk after their mother died, beating him and his brother when they were kids. The boys stayed out of his sight as best they could, but their peace never lasted long. Between beatings, he berated them and told them they were worthless and would never amount to anything. When tuberculosis took him, he suffered for a year and died a painful death. The constant abuse made Harry a timid and docile adult. It had the opposite effect on Harley. He had a violent temper, prone to fly off into a rage with very little provocation. He was six feet three inches tall, heavily muscled, and weighed upwards of two hundred and forty pounds. He and his brother both had baby faces when they were young; it had been a constant source of teasing and embarrassment to him growing up. They outgrew them, but Harley had remained self-conscious about it and grew a thick black beard. It made him look mean and tough, and people instinctively gave him a wide berth. A poorly stitched knife wound on his cheek gave him an even more menacing appearance.

The storm had moved on to the east, and the bright afternoon sunlight woke him. He shook off the dream, poured a little water from his canteen into his hands, and splashed it onto his face. He got out and stretched his stiff muscles, walked around the Beast inspecting for damage and prepared to head out. He started to climb back into the truck's cab when something caught his eye, shining in the bright sunlight high up on the side of the mountain. "What's this?" he asked himself out loud. "Ain't nothin' but black rock on that mountain!" He got his binoculars from the cab for a closer look. He nearly dropped them when he saw it—a wrecked airplane! It looked like it had flown directly into the face of the mountain. "Damn fool musta been flyin' in that storm and couldn't see the mountain in front of him!" he said.

Woolsey Peak was a hulking volcanic summit a little over three thousand feet high, surrounded by Sonoran desert vegetation with mixed varieties of cactuses, mesquite, and palo verde trees. It was steep and rugged, covered with black basalt boulders and outcroppings of jagged black rock, making it a challenging climb. Harley had climbed it several times, usually from the more accessible approach on the southwest ridge.

He was nothing if not an opportunist. There were several hours of daylight left, but not enough to go around to the southwest side, make the climb, and get down before dark. He studied the face of the mountain below the wreck for the best way up. It wouldn't be wise to be caught up there at night. He thought he could see a doable path up if he was very careful. It would be a tough climb and slippery going after the rain. But, he thought, it might be worth the effort. He strapped on his S&W .357 Magnum loaded with snake shot cartridges, looped a full canteen of water over his shoulder, put a length of rope in his canvas backpack, and grabbed a small pickaxe from the back of the truck. He might have to tie the rope off on a boulder to lower himself to the wreck; the pickaxe could come in handy to keep him from slipping. He studied his route again before picking his way through the creosote and cactus to the mountain's base and starting the climb.

It was even more brutal and more treacherous than it appeared from below. He used the pickaxe to drive into the ground for more leverage on the steepest slopes. The sun was dropping lower in the west, and the light was beginning to wane when he reached the wreck. He would have to work fast to get down before dark. The plane's fuselage had crumpled like an accordion when it hit and flattened somewhat when it flipped upside down. The door to the cockpit had blown off; it was a tight squeeze inside the cabin. He found two dead men inside, hanging limply upside down by their seat belts. They looked as if every bone in their bodies had been broken, and their faces were severely damaged. He could see the imprint of their heads' impact on the dash. He quickly removed each man's wallet and riffled through its contents. There were several hundred dollars between them, which he shoved into his pockets and tossed the wallets onto the cabin ceiling. He crawled further inside and found a large attaché case lying on the cockpit's ceiling behind the seats. It was partly covered by one of two duffel bags at the back of the cockpit. The other bag had split open, scattering clothes and toiletries around.

He quickly searched through the second bag, but it, too, contained nothing but clothes, nothing of value, and he tossed it aside. Harley gingerly crept back and stopped when the fuselage groaned and slipped a little under his weight. He backed out very slowly and deliberately, dragging the attaché case along and holding his breath as he crawled out the cockpit doorway. The case's latches opened easily. He was dumbfounded by the contents, unsure what to make of them. It was packed with some strange-looking paper certificates. They looked valuable—each one said to pay the bearer ten thousand dollars!

Harley didn't know what they were, but they appeared to be worth a lot of money. He couldn't take time to count them; he just closed the case. The plane shuddered and slipped a little further down the slope. It was lodged precariously against the side of the giant black boulder; it wouldn't take much to send it sliding further down the mountain. The light was fading fast, and he had to get down quickly now. The pickaxe made it awkward with both hands full. He tossed it aside to keep one hand free and carry the attaché case with the other. It wasn't easy going as he picked his way down through the maze of black rock and boulders that covered the face of the mountain. He slipped several times on the wet rocks and once banged up his left shoulder and hip. A large rattlesnake rattled angrily at the disturbance as he slid past it; he was thankful he was too far away for it to strike. The last light was fading to darkness when he stumbled back to his truck and tossed the attaché case and his gear into the cab. He was winded from the climb and just sat for a few minutes behind the wheel of the Beast. His shoulder and hip hurt like hell. But, he thought, it would be worth it. That attaché case was going to make him a very wealthy man.

He couldn't risk crossing the flooded washes in the dark and possibly getting stuck with the sheep in the back and an attaché case full of who knew what. The washes would be down by morning. Plenty of time to get his cargo to town. He ate some venison jerky and an apple, then settled in to wait for the morning sun to wake him.

⚜

The taxidermist's shop was in the little town of Cashion, between Phoenix and Avondale. Harley pulled around to the shop's back door at eleven o'clock the following day. He banged on the door until Snuffy Snyder showed up. He said, "All right, all right, hold your horses," then slid the back door open and looked at Harley. "You look like hell," he said with no preamble. "What'd you do...sleep in the Beast again?"

"Yep. Got caught in a flood out by Woolsey Peak and had to wait it out til mornin'."

"Back your truck inside the door, and let's see what you got." The shop had been a garage before Snuffy bought it. The wide door was helpful to keep prying eyes from his business. He had acquired the nickname Snuffy because he always had a wad of Copenhagen snuff bulging in his lower lip.

Harley backed in and stepped down from the Beast. "Damn, Snuffy! This place smells worse than the last time I was here. You oughta air it out."

The place had the distinctive aroma of stale blood, rotting flesh, and various chemicals. The odors were embedded in the walls, and no amount of cleaning could remove them. A more refined person than Harley would have gagged and made for the door.

"Aw, quit yer bitchin' and show me what ya got."

Harley opened the back of the Beast and said, "Wha'dya think?"

Snuffy whistled when he saw the bighorn ram. "Damn! That's a trophy if I ever seen one! Let's get it over on the workbench." He looked it over carefully and said, "I've got just the right buyer for this one. He's from one of them A-Rab countries."

"Same deal as before?" Harley asked.

"Yep. I'll let you know when the money arrives."

They shook hands, and Harley headed back to Buckeye.

CHAPTER 3

"Naw sir, I cain't tell you where they went." The old man spat a brown stream of tobacco juice onto the dirt.

"Can you think of anyone else who might know?' Sean asked.

"Naw, sir. I shorely cain't."

"All right. Thank you for your time, sir."

Deputy Sean O'Conner got in his Maricopa County Sheriff's patrol car and returned to the Avondale district office. He was frustrated—the old man was the final interview he had conducted to try to find Jennifer Stone's family. She was the last of the girls he had helped free from a human trafficking ring last spring. Sean had spent the last four months working with the county's social services department to try and find the parents of fifteen girls who had been kidnapped and forced into prostitution in Arizona before being sent to Detroit. He had been instrumental in bringing down the operation in Maricopa County. That led to the breakup of the organized crime ring in Detroit and sending the girls back to Arizona. Their families were all transient workers who had been working in the cotton fields to make money before moving on to California. Sean had been assigned to work with social services and had only been successful in finding the families of nine of the girls.

He had exhausted every possible lead, working long hours in addition to his other duties as a deputy county sheriff. It was a bittersweet relief to be done with the assignment and move on to other things. He worked late finishing his final report to the district commander. It would be on his desk in the morning.

That night, he met up with his best friend Ricky Martinez at the Wishing Well bar for burgers and beers. Ricky said, "You did a great thing finding families of nine of those girls. Maybe the others will turn up someday. Don't beat yourself up for not being able to find them all. Those people are on the move constantly."

Sean washed down a bite of cheeseburger. "I know you're right, Ricky. I appreciate it. I'm just frustrated by not being able to do more. At least now I can get back to more of my regular duties."

The two men reminisced about some of their adventures earlier that year in Sean's pursuit of the man known as the Weighmaster. He had been the man responsible for kidnapping all those girls. Ricky had helped Sean rescue the first of the girls from a brothel called the Orange Palace, where they had been kept. Then, he accompanied Sean deep into Mexico in pursuit of the kidnapper.

Ricky laughed and said, "You know, I'm still amazed we pulled that off without being arrested in Mexico!"

"Yeah, me too. I guess I'll never be able to show my face south of the border again!"

They ordered two more beers, laughed, and talked another hour, then called it a night. Sean had to be at work early the following day. He got home and fed Sarge, his chocolate labrador retriever, a late dinner. Then he went to bed, and the dog curled up on the floor beside him.

✤

The next morning, the district commander called all the deputies into his conference room. When everyone was settled, he asked Sean to stand. "Sean, the department appreciates all the hard work you've done locating those kidnapped girls' families. The sheriff wants me to present you with this commendation for your exemplary work. Congratulations!"

Sean was about six feet tall and around two hundred pounds. A prominently chiseled chin and wide cheekbones gave his face a rugged look. His naturally ruddy complexion turned bright red, made even brighter with the contrast against his blonde hair and green eyes. He was always shy about receiving praise. He shook the commander's hand and said, "Thank you, sir. But a lot of other people deserve credit for it, too. I just did the fieldwork." The other deputies gave him a round of applause, and the meeting broke up.

The commander said, "Sean, step into my office. I have a new job for you." Sean took a seat and waited for him to continue. "I received a call a little while ago of a reported airplane crash in the Buckeye area. A pilot from Luke Air Force spotted it on Woolsey Peak and radioed it in. The base commander passed it on to us. I know you're familiar with that area, and I want you to investigate it. Report back on survivors or casualties as soon as you can."

Sean thought for a minute before replying. "Sir, I do know that area. I hunted deer around there with my dad, and I climbed that mountain a couple of times years ago. It's very remote and rugged, and it isn't easy to get in there under the best conditions. We always did it on horseback. I expect the washes have all run deep with the rains we've been having, making it even tougher."

"What do you need, Sean? This is a priority. There may be lives at stake."

"Yes, sir. I understand. I'll need to use the four-wheel drive Jeep we just received. It's the only way I'm going to get in there."

The department had recently acquired two of the vehicles. One was placed in a district office in the eastern part of the county, the other in Sean's district.

"Sure, Sean. It sounds like what those rigs are built for. But try to bring it back in one piece."

"One more thing, sir. I want to request a partner to go out there with me. That mountain is hazardous under the best of conditions. Today, it will be slippery from the rains, and there's no telling where the crash site is on the mountain. It might take two of us to reach it."

The commander considered and said, "Alright. I'll assign Brad to go with you. Be careful and let me know what you find as soon as possible."

"Yes, sir. It may be late today. It's possible we could get trapped out there if there are more heavy thunderstorms. It could be tomorrow before we could get out."

"Do what you have to and be careful." The commander dismissed him with a nod, and he went to catch Brad before he left on patrol. Brad Jones was Sean's best friend in the department. They had worked together several times and trusted each other's judgment.

He caught Brad as he went out to his cruiser to start his patrol and said, "Hey, Brad, the commander just gave us an assignment to investigate a plane crash out by Buckeye."

"A plane crash! Wow! That's something different!"

"Yep, but it won't be any picnic. It's way out southwest of Buckeye on Woolsey Peak. It's some of the roughest country in the county."

"Yeah, I've heard of it. What do we need?"

"The commander approved using that new jeep in the parking lot. We need to load it with some supplies in case we get stuck out there and have to stay overnight. We can stop at a grocery on the way and get a few things. Grab your raincoat and canteen from your cruiser. And you're gonna need some hiking boots."

"My boots are in the trunk with my raincoat and canteen. I'll grab them now."

"It would be a good idea to follow me in your cruiser. We can park it beside the turnoff to the mountain. It's possible we could get stuck out there with all the rain we're having, and we might have to walk out."

Brad was a couple of years older than Sean. He had been deferred from the draft because he was married and working for the sheriff's department. Sean had spent some of his early training with him and developed a close working relationship. Brad's wife, Ann, was expecting their second child.

Sean loaded his gear into the Jeep, and they headed out. They stopped at a market in Buckeye and bought a few cans of food in case they were stranded overnight, then went to the Texaco gas station, where the department maintained an account. The Jeep was equipped with two five-gallon jerry cans carried in side holders. Sean filled one can with fuel and topped off the other with water. Then, they set out for the crash site.

During the war the only four-wheel drive vehicles were made for the military. The little Willys Jeep CJ-2A began production as the war was winding down in 1945, making it the world's first mass-produced civilian four-wheel drive vehicle. It looked pretty much like its predecessors used by the military. It had a canvas top and was open on the sides with fold-up doors that could be fastened on in bad weather. The department bought two of them and painted them in the department's vehicle colors. They sported the badge of the sheriff's department on the side. The little Jeep rode like the military version, too, and Sean felt every bump in the road.

They reached the turn-off to Agua Caliente Road at about nine a.m. and loaded the rest of Brad's gear in the back of the Jeep. Sean kept a sharp eye on the weather, with clouds already forming in the distance. He said, "Brad, I'm guessing today's liable to be a repeat of the storms we've been having. We'll have to move fast and try to get to the crash site before the storms fire up. It's gonna be a rough ride, so hold on!"

Brad laughed. "Hey, this ain't my first rodeo, pardner! I've been bucked off tougher rides than this!"

They had a good laugh and set out as fast as was safe on the rough road. The washes had flowed strongly from yesterday's rains; some were still running small streams of water. Sean nursed the little Jeep across them, thankful for the rig's four-wheel drive, then turned off on the dirt track that branched off toward Woolsey Peak.

They had a difficult crossing at the deepest wash they crossed. The floodwaters had eroded the banks, and they had to carefully maneuver the jeep over the edge and up the other side.

Brad said, "Whew! I wouldn't want to try crossing that thing when it's running a lot of water!"

"Nope. It's the main reason we might not get out of here today if there's more heavy rains."

They reached the peak's north side, and Brad said, "Look there, about a third of the way down from the mountaintop toward the west side. There's something white up in all that black rock."

Sean stopped and stepped out of the Jeep. "Yep, I see it. Has to be the plane. There's nothing else but black rock on that mountain."

Sean eased the vehicle out of the dirt track and picked his way through the heavy growth of creosote and cholla cactus to the mountain's base directly below the crash. They stopped beside a tall saguaro cactus with several arms reaching skyward and surveyed the scene, looking for the best route up to the crash site.

Sean said, "I always started my climb on the southwest side of the mountain. It's easier going up that long ridge on that side. But it would take too long. Those thunderheads are forming fast in the east, and we don't have time to spare. We gotta get up there, have a look, and get back down before we get hammered by one of those storms!"

"I think I see a possible route," Brad said. He pointed the features out to Sean.

"Probably the best we're gonna get. Let's load up our gear and get at it!"

They grabbed their canteens and slung them over their shoulders. Sean had brought a length of rope, and he draped it over his other shoulder. Then they set out, moving quickly but cautiously, picking their way through boulders, loose rocks, and the thick teddy bear cholla cactus that grew everywhere. It was still slippery from the rains the day before, and both men slipped occasionally, banging elbows and knees on the rocks.

It took them an hour and a half to reach the wrecked Stinson. Sean had a small Kodak camera and took several pictures before they searched the plane.

Brad said, "Look here, Sean. Someone's been here before us. Who do you suppose could have been here already? This was just reported this morning." He pointed to a pickaxe lying on the ground a little way from the wreck. Sean took a picture of that, too.

"It had to be someone who was near when the plane crashed. Maybe a hunter."

"No way anyone could survive a wreck like this, Sean. They must have hit going full speed. Probably caught in a storm and didn't see the mountain until they hit it. Crumbled it up like a toy!" They could see the plane's two passengers through the windshield.

"Let's see if we can find any identification for those guys," Sean said. "The wreck doesn't look very stable. We need to move slowly and carefully to avoid sending it on down the mountain with one of us in it!" He took the rope off his shoulder, tied a loop around his waist, and handed the other end to Brad. "You're my insurance, Brad, in case this thing slips on down the slope. I'll crawl inside and see if I can find some ID; you haul me out that door if it heads down the slope!"

Sean carefully started to crawl through the open door. The plane shifted a little with his weight, and he stopped to be sure it had settled. He could see both men's wallets lying open on the plane's ceiling below them. It was a disorienting and surreal scene—everything was upside down. He picked up the nearest wallet and found a Nevada driver's license but nothing else. The bill compartment was empty. He gingerly reached across to the other man's wallet and found another Nevada driver's license and an empty bill compartment. He put both licenses in his shirt pocket. A couple of duffel bags on the floor in the back appeared to have been gone through; clothes were scattered on and around them. It wasn't safe to try to reach them, and Sean doubted they contained anything other than clothes. He took several pictures inside and cautiously backed out of the plane's door. It gave another shudder at the shift of weight.

The men studied the licenses. Brad said, "Looks like both these guys lived in Las Vegas. What the hell were they doing flying over this country in a storm?"

19

"No idea. But I have a feeling they may have been up to no good to take a risk like that. And whoever was here before us ransacked their luggage and stole their money. That's gonna be a mystery for us to solve, too. There's nothing else we can do here now. We'll have to leave the bodies as they are and get help to remove them."

The men could see the clouds that formed earlier moving toward them. A lightning bolt flashed over a peak in the distance, and the thunder reverberated off the mountain. Sean caught a flicker of movement out of the corner of his eye and turned to look. He pointed a little distance up the slope and said, "Look at that, Brad! A bighorn ram!" The men stood still for a full minute, watching the magnificent animal as it stood watching them.

Sean broke the spell of seeing the ram. "We've got to get off this mountain as quick as we can. We don't want to be here when those storms arrive. Move as fast as you can and try not to slip. I don't want to have to carry you off this pile of rocks!"

Brad chuckled and said, "Same to you, partner."

Both men slipped several times, but short of some scrapes and bruises didn't do any permanent damage. The rain hit just as they arrived back at the Jeep. They grabbed their raincoats, snapped the doors in place, and headed back for the main road. The Jeep's single windshield wiper was nearly useless, and Sean frequently struggled to see what was ahead. The wind and rain beat at the Jeep's canvas top, and they sometimes thought the wind would rip it off the vehicle. The desert's soil was already saturated from previous rains, and this storm's runoff had already begun to flood the washes. The water rose fast as they carefully eased in and climbed out of the deepest wash on the track.

Sean said, "Damn! That was close! We wouldn't have gotten across in another ten minutes!"

They finally reached the highway and Brad's cruiser. They hopped in the car and waited for the storm to subside.

They tried to raise the district office on the car's radio, but they were at the fringe of its range, and the severe electrical storm raging around them created too much static. They could only wait out the storm and then head back to town.

Sean said, "You know, the Mexicans hit it on the head when they named this kind of country malpais. It means bad country."

"Yeah, I've heard this black rock around here called by that name, too."

"I wonder if seeing that bighorn was some kind of sign. He seemed to come out of nowhere and wasn't afraid of us."

Brad laughed. "Don't know. That's too deep for me."

Both men were ravenous and opened a couple of cans of Vienna sausages and a box of saltine crackers. It would tide them over until they reached civilization again.

CHAPTER 4

"Getting those bodies out of the wreck and off the mountain is going to be very difficult," Sean said. He, Brad, and the district commander sat in the commander's conference room. Sean continued, "It's on a steep face of the mountain, barely lodged against a boulder and very unstable. There's been a lot of rain, and the rocks are slippery; you have to be careful with every step. The plane will have to be secured before the bodies are removed to keep it from sliding further down the mountain."

"Do you think it's something we can handle within the department?" the commander asked.

Brad said, "I don't think so, sir. Getting the bodies out of the wreck is one thing—getting them down off the mountain is another. As Sean said, it's a tough climb. We had a rough time getting down with just our gear. Maybe someone with experience in that type of rescue could do it. I don't think anyone like that is available in the department."

"Another issue, sir," Sean said. "This weather we're having looks like it might hang around for a while. We barely got off that mountain before a strong thunderstorm hit. It would add another dangerous element to anyone on the mountain caught in one of those."

The commander thought for a minute. "I heard about a volunteer group that does mountain rescues. Perhaps they could help."

Sean said, "That would be great, sir. I have another idea that might help, too. A helicopter would be perfect to get the bodies off the mountain. Maybe the National Guard could provide one with a pilot."

"All right. Sean, I want you and Brad to take the lead on this. You'll be in charge of coordinating the work. Make any contacts you think can help. We can involve the sheriff if necessary. Give me a report by the end of the day. In the meantime, I'll assign someone to contact the Las Vegas police to try and contact any family those men have."

The meeting broke up, and the deputies got busy on their phones. They had a plan by the end of the day and presented it to the commander.

Sean began. "Sir, the volunteer rescue group is willing to assist. They are mostly guys who recently returned from the war in Europe and have that kind of experience. We would need to pay their expenses."

"The National Guard said they can make a helicopter available, but we would have to pay the expense for fuel," Brad added. "Also, they want a formal request from the sheriff."

The commander said, "I've already talked to the sheriff. He gave me the go-ahead with whatever we needed. I'll call him back and ask him to provide a written request to the National Guard. I want you two to coordinate this and lead the rescuers to the scene."

⁜

By the following day, the men had all the pieces in place. The volunteer rescue group had six men available, and the National Guard had a helicopter and pilot on standby. Sean and Brad arranged to meet the men at a coffee shop in Buckeye at eight a.m. to map out a strategy. They would then notify the National Guard of a time for the chopper to rendezvous at the site.

The commander motioned them into his office before they left. "The Las Vegas Police said the addresses on both men's driver's licenses were fake—there are no such addresses in Las Vegas. We tracked down the aircraft's owner through its tail identification number. It belongs to a casino in Las Vegas. A detective has been assigned to contact them for information. I'll let you know what we find out."

Sean and Brad left for Buckeye in the Jeep and met the volunteers. They were all trained in mountain rescues while serving in the Army or Marines. The two deputies described what they had seen at the crash site.

John, the leader of the volunteers, asked, "What do you guys think we need to secure the wreck?"

Sean replied, "At least two stout ropes, maybe a hundred feet long, and some heavy-duty steel pins to drive in the ground to secure them. You'll have to find the best way to secure them to the wreck. It's very unstable; it wouldn't take much to send it sliding down even further. And I hope your rigs have four-wheel drive. It's some rough country with a bunch of flooded washes."

"We have some sharpened three-foot lengths of rebar with eyelets welded on top. They should work to stabilize the wreck. And we have two military trucks with four-wheel drive," John said. "The National Guard loans them to us for rescue operations. A couple of our guys are Guardsmen, too. Let's get out there before more afternoon storms set in!"

"One more thing before we go," Sean said. "It's snaky country out there. Rattlesnakes den in those black rocks. Be careful!"

They headed out in the Jeep, with Sean and Brad leading the two trucks. Sean radioed into the district office and asked the clerk to contact the National Guard and have them send the helicopter to meet them in two hours. He had already given them the information for the location.

The dirt track was even slower than before. The heavy rains had eroded the washes' banks even more, making it difficult to cross them and get back out. Their tires spun in the mud in the bottoms, making it tougher to get across. After an hour of creeping across the washes, they arrived at the base of Woolsey Peak below the crash site.

The volunteers were unloading their gear when the helicopter showed up. The pilot got out, shook hands all around, and asked who was in charge. Sean stepped forward. "What do you need to know, sir?"

The men talked about the logistics of getting the bodies off the mountain. The helicopter was a two-passenger Sikorsky SR-5 that looked like a giant bug. But it was a very capable craft that had proven itself in the war. It was outfitted with a sling that was currently stowed on its side. The pilot explained how to unroll the sling's cable so that it would dangle below the helicopter when it was airborne. When he brought a body down, they would have to unload it and then make sure the sling's cable was clear of any snags. They didn't have radio communications with the men on the mountain, and Sean asked if any of the men had a pistol. All but one raised their hands. Sean continued, "Fire one shot in the air when you are ready for the pilot to come for a body. That will be the signal for him to lift off." Brad and I will stay here to remove the body from the sling when he returns." He paused and surveyed the horizon. "We have to work fast. Those clouds to the west are likely to move in soon, and you guys don't want to be on this mountain when that happens."

The pilot seconded that. "I can't fly this bird in a violent thunderstorm. I'll need to get out of here before one hits!"

The volunteers headed up to the crash site, moving in single file. Sean was impressed—it only took them forty-five minutes to reach it. The men first drove the deep stakes into the ground, tied two ropes onto their eyelets, and then secured their ends to the landing gear struts, which were now pointed skyward. They were bent up but still seemed strong. Each man kept a tight hold on the ropes as an added precaution.

John went into the cabin first. The bodies were rapidly decomposing in the heat; the odor in the confined space was almost overwhelming. He gagged as he unbuckled Cutter's seat belt, caught the body, and eased it down onto the cockpit's ceiling. Then he gripped the body under its arms. The plane groaned and shifted a little as the weight was moved around. John waited until it settled, then pulled the body out. Two other men helped him carry it a little distance from the wreck so the helicopter's sling could reach it without getting tangled in the wreck.

John said, "The other body is going to be more tricky. I'll have to move all the way inside to reach him." He pointed to one of the men. "Chuck, you need to follow me in. It will take two of us to get him out. Be prepared for the horrible odor and move real slow and deliberate. We don't want to turn this thing into a sled rocketing downhill!" He didn't have one hundred percent confidence that their two safety ropes would hold if the whole weight of the plane started sliding downward.

The two men worked slowly and cautiously. The wreck had shifted to the left of the boulder it was up against, straining the safety ropes they had attached.

"I'll grab him under his arms, Chuck. You unbuckle the seat belt and get under his legs. Then let's gently lift him and try to back out of here." Their movement started the wreck groaning and scraping against the boulder. The two men on the ropes were pulling for all they were worth trying to keep it from pulling free of the pins in the ground. The two men in the cockpit moved faster, attempting to get out before the worst could happen. Chuck had made it out and pulled Billy's corpse out with him just as the wreck gave a loud grinding screech against the boulder and shifted downhill. Both the restraining metal pins were jerked from the ground, and the ropes burned through the two men's hands holding them. Then, as if in slow motion, the plane started sliding downhill and rapidly picked up speed, bouncing over rocks and ricocheting off large boulders. John was trapped inside. The aircraft bounced over a large boulder, and one wing dug into the ground, causing the plane to cartwheel and slam onto the bottom of the fuselage. It finally came to rest about two hundred yards below the men.

The other volunteers left the corpses where they lay and moved down to the wreck as quickly as they could. They could see John lying unconscious inside the aircraft's cockpit. He was bleeding profusely from his head. Chuck yelled, "We've got to get him out before the damn thing goes any further! I'll crawl through the

26

door and try to pull him out. Two of you grab my ankles to pull me out if it starts sliding again!"

He carefully pulled John's unconscious body from the wreckage, and the men laid him off to the side of the wreck. One of them sat on the ground against him to keep him from rolling down the steep slope. Chuck said, "One of you get down to the 'copter and explain what's happened. Have the pilot come to us first. We need to get John down so we can treat him and get him out of here." One of the men took off, slipping and sliding, moving as fast as he could.

About twenty minutes later, the 'copter lifted off, and the pilot maneuvered the sling to them. They secured John as best they could and waved off the pilot. The men got him into one of the pickups the volunteers were driving as soon as he was on the ground. They cleaned him up and dressed his wounds the best they could. Then, the volunteer took off back toward civilization and a doctor.

The other men went back to the two bodies. One took out his pistol and fired a shot. The helicopter lifted off immediately, and they secured the first body in the sling. The wind was picking up, and the men could see an ominous-looking thunderstorm moving in their direction. The pilot noted it, too, and quickly returned for the other body when the first one was free. They repeated the process, and it was quickly over. The pilot landed, and the deputies helped him secure the sling in its holder. The pilot yelled over the noise of the idling engine, "It's been fun, but I've gotta get the hell out of here before that storm hits. Adios, buddies!" He climbed into the cockpit, lifted off, and headed fast toward Phoenix.

The men placed the two bodies into body bags and then laid them in the back of the remaining volunteer's pickup truck. Then they headed back towards the highway just as the first fat raindrops started to fall. It was a race against time to get across the washes before the water came up again. They drove too fast between the crossings, bouncing around and barely under control.

27

They managed to beat the flood. Sean called the district office when they were in radio range and asked to have a coroner's ambulance meet them in Buckeye at city hall to transport the bodies to the county morgue. After meeting the ambulance and transferring the bodies, the men all shook hands and beat each other on the back, blowing off some of their pent-up nervous energy. Sean thanked each of them in turn and told them to call on him if he could ever return the favor. He asked Chuck to keep him informed about John's condition. Then, the thunderstorm moved over the town, and they headed back home.

CHAPTER 5

Joe the Fish was head of security for the Lucky Joker Casino. He said, "Boss, there's two Vegas cops here to see you."

Tony Miller, aka Tony Two Guns, was the general manager. He replied, "Aw, crap, Joe. Whadda they want?"

"They didn't say, Mr. Miller. Just asked for the manager."

"Okay. Bring 'em on back."

Joe escorted the two suits down a long hallway off the casino floor. He stopped at the manager's door and knocked.

"Come in," said a deep voice. Joe opened the door and showed the two cops inside. Tony told Joe to stay and then introduced himself to the two officers.

"I'm Detective Black," one of them said, "and this is my partner, Detective Flowers."

The three men shook hands, and Tony said, "Have a seat, detectives. What can I do for you?"

Black said, "We need to talk to you about an aircraft registered to the casino." Tony's eyebrows raised, but he said nothing. The detective continued, "The plane was found crashed into a mountainside in the desert west of Phoenix. The registration is this casino. There were two men aboard, both killed in the crash."

"Oh my God," Tony exclaimed. "We didn't know the plane was missing. Our pilot is on vacation, so no one would have noticed it was gone. Who were the men that were killed?"

"Their Nevada driver's licenses identified them as Ryan Cutter and William Barnes. We went to the addresses on their licenses, looking for their next of kin, but both addresses were fake. Maybe you can shed some light on who they were and what they were doing with the casino's airplane."

Tony thought for a moment before replying, "Both those men worked for me. They were trusted members of my security team. I heard Billy had been taking flying lessons from our pilot, but I didn't know he was qualified to fly on his own. I have no idea why they would have taken our plane. Neither of them said anything about it to me, so I doubt they were on the casino's business. It's a damn shame to lose them, though. They were both valued employees."

Detective Black asked, "Do you have any information about their next of kin? Their bodies are being held in the county morgue in Phoenix."

Tony said, "Joe, go out and ask Doris to bring me the personnel files for Ryan and Billy."

The detective continued, "We also found a car parked by the hangar where your plane was kept. It had brain and blood spatter on the inside and outside of the passenger door. And just yesterday evening, a motorist reported a body lying alongside Highway 95 outside of town. The dead man's name was Ernest Bliss. He had been shot in the head at close range." He paused briefly and continued, "Would you know anything about that?"

Tony stood up from his desk and exclaimed, "Ernie's dead? What the hell's going on?"

"We're hoping you could shed some light on all of this, Mr. Miller," Detective Black said calmly. "Is Mr. Bliss' death somehow related to the two men who took your airplane? The bloody car at the airport is also registered to this casino. It would appear your employees were up to no good."

"I'm as confused as you by all this, detective. I assure you I will get to the bottom of it, and you will be the first to know what I find out."

Tony's secretary Doris knocked and came in with the two personnel files. Tony said, "We need to add Ernie Bliss to the stack, Dorothy." She got a puzzled look on her face and went to fetch the file.

Tony provided the three men's information to the detectives. Black said, "We'll notify these families. In the meantime, all three men will be kept in the morgue here and in Phoenix while we investigate their deaths." The two detectives stood up to leave. "Keep us informed. We'll coordinate with the Maricopa County Sheriff's Department in Phoenix to try and find out what happened." The two detectives left. There were no handshakes this time.

As soon as the detectives left, Tony went up to the casino hotel's penthouse to visit Mr. Bianco, the property's owner. He had a face like a bulldog with jowls hanging below his chin. Deep wrinkles on his forehead made him look older than his early sixties. His deep-set black eyes bored into Tony as he laid it all out.

Bianco said, "Those bastards made off with a million bucks in bearer bonds. Serves 'em right, flyin' into a mountain. But I hate losin' that airplane. What the hell happened to the bonds? Do the cops in Arizona have 'em? We need to find 'em, and quick. A lot is ridin' on that money. Put a team together and send 'em to Arizona to find it." He paused briefly, looked at Tony, and said, "And tell 'em to do whatever they gotta. Just don't get caught doin' it!"

CHAPTER 6

Harley was sitting on the living room couch at the house he shared with his twin brother in Buckeye, fingering the bearer bonds. His brother was still working in the shop. Harley picked up one of the bonds and looked it over carefully, then held it up to the light from a window to see if there were any watermarks. As far as he could tell, they were legitimate. He had never seen anything like the bonds, never even heard of them. He took them out and counted them, then put them back in the case. Harley whistled softly—there were a hundred of them! A million bucks!

He tried to think what it meant. What were those guys in the plane doing? Where were they headed? Did they steal it, or were they delivering it to someone else? No answers presented themselves. But, he thought, one thing was sure. Someone was likely to come looking for them—possibly someone very bad if criminals were involved. He would have to be very, very careful if he wanted to keep them for himself.

Harley was no businessman and had no idea how the bonds were used. He decided visiting his lawyer would be a safe move to get information. An attorney who had gotten him out of some tough scrapes in the past should be able to help and keep quiet about it. He picked up the phone and made an appointment for 9 o'clock the next morning.

🌵

The sign on the lawyer's door read "Michael Fishburn III, Attorney at Law." Harley thought it was a mighty fancy name, considering the office was in a run-down strip mall in Phoenix. But the guy had done right for him and kept him out of jail several times. He opened the glass door and stepped inside, and Shirley, the secretary, greeted him by name.

"Good morning, Mr. Henderson. Mr. Fishburn is waiting for you. Go right in."

She was an attractive woman, and Harley had once asked her out. She politely declined. He wondered briefly if he should try again but thought better of it. He had bigger things on his mind. Maybe she would be more receptive when he became a millionaire.

He stepped into the attorney's office, and Fishburn rose to shake his hand. He was dressed in a dark three-piece suit, making him look more affluent than he was. The lawyer said, "Good to see you, Harley. What have you gotten yourself into this time?" He smiled and pointed Harley to a chair in front of his desk.

"Well, I ain't in no trouble this time, Mr. Fishburn. But I got somethin' I need your help with." He slid an envelope containing one of the bonds across the desk. "I want to know what this is and what to do with it."

Fishburn slid the bond out of the envelope and laid it on his desk. His eyes were large with surprise. He gave a low whistle and said, "Where did you get this?"

Harley shuffled in his chair and said," I found it with a few others in a brown envelope layin' alongside Highway 80 a couple of days ago. I ain't never seen one before. Tell me what it is."

"Did the envelope have an address on it?"

"Nope. Just a plain brown envelope."

The attorney studied him for a few seconds and asked, "How many of these were in the envelope?"

"Well, they was four of 'em."

Fishburn knew Harley well enough to suspect there was more to the truth of this. His mind was rolling over possibilities about how he might be able to cash in on whatever the man had found. He said, "They are called bearer bonds. This one is worth ten thousand dollars, just like it shows. They can be cashed just like a check for the face amount. They are issued with coupons attached to them that can be cashed for interest. But it looks like the coupons have been removed from this one, and it has reached its maturity date. That means it now only has the face value. Do the others have coupons attached to them?

"No, I didn't see no coupons on 'em."

"Well, it sounds like you have found forty-thousand dollars' worth of them. That's a sizable chunk of money for someone to lose along the highway."

"Can I just take it to the bank and cash it?"

"Yes, you can. But you need to be careful because the bank might keep a transaction record. You could be liable for taxes. But I know a guy who deals in these bonds who could handle it for a fee. There would be no record of that transaction. I can help you with it if you'd like."

"How much is the fee?"

"Last time I worked with him, it was ten percent of the face value."

"I don't want to get mixed up with the tax people. I want you to handle it for me."

Fishburn struggled to keep from smiling. "I'll have to add another five percent for my fee. That would net you eighty-five hundred dollars for each bond."

"Damn! That's a big bite. Can't I do it myself?"

"Sure, if you want to risk the exposure. And it's possible whoever lost the bonds could come looking for them, and a bank is the first place they would try to find information."

Harley thought about it and said, "Alright. I'll bring in the others tomorrow, and you can handle cashing 'em for me."

"It will take me a few days to get it done. I'll call you when I have the cash for you."

They stood up and shook hands. Harley said, "Thanks, Mr. Fishburn. I knew I'd come to the right place."

"Thank you, Harley. I'm always here and ready to help you with whatever you need. I'll call you soon."

He watched the man walk out the door, then allowed himself a self-satisfied smile. Damn, he said to himself, this is going to be the easiest money I've ever made. It was Friday—he couldn't do much until the following week. He picked up his phone and called one of his friends at a bank, told him what he wanted to do, and made an appointment for the following Monday.

CHAPTER 7

Jimmy Rossi, aka the Fixer, sat in the back seat of his Cadillac, watching the countryside roll by. He was the go-to guy the casino used to solve problems that required more than a little business discussion. Two of his men, Lefty, and Frankie, were traveling with him in a separate car. Lorenzo, his chief lieutenant, was driving his Caddy.

Jimmy looked out the window and said, "God, I hate this country. Nothin' but sand and cactus. If it weren't for Vegas, the whole place would be worthless!"

"Yeah, boss," Lorenzo said. "I'd never leave town if I didn't hafta, unless I could get on a plane goin' back to Jersey." Rossi laughed and nodded his agreement.

"Just get us to Phoenix in one piece, Lorenzo. Maybe we can find somethin' to entertain us while we're there." The men laughed again and settled in to watch the endless miles of mountains, desert, and cactus roll by. Rossi pulled his new Stetson Wanderer down over his eyes and dozed off. The grey fedora matched his new Italian suit.

"Well, Sean, it looks like you've opened up another can of worms for us," Detective Johnson joked. "We've been looking for something useful to do since you busted up that Orange Palace operation a few months ago." Everyone around the table laughed, including the district commander. The group meeting in the commander's conference room included Detectives Johnson and Harper, the commander, Sean, and Brad Jones. The two detectives couldn't have looked less alike. Johnson was portly and pale, balding over a round face, with close-set black eyes; Harper was tall, skinny, and tanned. His hatchet-face, grey eyes, and curly black hair gave him a wolfish look. The detectives had asked for the meeting to discuss the airplane wreckage on Woolsey Peak.

Johnson lit a Pall Mall, shifted his ample belly into a more comfortable position, and continued, "The information we've gotten from the Las Vegas Police is beginning to paint a picture of something big associated with the wreck. It seems there was a murder in Las Vegas that may be connected to whatever was going on. They found a car where the man was likely killed parked next to the hanger where the plane was kept. We've learned that the car and the wrecked airplane belonged to the Lucky Joker Casino in Vegas. We also learned the two dead men in the crash were employees of the casino. According to the Vegas PD, the people who run the casino acted surprised about the whole thing."

The detective paused to let all that sink in, then nodded to Detective Harper. He ran his hand through his hair and said, "Our best guess is your boys who ran into the mountain were likely running from their bosses with some goodies—we think maybe they stole a bunch of money from the casino, then stole the plane to make a getaway. They were probably heading for Mexico when the mountain got in their way. We figure they'll send somebody looking for whatever they are missing."

Johnson looked at the other men and settled on Sean. "Sean, I understand you found evidence someone had been at the crash site before you and Brad. What can you tell us about that?"

"Well, sir, as I said in our report, someone had been inside the plane and went through the dead men's wallets. They probably took whatever cash was in them. Also, he or they had gone through a couple of duffel bags in the back of the cabin and scattered clothes around. We found a pickaxe on the ground beside the plane. We figured whoever it was must have taken something from the plane and needed to keep a hand free while they carried it down the mountain. It's rough and very slippery up there after all the rains, and you sometimes need a hand to catch yourself when you slip."

Johnson interrupted and asked, "Is that pickaxe still up there?"

"I'd assume it is, sir unless one of the volunteers who helped retrieve the bodies brought it down. I can find out."

"Please do, Sean. It could be a clue to who was there if we can find fingerprints on it. If none of the volunteers picked it up, we'll need you to go back up there and bring it in for fingerprint dusting."

"Okay, we'll do that. There's one other clue we found. There were fresh tire tracks near where we stopped before climbing the mountain. They were made by oversized tires on a heavy vehicle, pressed deep in the mud. They had to have been made after the rain that day, or they would have washed away. I took a couple of pictures of them."

The commander said, "That's great work. Those clues might lead us to find out what this was all about. I want you, Sean, and Brad to keep working on this. Anything you can find out will be helpful. Stay in touch with the detectives and coordinate information."

Both deputies said, "Yes, sir."

Detective Johnson said, "There's one more thing before we break up. Something very valuable was likely taken from that wreck. Those casino guys in Vegas won't take that lightly and will probably show up here looking for it. They are not nice guys, so be on your guard if they approach you. They'll be looking at anyone who might have what's missing and won't be bashful about trying to get information about it. They might even suspect you guys took it."

The two deputies spent a couple of hours chasing down the volunteers who had been on the mountain. Two said they remembered seeing the pickaxe but didn't think anyone picked it up. It was still likely lying where it was left.

Brad said, "Well, Sean, looks like we get another all-expense paid trip into the wilderness to climb that mountain again."

"Looks that way. Maybe we'll luck out, and the rains will back off."

"Yeah, sure…that's the way our luck has been running, all right!"

Sean laughed. "It's getting late in the day now. How about we head out there first thing in the morning? Maybe we can beat the afternoon rains. And, if we have time, I want to talk to some people in Buckeye. I have an idea who might have a heavy rig with those oversized tires."

Later that night, as Sean was preparing for bed, he got a call from Brad. "Sean, Ann's gone into labor. I'm at the hospital with her and will probably be here all night. I'm gonna have to miss our little outing tomorrow."

"Wow, Brad! That's great. Congratulations to you and Ann. Don't worry about tomorrow; I'll lasso someone else into going with me. Give Ann my best wishes and let me know who your new arrival is tomorrow!"

The men hung up. This was Brad and Ann's second child, and he sounded just as excited as with the first.

🌵

Rossi and his men had blown into Phoenix about sundown. They booked four rooms on West Van Buren Street, then met up in the motel's coffee shop for dinner. Lorenzo made a face and said, "Jeez, I've tasted dishwater that was better than this coffee! Let's find a better place in the mornin' for breakfast."

Rossi said, "Quit yer bitchin'. The boss is payin' for it."

"Well, I bet the boss wouldn't drink this swill, either!"

After they finished eating, the group got down to business. Rossi said, "I'm going to find out from the local cops who they sent out to the wreck, then pay 'em a visit to see what they know. I'll take Lefty with me. Lorenzo, you take Frankie with you out to that backwater town they call Buckeye and nose around. See if anybody knows anything."

The Vegas cops had told Rossi that the Maricopa County Sheriff's Department had investigated the crash site. He called the main office the next morning and was referred to the district office in Avondale. He and Lefty drove to the office, and Rossi went inside. The clerk showed him to the district commander's office.

Rossi said, "Thank you for takin' the time to see me. I work for the Lucky Joker Casino in Las Vegas. The owners asked me to look into what happened with the casino's plane that crashed recently. What can you tell me about it?"

The commander thought the guy looked like a Vegas hood. He wore an expensive suit and tie despite the temperature rapidly approaching a hundred degrees outside. A pricey-looking pair of black and white brogues set off the suit. Both his hands sported a couple of large gold rings, and an expensive gold Rolex "Oyster" watch dangled from his left wrist. Hell, the commander told himself, this guy's jewelry cost more than I make in a year! Rossi had steely grey eyes and black hair slicked back in a Pompadour style. A jagged scar cut across the left side of his face from his ear to the corner of his mouth. The commander later told his clerk that the guy looked like an East Coast gangster who had just stepped off a train from New York City.

"Well," the commander said, "We don't know a lot at this point. My deputies investigated it on what we think was the day after it happened. The wreck is on the side of a rugged mountain in a remote desert wilderness, and it's very hard to get to, especially with all the rain we've been having".

"Were your men able to see inside?"

"Yes, they found the two men inside dead. Someone had been there before them and had gone through the men's belongings. A couple of days later, we organized a party of volunteers to help bring the dead men off the mountain. They are both in the county morgue awaiting instructions from their next of kin."

"Thank you for taking care of our men. I'm sure their families will appreciate it."

"You're welcome."

"Did your men find any clues about who may have been there before them?"

40

"Only some tire tracks. They're currently trying to find information about them." The commander didn't think sharing information about the pickaxe left at the scene was appropriate.

"Would it be possible for me to talk with the deputies who were there? The owners asked me to find out all I can to help 'em figure out why the men took the plane and wound up here."

"One of them will be back in here around four o'clock. You can check back then."

Rossi rose to leave. "Thank you for your time, commander. I'll check back with your man later today."

The commander watched him leave and said to himself, that man's trouble with a capital T.

The commander had assigned Steve Riggs to replace Brad for the next trip to Woolsey Peak. Steve was new to the department and only recently completed his training. He had been one of the lucky soldiers sent home early after Germany's surrender in the war. He was a tall, lanky young man with a quick smile. He had wanted to become a professional rodeo cowboy, but the war changed that. The first thing he did when he returned to the state was marry his long-time sweetheart, Mary. He needed a job and applied to the sheriff's department.

Sean briefed him on what they needed to do. Sean again took the Jeep, and Riggs followed him in his department cruiser to the turn-off onto Agua Caliente Road. They left the cruiser and headed out in the Jeep. As Sean had feared, the road was in even worse condition from all the recent heavy rains. Some of the washes still had water in them; their banks had been further eroded by rushing flood water. Sean carefully nursed the Jeep through them; they barely made it through some of the worst. He heaved a sigh of relief when he got to their destination. They left the road, following his previous tracks, and stopped at the base of the mountain.

Sean said, "Man! I hope we don't get any more rain before we get out of here. Brad and I barely made it back to the highway the last time."

"Yep! So, let's get it done, Sean, and get the hell out of here!"

They loaded their canteens, and Sean slipped his backpack over his arms with a first aid kit, camera, notebook, and pencil inside. Then he looped a length of rope around his shoulder. He had learned in the army that you never knew when you'd need a rope on a mountain. "This thing's steep and slippery, Steve. Take your time and watch your footing. I banged the heck out of my hip and shoulder the first time I came up here."

They moved cautiously up the slope. Sean noted more thunderheads beginning to build in the distance, but he didn't mention it. Steve was already a little spooked, and Sean didn't want to make it worse by worrying about a storm. They passed the wrecked plane and continued up to the original crash site. The pickaxe still lay on the ground where it had originally been dropped. Sean put on gloves to handle it just in case there were salvageable fingerprints. They would likely be on the metal head, but he thought prints might be lifted from wood, too. He didn't want to take a chance of smudging them.

They started back to the Jeep. About halfway down, Steve slipped on a wet rock and tumbled a short way down, landing on a rock ledge. He immediately let out a scream and yelled, "Help, Sean! I'm snakebit." Then he screamed again. Sean dropped the pickaxe and carefully moved down to the ledge just in time to see a large, pale green Mojave rattlesnake slither into a crevice nearby. It had been sunning itself on the rock ledge and kept its rattle buzzing until it was out of sight.

"Oh my god, Steve! Where did it hit you?"

Steve could barely croak out, "My throat and my arm!"

Sean knew he had to work fast. The Mojave rattlesnake's venom was the most potent of all rattlers. He'd heard a doctor say that the venom was notorious for being able to cause paralysis and could cause a victim to stop breathing. Somehow, he had to get Steve to a hospital. The first aid kit in his backpack included a Saunders snakebite kit. He had some first aid training for snakebites in the Army but had never had to apply it—until now. "Try to stay calm, buddy! I'm gonna get you out of here." Steve groaned as Sean got the kit out. "Try to stay still, Steve. I'm going to use the vacuum extractor to try and get the venom out." He was worried about the amount of venom Steve may have gotten—the snake was angry at being disturbed and could have injected a large dose.

The first step was to put a tourniquet between the bite wound and the heart. Sean could put a tourniquet on Steve's arm, but there was no way to do it with the bite in his neck. He put the tourniquet on his arm, then removed one of the kit's iodine packets. He applied the iodine to the lancet blade, and both bites. He used the lancet to make cross-shaped incisions across the fang mark on Steve's arm.

The worst bite was on Steve's neck. Sean didn't know if he should try to open those fang wounds; it was dangerously close to the artery. But it was the worst place for the snake to have bitten him. He decided to risk it. Steve would likely die if Sean didn't do something, and soon. He carefully opened the wounds and used the suction syringe from the kit to try and extract as much venom as possible. He repeated it on both wounds several times, but there didn't appear to be much venom in the syringe. He loosened the tourniquet on Steve's arm for a few seconds, then reapplied it. The kit contained two adhesive bandages, which Sean applied to each bite.

Steve had gone into shock and didn't appear to be breathing. Sean applied mouth-to-mouth resuscitation, but Steve didn't seem to respond. There was nothing more Sean could do for him, so he carefully lifted him on his shoulder and started the grueling climb down. He shuffled along sideways, carefully placing each step. Steve's weight made it difficult to keep his balance, and he slipped and nearly fell several times.

He finally reached the bottom, having somehow miraculously avoided any falls. He laid Steve beside the Jeep while he studied what to do next. Steve couldn't set up, so Sean arranged a couple of blankets in the small back cargo space, picked him up, and laid him in the cramped bed. He had to open the Jeep's tailgate to allow some space for Steve's legs.

Steve was still not breathing, and Sean tried mouth-to-mouth resuscitation again. But he was unresponsive. Climbing into the driver's seat, Sean said, "Hang in there, buddy. This is gonna be a rough ride!" He was unable to contact the district office on the radio, but there was nothing they could have done to help anyway. Sean didn't have much hope for his friend. He had heard many stories about rattlesnake bites, and they all agreed on one thing—The Mojave rattler's venom was by far the most deadly, and Steve had gotten two doses from the angry snake's bites. All Sean could do was to try to get him to a hospital; the nearest was in Phoenix, a long drive from their location. He drove as fast as was safe on the muddy track, occasionally sliding and fishtailing in the mud. Steve's inert form rolled back and forth, but there was nothing Sean could do to prevent it. Each wash was a challenge, and there was no way to cross them quickly. He did the best he could, careful not to get them stuck. That would have been the end for Steve.

They finally reached the highway where Steve's cruiser was parked. Sean moved him onto the car's back seat and headed toward Buckeye. His color was ashen, and he showed no sign of life. He was finally able to raise the district office on the radio, tell them what happened, and ask an ambulance to meet him at the Buckeye City Hall. He kicked on his lights and siren and drove fast to the town.

The ambulance was there when he arrived, and the two medics moved Steve into the back of their vehicle. After a short time, one of them stepped out and shook his head. "I'm sorry, sir," he told Sean. "He's gone. There's nothing we can do for him."

"No! That can't be!" Sean yelled. "It can't be!"

The medic said, "I'm sorry. It looks like you did everything you could. You look like you're in shock, too. Let me get you something to take when you get home. Take a couple of these pills and rest. We'll take care of your friend."

Sean sat sideways on the cruiser's seat with the door open and his face in his hands. This was far worse than any battle he had been in with the Germans. He had to pull himself together and do what needed to be done. Steve was newly married, and Sean would have to tell his wife what had happened.

He returned to the district office and found a man in an expensive suit waiting for him. The clerk said the man wanted to discuss the plane crash with him. But first, she took Sean by the arm and said, "I'm so sorry, Sean. This is unbelievable. Are you all right?"

"I'm exhausted, Gloria. I've got to find Steve's wife and then get some rest."

The man in the suit stood up and offered his hand. "I'm Jimmy Rossi. I represent the owners of the airplane that crashed. Can I ask you a few questions about what you saw?"

"Look. I just watched a man die from a snake bite. Right now, I need to go to his wife to let her know. I'm off tomorrow; I'll be back on duty on Monday. How about we do this then?"

"Of course. I didn't know. Sorry about your man. Would nine o'clock work?"

Sean nodded his head. "Yeah, I'll be here." Rossi walked out and got in his Cadillac.

The commander came out of his office and put his hand on Sean's shoulder. "My god, Sean. What an awful thing. I know you did all you could. I heard it was one of those Mojave rattlers. They're the worst."

Sean nodded and said, "He never had a chance, commander. I did everything I'd been taught to do for him, but I think he died while I was carrying him off the mountain."

"Go find his wife Mary and tell her what happened. Then get some rest on your day off tomorrow. I'll send a couple of guys out to get the Jeep."

"Thanks, sir. I just need a good night's sleep. The medics gave me something to help with that."

Sean left in his pickup and drove to Steve's house. The couple had only been married a few months. They had recently bought a little two-bedroom home in Goodyear. Steve had told Sean he was saving money, and they planned to start a family soon. Mary answered the door and looked at Sean standing there with his hat in his hand. She burst into tears and fell into his arms; he let her cry. Finally, she raised her head and said, "What happened?"

They sat on the living room couch, and Sean recounted the whole story. When he finished, he said, "I'm so sorry, Mary. There was nothing more I could do."

"I know you did all you could, Sean. Thank you for coming to tell me."

"Do you have someone you can be with tonight?"

"I'll call my mother. She lives close by."

They stood, and Sean held her again for a minute. "Call me if there's anything I can do for you. Anything."

She gave a tearful nod, and Sean left to go home. He thought it was the most painful thing he'd ever done. His dog Sarge was waiting for him, wagging his tail and excited for him to be home. It was the only bright spot in his day. The dog seemed to sense Sean was in pain and stayed close to him as they moved through the house. Sean fed him, put fresh water in his dish, and said, "I'm beat, Sarge. I'll see you in the morning." He swallowed the two pills the medic gave him and immediately fell into a deep sleep. Sarge finished his dinner, then curled up on the floor beside his master.

Sean was awakened before daylight by a warm tongue sliding down his face. He opened his eyes to see Sarge watching him. He scratched the dog behind his ears and said, "Good boy, Sarge. You're a real good boy!" Sarge's tail beat a rapid rhythm on the bed, and Sean put his arms around the dog's neck and hugged him.

It was one of those damned dreams—the first one Sean had experienced in a couple of months. His thrashing and moaning always alerted the dog, who jumped on the bed to wake his master. In this dream, Sean had been back on the C-47 transport over Normandy on D-day. He jumped out the door and saw Steve Riggs jump out behind him. Sean's parachute opened, but Steve's did not—he sped by Sean, and he watched helplessly as the man hit the ground at a hundred sixty-five miles per hour. In the dream, he could hear the man's screams until he hit the ground. That's when Sarge heard Sean moaning and flailing around. Licking his master's face was the only way the dog knew to help him.

Sean was part of an elite paratrooper team during the Normandy invasion in 1944. He received multiple wounds and suffered a severe concussion during that action. The horrible nightmares about his wartime experiences started after he regained consciousness in a British hospital. The doctors called it battle fatigue and prescribed a medication, but Sean found the effects of the drug to be worse than the nightmares. He decided to endure the dreams rather than move around in a daze caused by the pills.

He figured this dream was a result of the extreme stress of trying to save his friend on the mountain after the rattlesnake bit him. He couldn't get back to sleep, so he got up and made a pot of coffee. It was his day off, and he would get an early start on some of the chores he had been putting off around his house.

CHAPTER 8

Sean was busy at his desk Monday morning writing his report from Saturday's disaster. The man in the fancy suit showed up at precisely nine a.m. and asked if there was somewhere private they could talk. Sean took him into the conference room.

"What can I help you with, Mr. Rossi?"

"I understand you were the first to reach the crash site. What can you tell me about it?"

"Well, sir, I and another deputy, Brad Jones, were sent to investigate. The plane was in bad shape, upside down and crumpled up like an accordion. It looked like they had flown straight into the face of the mountain. We found the two men dead in the cockpit; they probably died instantly. We think the pilot was probably disoriented in a storm because there was severe weather on the day of the crash."

"What did you see inside the plane?"

"The two men were hanging upside down by their seat belts. It looked like every bone in their bodies was broken. Someone had been there before us and gone through their wallets. We found their driver's licenses, but there was no money; we assumed the person had stolen it. There were two duffel bags which had also been gone through."

"Do you have any idea who the other person was?"

"No, sir. To be honest, we haven't had much time to investigate that."

"Would it be possible for me to speak with the other deputy who was with you?"

"Not today, sir. His wife had a baby yesterday, and he's off tending to her."

Rossi nodded, rose from his chair, and said, "Thank you for your time, Deputy. This has been very helpful. I'm sure your department will let us know when you find whoever stole from

48

our men on the plane. He handed Sean a card with only a phone number on it. "Please let me know if you find out who was there before you. The number on the card is for my office in Las Vegas. They'll know how to contact me."

The men stood and shook hands, and Sean watched Rossi leave. The commander had also watched him go and said, "What was that about, Sean?"

"He wanted to know what I saw at the crash site. He's kind of a creepy guy with those fancy duds and all that jewelry. And, oh, he wants us to let him know if we find out who was there before us."

"There's more going on here than we know, Sean. He could have learned what you told him with a phone call. He made that long drive from Las Vegas instead—he's looking for something. Maybe the early visitor found more than a little money in the dead men's wallets."

"I hadn't thought about that, commander. But you could be right. There's a reason he dropped the pickaxe. He must have needed a hand to carry something he found in the wreck while keeping the other hand free to catch himself when he slipped. I need to go back out there to get that pickaxe. I dropped it when the snake bit Steve."

"Brad will be back tomorrow. Take him with you. And both of you, be careful. No more snake bites!"

Sean started back to his desk, and the commander said, "I've got a feeling we haven't heard the last from that Vegas guy, Sean. Be alert—he looks like the kind of man who could cause trouble."

Rossi and his men met up at Joe's Coffee Shop in Goodyear. They took a back booth away from other customers. They all ordered coffee and agreed it was much better than the dishwater the motel restaurant passed off as coffee.

Rossi had cut his teeth working for the Jersey mob. He started as an errand boy and slowly graduated to collecting protection money from local businesses. His reputation grew as a man who didn't accept excuses, and the shop owners grew to fear him more than the others who came to pick up payments. He had severely beaten a couple of owners who claimed they had no money; one of them nearly died in the hospital. No one was ever short on their payments after that.

He gradually worked his way into the bosses' inner circle. They tested his loyalty by sending him on his first assassination job. It involved one of the organization's lieutenants who had been skimming money off their drug racket. "Make it ugly, Jimmy," the boss had said. "I want to send a message to anybody else that thinks they can steal from us."

Jimmy found the man eating lunch in an Italian restaurant. He walked up to the man without saying a word, pulled his Smith and Wesson .38 Police special, and fired all six rounds into the mobster. The last two rounds were headshots. It was certainly ugly…blood was splattered on the wall behind the man, and he had fallen forward with his face in a plate of spaghetti. Blood and brain matter oozed onto the plate, comingling with the red spaghetti sauce.

After that initiation, Rossi became one of the mob's main enforcers. He was a deadly and efficient killer and utterly loyal to his bosses. They sent him to Las Vegas when they got into the casino business. His job was to take care of any significant problems that surfaced and to ensure his work left no connection to the casino. He proved himself to be very good at his job.

"I smell a lie," Rossi told his men. "It seems too convenient that some mysterious person was there before those two deputies and robbed the two dead men. I think maybe the deputies found the bonds and cooked up a story to deflect any attention from themselves. I bet one of them has them stashed under their bed right now."

The men all nodded in silent agreement. "What's next, boss?" one of them asked.

"We need to find out where they live and search their houses. Should be easy while they're working. We can start with Deputy O'Conner. Lorenzo, you saw me talking to him this morning, and you know what the guy looks like. I want you and Lefty to watch for him when he gets off work this evening and follow him to find out where he lives. Then take Frankie and the three of you go in there tomorrow morning when he leaves and toss the place from one end to the other. I'm bettin' our boy's got those bonds stashed somewhere inside."

Early the following day, Lorenzo and the other two men were parked down the street from Sean's house, watching for him to leave. They waited half an hour after he was gone, and Lorenzo pulled the black Chevy sedan up in Sean's driveway. He got out and nonchalantly walked up to the door, looked around, didn't see anyone watching, and put his shoulder into the door. The old lock gave way easily. He motioned the others to follow and stepped inside.

Sarge had been in the backyard and heard the commotion at the door. He went through his back door access and charged through the house, barking. Lorenzo looked up just as the big dog hit him and bit into his left thigh. He hit Sarge in the head with his fist; the dog turned loose of the leg and immediately went for the other one. Lorenzo pulled his .22 revolver from its holster and fired two rounds into the dog's head. Sarge collapsed by the door.

The other men pushed through the door and stepped over the dead dog. Lefty looked at Lorenzo and said, "Holy shit! You're bleedin' to beat hell on your left leg. Better get somethin' on it!"

"Yeah, yeah. You guys get busy tossin' the joint while I find somethin' to put on my leg. And hurry up—I expect the neighbors might be callin' the cops about now. We need to be out of here in ten minutes or less. Jump!"

Lorenzo tracked blood from the front door across the living room, leaving a trail from Sarge's body. He found a towel in the bathroom and tied it around his leg to stop the bleeding.

51

The men started with the two bedrooms, pulled off the bedding, checked the mattresses, and looked under the beds. Then they pulled everything out of the dresser drawers and checked behind the furniture. Two men went through the kitchen cabinets and scattered pots, pans, and dishes, heedless of breaking Sean's mother's prized China. Lorenzo and Lefty checked the living room, looked under all the cushions, and felt for anything hidden inside the couch or chair. The last place they looked was the garage. They pulled everything off the shelves, grabbed a step ladder, and looked in the attic—they came up empty-handed.

A siren's wail in the distance was coming toward them. They made a quick exit from the house, jumped in their car, and squealed tires when they hit the street.

They were long gone when a sheriff's deputy arrived. He saw the door standing open, drew his service revolver, and cautiously stepped inside. Sarge lay in a puddle of blood around his head, and the deputy stepped around his body. He went through the house, checking each room. There was no sign of the burglars. The place was a mess, with broken dishes, furniture cushions, bedding, and clothes scattered around.

A woman who lived across the street stuck her head in the door and called, "Hello?" The deputy came out of the bedroom, and the woman said, "I'm the one who called, deputy. I know Sean, and those men didn't look like any of his friends. There were three of them." Then she saw Sarge and gave a little squeaking cry. "Oh, my. Sean loved that dog more than anything!"

The deputy thanked her for calling and asked her to wait outside. He picked up Sean's phone in the living room and called the district commander. The deputy said, "Sean's house is a huge mess, sir. Somebody was looking for something and turned everything inside out. And they shot his dog, too.

"Stay there," the commander said, "And don't touch anything. I'll get a crime scene crew out to evaluate it. Keep the neighbors out; don't answer any questions. I'll be there shortly."

The commander tried to contact Sean on the radio but couldn't reach him. He and Brad had left early that morning to retrieve the pickaxe where Sean had dropped it on the mountain to tend to Steve's snakebites. Radio reception was frustratingly spotty in the far reaches of the district. He instructed Gloria, the district clerk, to keep trying to reach him. Then he left for Sean's house.

It was mid-afternoon when Sean got to his house. He was shocked when he looked around. He sat down on a living room chair and stared at Sarge's body still lying just inside the door. His shock evolved into anger.

The commander had stayed with the crime scene crew, waiting for Sean to return. "Sean, this looks like the work of that Las Vegas guy. He must have a crew that he used to toss your house. The crime scene guys are finding plenty of prints—we'll find the bastards that did this."

Sean nodded and said, "I can replace everything but Sarge. He was my best friend. He sat and shook his head and continued, "He even saved my life when the Weighmaster's crew tried to kill me. I'd be dead if it weren't for him."

"I understand, Sean. Take whatever time you need to clean up here and care for Sarge."

Sean jumped to his feet and said, "Brad! Commander, they know Brad was there with me on that first visit. We need to warn him right now!"

"You're right, Sean." The commander picked up the phone and called the district office. Brad was still there, writing their day's report. He explained what was happening and said, "Brad, you need to get home right now and check on your family. You could all be in danger. Can your wife and children stay somewhere until this is over?"

"Yes, sir. My wife's family is nearby. I'll move them there as soon as I can get home!"

"Call me when you get there and let me know if they're okay."

"Yes, sir, I will."

"One more thing, Brad. I'll arrange to have a deputy watch your house as long as necessary. We'll find the people responsible for this."

✤

Sean's friend Ricky Martinez came to help put the house back together. He found Sean in the backyard, finishing the burial of his dog.

"I'm so sorry, amigo. Sarge was a great dog."

"Yeah, he was, Ricky. I'll never be able to replace him. Come inside, and let's drink a beer to toast his life."

Sean had gotten Sarge as a pup, and his family had taken care of the dog when Sean went into the Army. When he returned, the bond with the big lab was as strong as ever. He stayed close to Sean when he was home, sleeping beside his bed. The dog was highly protective of him and had saved him from being killed when a hitman broke into the house a few months earlier.

The friends sat in silence in the living room, sipping their beers.

"I'll find who did this, Ricky. And, when I do, I'll make them pay."

"I hope you can, amigo. Can I help you clean up this mess in the meantime?"

"Yeah, thanks, Ricky. I still have to live here. I appreciate you coming."

"No problema. I'm happy to help."

The men set to work. It took them until midnight, including a couple more beer breaks. Sean finally got to bed, but he wasn't able to sleep. His mind kept churning over what was going on. It occurred to him that the lock on his front door was broken. What if whoever trashed his house came back? There was nothing here for them to find, but they may try to beat information out of him if they think he took whatever they were looking for. He no longer had Sarge to warn him. He got up, went into the kitchen, rummaged in his trash can, and found their empty beer cans from earlier that night. Then he took a kitchen chair into the living room, sat it in front of the door, and arranged the six cans along the edges of the chair's seat. That ought to make enough commotion to wake me if someone opens the door, he said to himself.

He wouldn't be able to rest until he found out who had trashed his house and brought them to justice. Then, he drifted off into an uneasy sleep.

❧

Rossi told his men to return to Deputy O'Conner's house that night. His orders were to squeeze the deputy until he admitted to taking the bonds. He said, "That deputy and his partner are bound to have the bonds. I don't give a rat's ass what you do or how you do it. But don't come back without the bonds or information on where they are."

The three men stood up. Lorenzo was limping a little from the dog bite on his thigh. He had gone to a local emergency room when they left the deputy's house that morning and got some stitches and a bandage. He figured an opportunity would come up tonight for him to thank the deputy for his damn dog.

They parked the Chevy a block away from Sean's house and walked back to it, keeping in shadows where they could. It was two o'clock in the morning, and no lights were visible from the neighbors' houses. There were no sounds except Frankie's heavy breathing. He weighed about three hundred pounds, and his main exercise was shoveling more food into his mouth.

Lorenzo stood at the front door, listening. The house was dark, and there were no sounds inside. He motioned for the men to be ready. They knew the layout of the house and planned to rush into Sean's bedroom and grab him before he could resist. Lorenzo raised three fingers and started a countdown, dropping one finger at a time. He hit the door on three.

There was a terrific clatter as the chair fell over, and beer cans hit the linoleum floor and rolled around. Sean wasn't fully asleep. He bolted out of bed, grabbed his model 1911 Colt .45 automatic off the nightstand, and stood inside his bedroom door. He heard loud, whispered curses and more cans rolling around in the living room. He stole down the short hall, reached around the wall, and hit the light switch.

It would have been funny under other circumstances. Three men were on the floor— in their rush through the door, two were tangled up with the chair and each other, and the third was getting on his feet. The man grabbed his pistol from its shoulder holster, but Sean shot him twice before he could bring his weapon to bear. The man got off one shot that went wild; the bullet lodged in the living room wall. The heavy .45 slugs from Sean's pistol tore through the intruder's chest and all but obliterated his heart. He was dead before he hit the floor.

Lefty was reaching for his weapon, and Sean said, "Don't." His voice was quiet and icy calm as it cut through the stillness in the room. The man had frozen in place, his hand near the inside of his jacket. "I will kill you if you so much as twitch," Sean continued. "Move your hand slowly down to your side." Lefty did as he was told.

Frankie stumbled to his feet and found himself looking down the big bore of Sean's .45. He pointed the pistol at Lefty and said, "You first. Slowly take out your weapon using two fingers and toss it over here by me." He did as he was told, and then Sean pointed at Frankie and said, "Now you. Two fingers, nice and slow." The man growled but tossed out his revolver.

"Now, both of you, right here on the floor in front of me, hands behind your back. I swear I'll shoot you if you move." The men did as they were told, and Sean noticed for the first time that blood was seeping through the pant leg of the man he shot. He nudged Lefty with his bare foot and said, "You're the bunch who were here this morning, aren't you." The man said nothing, and Sean continued, "And I suppose this guy with the bloody leg is the one who bled all over my house after my dog bit him." Both men on the floor shifted slightly. "Well, he got what he deserves. Son of a bitch killed my best friend. I only wish I could have had a few minutes alone with him."

Sean backed over to his couch, keeping his gun trained on his two prisoners. He picked up the phone, cradled the receiver to his ear with his left shoulder, and then dialed the sheriff's central dispatch with his left hand. He told them what had happened and to send a couple of deputies and an ambulance. He already heard a siren in the distance. It would be whoever was on shift from the district office that night. The wait wouldn't be long.

Sean flashed back to the night a few months ago during the Weighmaster investigation when the Detroit mob's hit men had tried to kill him in his house. Sarge had attacked the shooter as he stood in the front doorway and caused him to stumble backward into the front yard. The man already had a pistol drawn, but Sean shot him before he could aim. The man's pistol discharged at the same time and sent a bullet into the woodwork around the door. His accomplice was waiting in their getaway car and took off before Sean could identify the vehicle or license plate.

This night was like déjà vu for Sean: Cop cars and an ambulance parked in the street and in his front yard, their lights flashing; half-dressed neighbors milling around with a constant babble of voices; a dead man being carried to the ambulance on a stretcher; the crime scene crew working in his house; and two detectives with the district commander asking him questions. The two men Sean had disarmed had been handcuffed and locked in the back of separate patrol cars.

The commander said, "My god, Sean! Twice in the same year. Most deputies work an entire career and never shoot a man."

"I hope it's the last time for me, sir. My neighbors do, too. This kind of stuff doesn't make me too popular around here."

"I'm glad you're safe, son. Pretty clever door alarm you arranged. I always knew empty Coors cans must be good for something."

Sean and both detectives chuckled. Detective Johnson said, "We'll interview these two mutts tonight. Try to find out who sent them before they lawyer up."

"I have a pretty good idea who sent them. That guy Rossi who interviewed me — this is his doing," Sean said. He explained his suspicions to the detectives while they made notes.

The commander agreed with Sean's assessment. "Try to get some shut-eye, Sean. Come in late if you need to. It will be a busy day tomorrow."

"Not much chance of sleep, sir. I will see you in a few hours."

The scene was wrapping up, the ambulance and the patrol cars left, and the crime scene crew was packing their gear. They had done Sean the favor of cleaning up the blood on his floor. He was again left with the task of comforting his neighbors and explaining what had happened in their quiet neighborhood. He could tell some weren't thrilled to have him living there. He went into his house, brewed a pot of coffee, and sat sipping it until dawn. A shower helped wash away the stress of the night. Then he dressed and headed for the district office.

CHAPTER 9

The sheriff's department's crime lab had found some clear fingerprints on the head of the pickaxe. Their technicians combed through their print collection, looking for a local match. They would find them if the person had ever been printed in the county.

In the meantime, detectives Johnson and Harper were contacting local motels and hotels looking for a guest registered under the name Rossi. They doubted the man would have used his real name, but they had to check. The clerk at the district office had seen Rossi leave in a late-model black Cadillac after he visited with Sean. The detectives added that to the description they were using. It was slow work, but they were making progress. The two men Sean had captured the night before refused to answer any questions about Rossi or anything else until they saw a lawyer.

Sean went back to the town of Buckeye to see if he could get a lead on someone who had a truck with oversized tires. He had a couple of ideas of who might have such a rig, and his questioning of the managers in the local gas stations confirmed his suspicions. They all said the same thing—the only rig in town like that belonged to Harley Henderson.

He knew where the Henderson brothers' shop was and paid it a visit. He found Harry, Harley's twin brother, busy welding something onto a tractor. He raised his welder's helmet when Sean spoke to him and squinted to focus his eyes on the light. He said, "Hello, Sean. I haven't seen you in a while. How ya doin'?"

"I'm okay, Harry, thanks for asking. I'm looking for Harley. Is he around?"

Harry's face wrinkled up in suspicion. Harley had warned him never to tell the cops or anyone from the government anything if they came looking for him. "What ya need Harley for? He do somethin' wrong?"

"I just need to talk to him. Can you tell me where I can find him?"

"Well, he don't usually tell me where he's goin'. He shows up when he shows up. I reckon he's out huntin' somewhere. 'Bout all he does instead of helpin' me with the shop. Hell, his name's on the place, too. You'd think he'd help out more."

"Do you know where he might be hunting?"

"Aw, hell. Could be anywheres. You know how he is—he'd rather be out in the desert than hangin' around here."

"Okay. Thanks, Harry." He gave Harry one of his cards. "Ask him to call me when he shows up."

"Sure thing, Sean. See ya."

Sean figured Harry was covering for his brother. He was all but certain it was Harley up at the wreck. But he couldn't prove it without some solid evidence. Maybe, he thought, the lab would find his prints on that pickaxe.

🌵

Rossi was drinking coffee in his motel room, wondering where his guys were. Their car was not in the motel's parking lot, and no one answered the phone in either of the two rooms they were staying in. Then, he got a call from the boss in Vegas. "Hey, Jimmy," Mr. Bianco said. "I just got a call from Frankie—one of your guys. He said him and Lefty are in the county lockup down there, and Lorenzo is dead! What the hell's goin' on?"

Rossi nearly dropped the phone. "I don't know, Mr. Bianco. I sent those guys out last night to shake down the deputy we think has the bonds. I just found out they didn't come back last night."

"You don't know…you don't know! What the hell kinda operation you runnin' down there, Rossi? This was supposed to be a clean and simple operation to find those bonds. All you got to show for it is a dead man and the rest of your crew in jail. I'll have our people call a lawyer to get them out of jail and put 'em on a plane back east."

There was an ominous silence on the phone. Then Bianco said, "I thought you was better than this, Rossi. You got one chance to get this right!" The phone went dead.

Rossi was stunned. How the hell had this happened, he wondered. My men were damn good—how'd they get taken down by some hick sheriff's deputy? He picked up the phone and dialed a number in New Jersey.

❧

The commander got a call from the lab late that afternoon. They had found a match for Harley's prints on the pickaxe. He had been arrested a few years earlier and booked for assault with a deadly weapon. It was the first good news they had gotten since the whole mess started. He called Sean and Brad into his office.

"That pickaxe wasn't worth a life— but it's helped us get closer to closing this case. There were prints on it, which belonged to a guy named Harley Henderson, last known address in Buckeye. He'd been booked on an assault charge a few years ago."

Sean exhaled and said, "Damn. I was just at his place earlier today. I suspected it might be him because of the oversized tire tracks. But he was nowhere around, and his brother wouldn't tell me where he was— if he knew."

"That's unfortunate, Sean. His brother may tell him you were there, and he'll go into hiding."

"That's possible, sir. I knew this guy when I lived in Buckeye. He's a little older than me; he graduated from high school two years ahead of me. He was always a loner, always in trouble for fighting and ditching school. He spent all his time hunting and fooling around in the desert. I heard once that he was poaching game, but I don't think he was ever caught. He's probably got a camp somewhere he uses to hunt. That's likely where he would go if he learns we're looking for him."

61

The men were quiet while they considered this. Brad said, "Sean, remember that bighorn sheep that was watching us by the wreck on the mountain?"

Sean nodded, and he continued, "There's lots of those sheep in those mountains. I've heard people will pay big money for a trophy bighorn's head. Maybe he hunts them and sells the heads."

"We should check with the game warden to see if he might know anything about that. He might know where Harley's camp is, too," Sean replied. "Harley's apparently got a big truck that might allow him to go about anywhere. We need to narrow down the possibilities."

The commander said, "This is a priority for both of you. I want you to stay on this until you find him."

They broke up, and Brad tried to get hold of the game warden. He was out, and they would have to wait until the following day to reach him.

Sean said, "Let's head for Buckeye early tomorrow morning. We should take two cars in case we need to split up. Maybe we can find out where he lives, too. He's bound to have someplace he sleeps when he's not hunting."

"Sounds like a plan. What time do you want to go?"

"How about 6:30. We might accidentally catch him if he's around."

🌵

Harley spent the night with Ruby Reynolds at her place north of town, a small two-bedroom house she rented from a farmer. She made her living waiting tables at the diner in town and occasionally filling in at the Alibi Lounge when they were short a waitress. She was a little chubby, but Harley thought her soft curves made her a real dish. The whiskey gravel in her voice made her even sexier, in Harley's opinion. Her peroxide blonde hair set off her striking blue eyes and red lipstick. She painted her fingernails a bright shade of red to match the lipstick; the nails looked like drops of blood on her fingertips when she laid her hand on her white tablecloth.

She and Harley had been an on-again, off-again couple for three years. She put up with his frequent disappearances and looked forward to his return but made him bathe as soon as he entered her house. He always complained but did as she asked—she was worth the trouble.

Harry called Ruby's house earlier that night. He figured Harley would be there unless he were off in the desert somewhere. Ruby gave the phone to Harley. "What is it?" he growled. "Couldn't it wait til tomorrow?"

"There was a cop at the shop today looking for you. You in some kinda trouble?"

"Naw. What kinda cop was he?"

"Deputy sheriff. You remember him— Sean O'Conner. We went to school with him. He gave me his card."

Harley was quiet for a minute while he thought about what this could mean. Could they somehow have figured out he was at that wreck? He didn't see how. He couldn't think of any other reason they wanted to talk to him. He said, "If he comes back, tell him you ain't seen me and don't know when I'll be back."

"What'd you do, Harley? You gonna get both of us in trouble?"

"Don't worry about it. I'm gonna stop at the shop first thing in the mornin' to grab a few things. Then I'll disappear for a few days. Whatever this is will blow over."

He hung up and pulled Ruby up close. "I'm gonna have to bug out for a while. But I don't wanna waste that bath you made me take. Let's make this night worthwhile!"

CHAPTER 10

ean and Brad arrived at the brother's machine shop about seven a.m. Harley's truck was backed up to the open door. Sean pulled in front of it to block its exit and motioned Brad to go around the back of the shop. Sean got out, drew his sidearm, and cautiously approached the open door. He looked around the edge of the door and saw Harley running for the back door. He yelled, "Stop, Harley! You're under arrest!"

Harley reached the back door and flung it open only to find another deputy there with his pistol drawn and pointed at his chest. Brad said, "Put your hands up and stay right there!" Harley was like a caged animal, nervously looking around for a way to escape.

Sean came up behind him and said, "Take it easy, Harley. We don't want to have to shoot you. Put your hands behind your back."

Harley growled, "I don't know what this is about, Sean. But I'll get even with you."

"I'll only say this one more time, Harley," Sean replied. "Put your hands behind your back!"

Harley finally complied, and Sean put his handcuffs on. The man's wrists were so big the cuffs barely closed around them.

"What the hell's this about, Sean? What's goin' on?"

"You are under arrest for theft from the airplane that crashed on Woolsey Peak."

"What? I don't know nothin' bout no airplane crash!"

"Save it, Harley. We found your fingerprints on the pickaxe you dropped when you left the scene. You can explain it all to the detectives at the county jail."

Harley started cursing both men. He shook off Brad's arm as they were taking him to his cruiser.

Sean said, "Settle down, Harley. We don't want to hurt you, but if you try to run, we will shoot you." He shut up, and Brad put him into the back of the patrol car.

"Whew, Sean! I thought there for a minute we'd have to wrestle that bear into the car. I'll be glad to get him to the lock-up!"

Harley's big, heavily muscled frame and scruffy beard gave him a very menacing look.

"Yep, he's a big one, all right. And tough as they come. The guy would pick a fight with the sky if he didn't like its color! I heard the Army classified him as 4-F because he attacked one of the doctors who examined him for the draft. Kept him out of the war. I'll follow you into town and help get him into the jail."

The men headed for the county jail in Phoenix. Harley sat in the backseat of Brad's cruiser, seething like a volcano on the verge of eruption.

🌵

Rossi gathered his things and checked out of the motel. He didn't bother with whatever his men had left in the other two rooms. The motel could deal with it. He drove to a different motel a mile away and booked two rooms under a different name. The second room would be for the reinforcements he expected to arrive by plane early in the morning. He called Bianco's secretary at the casino, told her he had changed locations, and gave her the new telephone number. "I checked in using another alias," he said. "Tell the boss to ask for Mr. Martin. I'm in room one fifteen."

The redeye flight his two new assistants were booked on was scheduled to land at seven thirty the next day. He drove to Sky Harbor Airport in Phoenix and met the men in the lobby. They came through the gate carrying mid-sized suitcases. He had told them to bring suitable clothes for the desert.

One of the men said, "Hello, Mr. Rossi. Long time, no see!"

The two men shook hands, and Rossi said, "Hello, Angelo. It's good to have you here." Then he turned to the next man, shook his hand, and said, "Marco! It's great to see you again! Grab your

65

stuff, and let's get out of here." The three men chatted and laughed about old times. They had come up together in the organization, and Rossi trusted each of them with his life. The men were highly skilled and efficient killers, exactly what Rossi thought he needed. This Arizona thing was about to get messy.

They rented a Chevrolet sedan for the men at the Hertz rental car desk and Rossi had them follow him back to the motel. He got a call from the boss while the men got settled in the motel room. Bianco got right to the point. "Our banker guy did some checkin' around Phoenix, checkin' to see if anybody had cashed any bearer bonds lately. Got a hit with one of 'em—turns out some second-rate lawyer brought in four of 'em recently. The description fits, too. The lawyer's name is Michael Fishburn the Third. Sounds pretty fancy for an ambulance chaser."

"I'll find him today, boss. Find out what he knows. I think those sheriff's deputies were a dead end, anyway. This sounds like the break we need."

"Keep me informed, Rossi...and don't screw this up." The line went dead.

He found Fishburn's information in the phone book, called and made an appointment that afternoon, then rounded up his men. "We got a lead on an attorney that cashed some of our bonds. I'm going to see him this afternoon."

They parked in front of the office in a shabby strip mall. Rossi said, "Angelo, I want you to come into the office with me. Marco cover the back of the building in case he tries to duck out."

Rossi and Angelo walked into the lawyer's office at 2 p.m. sharp. Shirley, the secretary, took one look at the men and sensed trouble. She said, "Can I help you?"

Rossi said, "Just stay put, Missy. Angelo here will keep you company while I have a friendly chat with your boss. He's expecting me." Angelo looked at her with a smile that made her blood run cold. All the color drained from her face, and she busied herself with some typing to keep from looking at the man.

66

Rossi walked in Fishburn's private office unannounced, took a look around, and introduced himself. Then he sat down and studied the attorney.

Fishburn fidgeted in his chair and said, "What can I do for you, Mr. Rossi?"

"I wanna talk to you about some bearer bonds, Mr. Fishburn."

"Certainly, sir. I can help you with your bonds."

"Well, you see, Mr. Fishburn, what I wanna know is who brought you the bonds you recently cashed."

"Oh, I can't divulge information about my clients, sir. I'll have to ask you to leave."

Rossi shifted slightly so that his jacket moved to the side, revealing the revolver in its holster under his shoulder. The lawyer's eyes went wide, and he started stammering. "P P Please sir. I really can't..." Rossi cut him off with a wave of his hand.

"Here's how this will go, lawyer-man. I'm pressed for time to find out who had those bonds. They belonged to my employer. He is not a patient man, and neither am I. You can give me the name and where to find this person right now, or I will escort you from this office to a more private location. My men will encourage you to cooperate in the strongest terms. Maybe we'll bring your secretary along to watch, too. And you will cooperate, Mr. Fishburn... the Third."

Fishburn was visibly shaking and looking around the room for a chance to run. "I have a man at your back door and a man out front. You won't get far. So, what's it gonna be? The easy way, or..." Rossi's voice trailed off and left the other option unspoken.

"Alright, alright. You don't have to get ugly about it." He opened a file drawer in his desk and started to reach in.

"Easy." Rossi's hand was on his pistol.

Fishburn slowly brought out a file folder. He copied Harley's name and address and handed the paper to Rossi. He said, "I understand you cashed four of our bonds for this man. Did he say anything about having more of them?"

"N No, sir. I believe they were all he had."

"Alright. I'll pay you another visit if I find out you gave me bad information." He stared at him for a few seconds and said, "It won't be so friendly."

He stood up and walked out, leaving the attorney sitting behind his desk. Fishburn sat there for several minutes until he quit shaking. He went out and told his secretary to cancel his later appointments.

"Who were those men, Mr. Fishburn?"

He ignored her, returned to his office, and slammed the door.

Rossi gathered his men and told them they had a lead on the bonds, and they would head out early in the morning for the town of Buckeye.

✦

Harley was grilled relentlessly by two detectives at the county jail. He lost his temper a couple of times because they kept asking the same questions in a slightly different way. He jumped up once and nearly overturned the table he was handcuffed to. He shouted, "You guys ain't got shit on me. I want my lawyer. I'm done talkin' to you!"

Detective Johnson said, "Take it easy, Harley. We know you were at that crash site because you dropped a pickaxe beside it, which had your fingerprints on it. We know someone had gone through the two dead men's wallets before our deputies got there and riffled through their luggage. And we know there was something else very valuable on the plane with them, which you took."

"Yeah, yeah. So you keep sayin'. So, I was there. I didn't take anything. I ain't no thief. Somebody else musta been there after me. You ain't got no evidence, so you ain't got shit. I got nothin' else to say. I want my lawyer."

The detectives finally turned him over to the jailer and told him to let him have his phone call. Harley had to look up the number in the well-thumbed and filthy phone book chained to the wall by the phone. He called Fishburn and explained the situation.

Fishburn told him to sit tight and that he would be there as soon as he could.

Fishburn got him out a couple of hours later. It wasn't difficult—the cops had no solid evidence that he had committed a crime. When they were in the lawyer's car, he said, "What the hell have you gotten me into, Harley? Some mafia-type gangster was in my office this afternoon looking for information about those bonds. Somehow, they found out I had cashed them."

"What'd you tell them?"

"I had to tell them who you were! They said they would come back and kill me if I gave them the wrong information!"

"What? What the hell, Fishburn! Where's your spine? I thought lawyers was supposed to keep stuff secret. I oughta wring your scrawny neck right now! "

Fishburn said nothing, and the men rode in silence for a few miles. Then Harley said, "There was a million dollars worth of them bonds I found in a plane that crashed past Buckeye. You probably heard about it. I figured someone would come lookin' for 'em sooner or later. There was two dead guys on the plane with Las Vegas addresses on their driver's licenses. That oughta tell you somethin'— We're in this together, now."

"A million dollars? Good lord! Why didn't you tell me sooner? I could have helped you find a better way to deal with it."

"Yeah, I'll bet. But look—you're in the shit with me now. Those guys who came to see you ain't the kind to leave loose ends. They'll kill us both if they get their hands on those bonds. So, you better start thinkin' of ways to help me with this."

"I...I don't know what I can do."

"You're a lawyer. Figure it out. Do it right, and I'll make it worth your while. Now take me back to Buckeye so I can get my truck and deal with this mess you got me into."

It was dark when they got to the town, and Harley directed him to the machine shop.

"Shine your headlights on the front door so I can unlock it." He didn't have his keys—the cops didn't let him grab them before they hauled him away. The brothers kept a spare key for the door's padlock under an old, rusted-out gas can on the side of the building. He got the door open and smiled to himself. Harry had pulled the Beast inside when Harley hadn't come back for it. His keys were still in it.

He returned to Fishburn's car and said, "Okay, I'm good. I'm gonna lay low for a few days. I'll call you when I can. In the meantime, you better come up with a plan to save both our asses."

The lawyer watched him walk inside to his truck. He shook his head, wondering where this was going to go. A million dollars! Unbelievable! Then he headed back to Phoenix.

Harley found his brother at the house they shared. "Thanks for putting the Beast away," Harley said.

"What happened? Did the cops catch up with you?"

"Yeah, but they didn't have nothin' on me, and my lawyer got me out of jail."

"What are you into? What's goin' on."

"You're better off not knowin'. But I'll tell you this—if we play our cards right, there's gonna be good money in it for you. Just keep your head down, and don't tell nobody nothin'. There's likely gonna be some guys nosin' around askin' questions. Just play dumb; you don't know where I'm at or when I'll be back. I'm gonna bug out for a while. I'll check with you when I can."

Harry tried to get him to tell him more about what was going on. But Harley told him he couldn't tell him anymore yet. "It's for your own good, Harry. Just do like I told you, and everthin' will be fine. I'll see you in a few days." He left to pay a visit to Ruby and spend the night.

CHAPTER 11

Sean shook off another nightmare. He turned on his bedside lamp, and the clock showed four a.m. This dream was another one of many which involved his fiancé, Annaleigh, who had been killed a few months earlier by a car bomb meant for him. He was back in Normandy on D-day, racing through enemy fire to try and rescue Annaleigh, who was sheltering behind a disabled truck. He was almost there when a German mortar round hit the truck, and it exploded in flames. He could hear Annaleigh's screams, but when he reached her, she was lying on the ground, consumed in flames from the truck's gasoline tank when it ignited. It was a gruesome scene, and it kept repeating over and over until he awoke in a cold sweat.

He sat up to clear his head. He missed his dog, Sarge—the dog would have awakened him from the dream as soon as he started thrashing around. Instead, he endured the repeating nightmare more times than he could remember. He went into the kitchen and made a pot of coffee, then sat at the kitchen table thinking about the day to come.

This day, too, was going to be another déjà vu experience. The funeral for his friend Steve Riggs was to be that afternoon. It seemed like only yesterday that Sean had attended funerals for Annaleigh and the district's clerk, who had both been killed by the bomb blast in front of the district office. He carried the weight of responsibility for both women's deaths. He had been targeted by the bomb placed by the Weighmaster's associate; fate intervened, and Annaleigh took his place. Now this. Somehow, he felt responsible for his friend's death. He reminded himself he had done everything he could to save him after the snakebite. But it wasn't enough. Now, he had to console Steve's family and young widow as best he could.

The funeral was held at an Episcopal church in Phoenix. There was a large crowd of mourners, most unknown to Sean. He joined his district commander, Gloria, the clerk, and several other deputies in a pew toward the back of the chapel. The minister led the congregation through the traditional church ceremony, and then Steve's father gave a eulogy to his son. He didn't mention the cause of his death, but he did recognize Sean's role in trying to save his life. It was almost too much for Sean.

The Sheriff's Department employees were the last to offer their condolences to the family. Mary ignored Sean's offered hand, embraced him, and started sobbing again. He waited for her to finish; he didn't know what else to do. Steve's father invited Sean to join them at home for dinner after the service. It made him a little uneasy, but he couldn't refuse the invitation from his friend's father.

Sean was the only representative from the department there. He shook everyone's hands and tried to remember all the names as best he could. After the meal, Mary walked him to the door. She said, "Sean, I can't thank you enough for what you did. All my family feels the same way. Please don't be a stranger." She embraced him again, then watched him walk toward his truck.

CHAPTER 12

Rossi and his men grabbed a quick breakfast at the diner next to the motel the following day. He said, "We'll take both cars so we can split up later. Be ready for anything. If we find our guy, I want you men to tie him, gag him, and throw him in the trunk of your car. Then we'll find a quiet

place to find out where our bonds are."

They headed for Buckeye to find the address the lawyer provided. It turned out to be a machine shop. A beat-up Ford pickup truck was parked in front of the building, and the door was open. They could see a man inside working on some farm tools; the three men got out of their cars and walked inside.

Harry said, "Mornin'. What can I do for you fellas?"

"Are you Harley Henderson?" Rossi asked.

"No sir, I'm his brother Harry. Can I help you with somethin?"

"Where is your brother, Harley?"

"I can't rightly say, sir. He don't tell me where he's goin. He's likely off in the desert huntin' somewheres."

Rossi nodded to his men, and they quickly grabbed Harry by each arm. He said, "Hey! What's goin' on here? Who the hell are you guys?"

Rossi nodded again and said, "Grab his wallet."

"Look! I ain't got much money, but you're welcome to what I got. You don't have to do this!"

"Shut up." Rossi took the wallet and looked at the driver's license. "Well, at least you didn't lie about who you are. Now tell me where your brother is."

Harry struggled against the two men holding him. Like his brother, he was a big man and strong from years of hard work. But the two men holding him were big and muscular, too, and he couldn't break free.

73

Rossi pointed to an ancient oak desk chair sitting by a desk. "Put him there, and we'll have a long talk," he told the men. They found a coil of rope hanging on the wall and tied Harry to the chair.

"Now," Rossi said, "one more time. Where is your brother?"

"I told you I don't know! Let me go!"

Both of Rossi's men had pulled on leather gloves. He nodded to Angelo, and the man hit Harry hard in the jaw.

"Last chance," Rossi said. "We've got all day. This will get a lot worse for you if you don't tell me what I want to know."

Harry spat out a mouthful of blood. "I can't tell you what I don't know!"

Rossi nodded again, and both his men took turns pummeling Harry. They needed to keep him conscious and were careful to direct their blows to instill the most pain without knocking him out. Rossi let it go on for ten minutes, then waved his men off.

"Is your memory any better now?" he asked.

Harry suddenly went rigid, his body straining against the rope, and then he collapsed against his bindings. His head lolled forward.

"What the hell?" Rossi said. "What'd you guys do to him?"

"You saw what we did, boss. He shouldn't be out."

Rossi grabbed Harry's hair and jerked his head up. His eyes had rolled up in his head, and he was completely unresponsive. The man wasn't breathing, and Rossi checked for a pulse and found none. He said, "Shit! The guy's dead! Musta had a heart attack or something. Let's get the hell out of here. I saw a coffee shop on the main drag. Let's meet back there and figure out what to do next."

They left Harry's lifeless body sitting there in the chair. A farmer came in a while later to check on the job Harry was doing for him. He saw him sitting there tied up in a chair and said, "Harry! Harry! What's happened?" He could see the man was dead. He rushed over to the phone on the desk and called the police.

4

Rossi and his men were at the coffee shop when they heard several police cars go by with their sirens wailing. Rossi said, "Sounds like somebody found the body. We're gonna have to move fast now. The cops will be looking for strangers in town."

"What do you want us to do, boss?" Angelo asked.

"Somebody in town knows where that brother is. We're gonna start at one end of the main street here and ask everyone we see if they know where we can find Harley Henderson. Tell them you have something that belongs to him. I'll work one side; you two take the other. Come find me immediately if you learn anything."

Rossi thought that his Cadillac might swing a little weight with these farm town rubes. He pulled into the first gas station he came to. The manager came out, looked the car over, and said, "This is a really nice car. Filler up?"

He struck Rossi as the chatty type and said, "Yes, please. And check the oil, too, if you don't mind."

"Sure thing, mister. Where ya from?"

"I'm from Nevada, just passing through. But I have a couple of cousins here I haven't seen in a long time—the Henderson boys. Wanted to stop and say hello. Do you know them?"

"Oh…I'm sorry, mister. I have terrible news. Harry died just this morning!"

"What? What happened?"

"I don't rightly know the details. I heard someone beat him up pretty bad, and he may have had a heart attack."

"Oh, no! Can you tell me where to find Harley? I couldn't find a phone number for him."

"You bet. He was just here this morning. I can give you his address if you like. He has a charge account here."

"That would be very kind. Thank you."

He went inside and returned shortly with the address written on a scrap of paper. Then he gave him directions on how to get there and said, "That'll be two-fifty for the gas, sir. Your oil looks fine."

Rossi paid for the gas and thanked him again. Then he left to find his men. They didn't need to talk to anyone else.

They found Harley's house and did a slow drive-by. There wasn't a vehicle there, and the curtains were drawn. Rossi said, "We'll come back tonight. I want the element of surprise on our side. We'll go in fast, don't give him time to react. And remember, we need him alive!" They went to a seedy-looking motel at the edge of town and rented a couple of rooms. They met in Rossi's room and went over their plan again. "We'll move after it gets dark. Get a little shut-eye. I'll let you know when it's time to go."

4

The Buckeye police had responded to the farmer's call, but the machine shop was not in the city limits. They called the Maricopa County Sheriff's Office. Sean was on patrol in the area and was the first deputy to respond.

The Buckeye patrolman was still there when he arrived. "Hey, Sean. Good to see you!"

"Hi, Leo. What happened here?"

"Looks like somebody beat Harry Henderson to death. Poor guy. Do you have any idea about what's going on? Who would do something like that?"

Sean walked inside the machine shop and studied the scene. "Leo, I can't say for sure, but this may have something to do with that plane that crashed on Woolsey Peak a few days ago. I arrested Harry's brother Harley yesterday because we found evidence he had been at the crash site, and something was missing. His lawyer got him out yesterday. Some people around have been asking questions about it; my guess is that they may be responsible."

"Wow! Can we help?"

"Keep an ear to the ground for anyone nosing around asking questions about the crash or Harley. They'll still be around if they didn't get what they needed from Harry."

"Will do, and I'll put the word out in our department."

76

Sean got on his radio and requested the department send a crime scene crew and an ambulance to the shop. He tried not to disturb the scene more than it had been and waited for the crew. The editor /reporter of the Buckeye Sun newspaper showed up and started asking questions. He was gawking around Sean and started inside the shop. Sean put a hand on his chest and said, "I'm sorry, sir. This is a crime scene under investigation, and I can't allow you inside."

"Just let me take a picture, and I'll be on my way," the reporter said.

Sean again blocked his way. "I'm sorry, sir. I can't let you inside."

"Aw, c'mon. The Buckeye boys would let me in. I hear Harry Henderson is tied to a chair inside, deader than a doornail."

"Sir, I'm not one of the Buckeye boys, as you call them. I'm a Maricopa County deputy sheriff. I'll have to ask you to wait by your car until we're through here."

The man grudgingly walked back to his car, mumbling about freedom of the press.

Detectives Johnson and Harper showed up an hour and a half later with the crime scene crew and ambulance. "Damn, Sean. There seems to be a lot of stuff going on here for such a sleepy little farm town. What do you know about what happened here?"

Sean explained what he had found at the scene. "The Buckeye policeman didn't know anything about this," Sean said and continued, "My best guess is it's connected to whatever his brother Harley removed from that crashed plane. I'd say that guy Rossi and some of his thugs beat him, and he died. I remember hearing in high school that Harry had a bad heart."

Johnson said, "It's getting ugly, Sean. It sounds like that Vegas bunch is getting desperate to find whatever Harley took from the plane and tried to force this guy to tell them what he knew. It doesn't look like they roughed him up too much by the looks of his face. Could've been a lot worse. As you said, maybe the guy had a heart attack or something. We'll find out from the medical examiner."

The men stood back and watched the crime scene crew work. They wrapped it up at noon. The medical examiner had sent Harry's body to the county morgue and would do an autopsy later that day to determine the cause of death. Sean found Harry's keys on the desk and found one that fit the padlock on the door. They closed and locked the shop, then put crime scene tape around the entire building. The Buckeye Police were checking to see if anyone had seen the men who had beaten Harry. Sean and the detectives went to the district office in Avondale to prepare reports.

✦

Ruby was making a late breakfast for Harley and herself. She had convinced him to sleep in a little before he took off for who knew where. The phone rang as they were sitting down to eat. It was her friend Meg from the diner where they both worked. Ruby's shift didn't start until noon.

Meg said, "Ruby! Have you heard?"

"Heard what, Meg?"

"They found Harry Henderson dead in the shop a little earlier. I heard he'd been tied up and beaten to death. I thought you should know."

Ruby dropped the phone. Harley looked at her and said, "What is it?"

She was speechless for a moment and finally said, "Harry's dead! Meg said they found him tied up in the shop, beaten to death."

Harley dropped his fork and jumped up, nearly knocking the table over. "I've gotta get down there." He reached for his cap and started for the door.

"Wait! You can't go down there! Stop and think. I don't know what kind of trouble you've gotten yourself into, but it sounds

78

like this might be part of it. The police would likely take you in for questioning again!"

Harley stopped and stood silent for a full minute. Finally, he said, "You're right, Ruby. I'd prob'ly make things worse. If Harry's dead, there ain't nothin' I can do for him. I've got an idea who did it. They're lookin' for me, and it sounds like they tried to beat some information out of Harry. His heart couldn't take it— the doctor told him not to strain himself, or he could have another heart attack worse than the first one. A beating was all it would take."

Ruby stepped up and hugged him. "Then you had best leave. I don't want anything to happen to you. And I don't want to know where you go."

"I'll find those bastards, Ruby. Harry didn't deserve that; he didn't do anything." He stormed out of the house, got in the Beast, and roared out of her driveway. She watched him go, shaking her head, wondering what kind of trouble he was in. It must have something to do with that airplane crash on Woolsey Peak.

Harley headed for the Texaco station in town to gas up the Beast and fill his extra gas cans strapped to the side of the truck. The first seed of an idea struck him while he waited —a way he might get back at the scum who killed his brother.

Chester, the station's owner, was the town's biggest gossip. He said, "I heard about your brother, Harley. What an awful thing! Do you know who did it?"

"Naw, Chester. I ain't got any idea. Everybody liked Harry. I don't know who'd wanna hurt him."

"My condolences, Harley. I can't imagine how you feel. That reminds me, Harley. There was a guy here earlier looking for you. He was driving a black Cadillac; said he was from Nevada. I gave him your and your brother's address. I hope that was all right."

"Thanks for lettin' me know, Chester. I'm gonna go to our house and try to sort out our stuff, figger out what to do about a funeral and such. Anybody else asks you, tell 'em they can find me there."

"I'll surely do that, Harley. Again, my condolences. And you take care of yourself!"

A slight smile turned up the corners of his mouth as he drove away. So, the Nevada bunch has found me, he thought. He stopped at the market and picked up some supplies. The almost identical conversation he had with the gas station manager played out again with the store owner. Harley again emphasized where folks could find him. Then he drove back to the house he had shared with his brother since their father died. He started making preparations for the visitors he was sure would come soon.

He figured they would come for him after dark, thinking it would give them an advantage. But he had a different advantage in mind. There was a gnarled old tamarack tree in the front yard. Harley and his brother had played in the huge tree's brittle branches as kids; the old rope swing they made still dangled from one of the thick branches higher up. A rough branch grew off the main trunk at a right angle about five feet off the ground.

He took his lever action Winchester .30-30 rifle from the rack in his truck along with his Smith and Wesson .357 magnum pistol. Extra rounds of ammunition for both firearms went into his pants pockets. Then he stepped off the distance from the house's front door to the tree's trunk. He made it to be roughly seventy-five feet. Twenty-five yards was nothing for a rifleman of Harley's caliber.

The fork of the trunk made a perfect rifle rest, and the massive trunk gave him good cover in case any of his quarry was quick enough to return fire. He spread a tarp on the ground, laid his weapons on it, entered the house, and turned on several lights. Then he went back to his hide, picked up the rifle, and laid its barrel in the notch formed by the right-angle trunk. The .30-30 had an open sight, ideal for a well-lit target under the porch light. He sighted along the barrel for a few seconds. Perfect, he said to himself. Then he settled down on the tarp and waited. He'd wait all night if he had to, and the next night, and the next—until the men who killed his brother showed up.

Rossi and his two men stopped at a burger joint for a quick dinner. The sun was setting; it would be full dark soon. They took their time with the greasy burgers and fries, joking about the old days in Jersey. Rossi was in exceptionally high spirits—his prey would be his soon. Then they could recover the bonds and get out of this god-awful hick town.

The men hung out until it was fully dark, then headed for Harley's house. They used the Chevy rental car; it was less noticeable than Rossi's Caddy. All the men carried pistols in shoulder holsters, but Rossi had warned them not to use them unless they had no choice. But if they did, they were to shoot to disable the man. They had to take him alive.

Rossi drove carefully, obeying the speed limits and traffic signs. Their target was at the far north end of the town, one of a half-dozen nondescript houses on the street. Rossi judged Harley's neighbors were likely the kind to stay in their houses with the curtains closed if they heard any disturbance. All the roads in the neighborhood were gravel. They turned onto Harley's street, killed the car's lights, and crept toward their target. The plan was for Angelo and Marco to break through the door and subdue Harley. Rossi would stay in the car until they grabbed him, then swoop in and they'd shove him in the trunk of their car. It was a short drive out of town to one of the many secluded areas among the farm fields. They could take their time with him there without worrying about a possible snoopy neighbor or someone coming to pay their respects to the bereaved.

Harley heard the crunch of a car's tires on gravel as soon as they neared his house. He couldn't see any headlights on the car, a sure sign his pursuers were headed for his ambush. He stood up and placed his rifle in a comfortable position in the notch of the tree.

The car stopped just short of his driveway. The Beast was clearly visible from the street, part of the carefully arranged bait. It was backed into the driveway. Harley saw two men get out of the car in the dim glow from his porch light. A driver stayed in the car. The two men were both big guys. Easy targets, Harley thought.

Angelo and Marco reached the front step and poised themselves to break through the door. Harley sighted on Angelo's head—he had a weird image of shooting pumpkins as a kid. Angelo's head was perfectly framed in front of the porch light. It exploded in a spray of blood almost instantly after Harley pulled the trigger. He jacked in another round as the second man turned toward the sound of the shot. Harley shot him through the heart and quickly reloaded and fired a second time into his chest to be sure. Then he swiveled the rifle's barrel toward the car on the street just as the driver hit the gas and took off in a shower of gravel. He got off one shot, but it was short of the driver's window, and the car sped off into the night. He cursed himself for not taking out the driver first, but he had been too intent on the men standing on his front porch.

He had to be quick now before the neighbors or the cops showed up. He opened the Beast's tailgate, raised the camper shell's hatch, and lifted each man onto the tarp he had spread on the truck's bed. They were each well over two hundred pounds, but Harley was too adrenaline-charged to notice the weight. Then he closed the tailgate and hatch. Next, he turned on the garden hose by the step and washed off as much blood and gore as he could see just as his next-door neighbor showed up.

"You okay, Harley?" he shouted. "I heard gunshots. What's goin' on?"

"I don't know, Ed. I was standing here rinsin' out the bed of my truck, heard a car comin' down the street, and next thing I know, there's gunshots, and I hit the deck. Don't know if they were shootin' at me or what. May have just been some damn kids out raisin' hell for fun."

"Well, I hope nobody got shot inside their house! I'm callin' the cops!"

"Good idea, Ed. Might want to stay inside til they get here."

Harley hurriedly finished rinsing away any blood he could see, turned off the lights in his house, got in the Beast, and headed out of town. He drove about ten miles to a desert track that went out past the White Tank Mountains north of the town. It was only accessible by a four-wheel drive vehicle and had virtually no use; he had used it a few times scouting for game. He went slowly in the dark, the track barely discernible in his headlights. This was no time to end up nose down in a wash. He stopped and got out a couple of miles from the main road. He recognized the spot he wanted by a big ironwood tree with branches overhanging the track. Good a place as any, he said to himself. He carried each of the bodies about thirty yards away from the track to a small desert wash, then dumped them unceremoniously into its bottom. He figured buzzards would find them early in the morning, and then the coyotes and maybe a mountain lion would come along for the party. There wouldn't be much left but their clothes in two or three days. He went another quarter mile, dumped the bloody tarp from his truck bed in some brush, and turned the truck around—he didn't want to leave any tracks near the dump site, just in case. Then he headed back to town to look around. Maybe he could spot a car with the glass shot out of the rear door. That guy Rossi must have been driving the car, he thought—so this ain't over!

All the houses were dark by the time the police cruised by Harley's neighborhood. This part of town was not within the incorporated city limits, and the town's police only responded as a courtesy. Nobody was hurt, and the officer wrote it off to kids having too much fun. It was a pretty common thing, especially if there had been a beer party nearby—no reason to notify the sheriff's department.

Rossi had driven quickly back to the motel and dumped the rental car in its parking lot. The shooter's bullet had shattered the window in the back door behind him, then exited through the windshield. It left a spider web of cracks with the bullet's hole in its center. He was lucky that the shot hit the car at an angle; otherwise, he would be dead instead of picking out a few shards of glass that had stuck in the back of his neck. He took out his handkerchief and dabbed at the blood on his neck, then carefully wiped down the steering wheel and any other surface he might have touched. His room got the same treatment: door handles, bathroom fixtures, and light switches. He didn't bother to check out of the motel; he used a fake name, and there was nothing to lead back to him. The Cadillac felt like an old friend when he settled behind the wheel and drove back toward Phoenix. It had been a very close call and a long night.

He tried to calm his nerves as he drove. This guy was tougher and smarter than he thought. He had carefully laid a trap and suckered them into an ambush. That took planning. He wouldn't underestimate him again. How the hell was he going to explain this to the boss? It could cost him his position in the organization. It could also cost him his life. He was replaceable if the boss determined he couldn't be trusted to do what was needed. Life was cheap in his line of work.

The solution was to present a workable plan along with the bad news. It was the only way he could think of to redeem himself in the boss's eyes. There was one possibility. He mulled it over as he drove. He would make some calls when he returned to the Phoenix motel. Hopefully, he would have a workable plan when he called the boss in the morning.

CHAPTER 13

It was two o'clock Sunday morning when Harley got back to his house. The neighborhood was dark and quiet. He went in the house, got a scrub bucket and some rags, turned on the porch light, and cleaned up all the remaining blood and bits of brain he could find. He hoped it would be enough if the cops came snooping around the house.

He had the Beast backed up by the front porch and loaded up any supplies he thought he might need. He figured the Las Vegas bunch would regroup and come after him again, and he needed to be ready. He cleaned out all the canned foods. There wasn't much in the refrigerator, and he left it. He pulled some extra blankets from the bedroom's closet; it could get cold in the desert at night, even in summer. Two more guns: a Winchester .308 and a Remington 12 gauge shotgun. They joined the others in the cab of the Beast, along with all his stockpiled ammunition from the house. He could fight a small war with these, plus others he had stashed in his desert bunkers.

Then he went to the machine shop. With his brother dead, it was now his shop. He hadn't thought about that until then. He tore off the cops' crime scene tape and went inside. There were a few more things he was going to need. He worked until the sun was coming up. Then he locked the door and looked at the metal building one last time as he drove away. The shop was his brother's thing, not his. He would arrange to sell it when he could. Then he headed for Ruby's house to say goodbye, maybe for the last time.

⚜

The Buckeye motel manager called the police when he noticed the Chevy in the parking lot with a side window shot out and a bullet hole in the windshield. He told the responding officer it belonged to two men who had arrived yesterday afternoon and another gentleman in a black Cadillac who had registered and paid cash for two rooms. The Chevy was sitting where it was when he came out that morning. There was no sign of the Cadillac or the three men. The officer looked the car over, not touching anything. It seemed very suspicious, so he called the police chief to have a look at it.

The chief arrived, got out of his car, and hitched his gun belt up under his ample belly. He pulled his billed policeman's cap down to shade his eyes from the bright morning sun and walked slowly around the car, checking out the bullet hole and shattered glass. His patrolman said he hadn't touched anything because of the bullet hole and all. The chief grunted and turned to the motel owner. "Show me the rooms," he said without preamble. The owner took him to the first room, and the chief said, "Stop! Don't touch anything!" The man jumped back like someone had shot at him. "Give me the key to both the rooms." The owner complied, and the chief took out his handkerchief and used it to open the first door. He didn't go in; he just stood at the threshold looking around. "Don't look like it had much use," he said, then went to the next room and repeated the process. He told the owner to keep the rooms closed and not to enter. He was going to have the rooms dusted for fingerprints. He said, "I need to use your phone." The owner led him into the motel office. He called the district sheriff's office and described the scene to the commander. "This might have something to do with that machine shop murder. Can you send your crew out to look for prints and such?" The commander agreed, and the chief hung up. The owner was staring at him wide-eyed. Nothing like this had ever happened at his quiet motel.

Two hours later, the sheriff's department crime scene crew, the district commander, and two of his deputies showed up. The commander was short-handed on a Sunday and had called in Sean and Brad on their day off. He said, "You deputies rope this area off with crime scene tape, then I want you to keep the looky-loos away while the crew does its work." Other motel guests had come out to see what the commotion was about, and a few townspeople were milling around.

The same reporter showed up that Sean had met at the machine shop and started taking pictures and firing off questions at him: "Is there somebody dead in one of those rooms? Does this have anything to do with the machine shop murder? Whose car is that?" He started to step over the crime scene tape, and Sean stopped him. "Hey, I just want to get some close-ups of that car with the bullet holes!"

"I'm sorry, sir," Sean said, "but you'll have to wait until our people finish the investigation. Do not cross this crime scene tape."

"Crime scene? What's the crime?"

"I don't have any information, sir. Please stay back."

The man walked off, grumbling to himself again about freedom of the press, stopping every few feet to snap a picture of the scene and the crowd.

The head crime scene technician told the commander, "The first room had been wiped clean. We pulled some good prints off the dash and upholstery in the car and from the second room. The registration shows this as a rental car, so there could be prints from previous renters. We'll get these prints back to the lab to sort them out; hopefully, some of the prints from the car will match those we found in the room. I'll let you know what we find."

"Thanks for your help," the commander said. "One more thing—have Detective Johnson send a copy of the prints to the Las Vegas police and the FBI." "Will do," the technician said and walked to his van.

The commander said to Sean and Brad, "We're done here. Pull down the tape and send these folks home." Then he thanked the motel owner for his help. He told the town's police chief he would inform him of what they learned from the fingerprints and

87

headed back to the district office. The reporter was still taking pictures of everything and everyone in sight.

One of the Buckeye patrolmen caught up with Sean as he was preparing to leave and said, "Hey, Sean. Last night, we had reports of gunshots in the unincorporated part of town up north. I drove through the neighborhood, and everything was quiet, so I wrote it off to some kids joyriding and making noise. But seeing this car with the bullet holes got me thinking—what if the shots had something to do with this?"

"Could be, Leo. Tell me more about where the shots were reported."

"Well, you know that area we call Valencia?"

Sean nodded.

"It was up in the north end of that."

"Isn't that the same area where Harry and Harley lived?"

"Hey! It sure is! Think there's a connection?"

"Let's go have a look. Park on the street—we don't want to disturb possible evidence."

Sean followed the patrolman, stopping in front of the Henderson twins' house. They could see the tire tracks left by the Beast in the dirt driveway. Sean recognized them as the same ones he had seen in the mud near the plane's crash site. He said, "Looks like Harley has been here very recently. I recognize these tracks; they were made by his truck. They're fresh, probably from last night."

They walked up to the cement slab that served as a porch. "Look here, Leo. These look like fresh blood stains," Sean said. He pointed to a couple of streaks on the wall by the door, then at some spots in the dirt beside the porch, and continued, "I think this is where the shots the neighbors reported came from. We'll need the crime scene guys to come back and evaluate this. I'll call to get a warrant to search the house, too."

They walked around the house and the yard. Sean spotted a glint of something shiny under the big tamarack tree in the front yard. It proved to be an empty shell casing, and three more were scattered around the bed of needles from the tree. He put on gloves and got an evidence bag and camera from his cruiser. He photographed the shells and surrounding area, then carefully gathered the shells. They were for a .30-30 caliber rifle—no doubt from the shooter's weapon. Then he radioed the district commander, who was on his way back to the office. The commander said he would get a subpoena and alert the crime scene crew. Once the subpoena was signed, they would go over the property inside and out.

CHAPTER 14

Rossi had returned to his motel in Phoenix after dumping the rental car at the motel in Buckeye. He slept a few hours, then checked out of the two rooms he had there. He didn't bother with whatever was left in the room his two assistants had used. He drove a few miles to a different motel and checked in under a different name. Then he made a call to Mexico. His friend Jose Rodriquez answered on the second ring.

Rodriquez was an operative in a drug cartel in Mexico who had been looking for a path into the lucrative casino business in Las Vegas. They needed an insider, someone known and respected, who could help them develop a distribution network for heroin, cocaine, marijuana, and whatever else might come into favor. Several discreet inquiries among the cartel's networks in other areas turned up Rossi's name. Rodriquez had contacted him, and the men reached an agreement. Rossi would open the right doors for the cartel; the cartel would give Rossi a significant cut. It had worked well for three years, and he had become good friends with Rodriquez.

"Buenos dias, Jose," Rossi said. "This is Rossi. Do you have some time to talk?"

"Si, amigo. Is there a problem?"

"I need a favor I hope you can help me with. It doesn't involve our business but is very important to me."

"Of course, amigo. Tell me how I can help."

Rossi laid out his problem. "I might lose my position with the casino if I can't recover the lost bonds. That would be a problem for both of us. My boss is losing patience, so I gotta act fast. This man I'm after just killed two of my top men. He's a hunter and used a rifle to take 'em out. I need some trusted people who can operate in the desert. They'll need tracking and hunting skills to find this guy. It could involve a firefight if he's holed up somewhere."

Rodriquez was quiet for a minute. Then he said, "I think I have just the men to help you out. They've done a lot of business for me in northern Sonora, so they are used to working in the desert. Right now, they are in Hermosillo. They just finished a job there and can be to you tomorrow. I'll contact them as soon as we finish this call."

"That's great news, Jose. I really appreciate your help."

"De nada, amigo. Glad to help out."

Rossi gave him the phone number and address of the motel where he was staying. They discussed a little business in Las Vegas before the call ended. Rossi heaved a sigh of relief. These guys should be able to run this redneck rube to ground.

Sean was back at the district office working on reports when Gloria, the clerk, rushed around yelling for everyone to listen to the radio. Sean walked to her desk to hear just as President Harry Truman began making an announcement. What he said seemed unbelievable. An atomic bomb? Sean had never heard of such a bomb. The President said that it caused incredible damage and killed many Japanese in a city called Hiroshima in Japan. He finished his address, and everyone was silent for a few minutes. Then the office erupted, with everyone talking at the same time. They all wondered what it meant for the war— surely the Japanese would surrender, and the war would end. Nobody knew what an atomic bomb was, but it was all anyone talked about the rest of the day.

Ricky called Sean just before he left the office. He said he needed to talk to him, and the men agreed to meet at their regular watering hole in an hour.

"Did you hear the news, Ricky?" Sean was still excited by the President's announcement.

"No, what news?"

"The President just announced we dropped an atomic bomb on Japan! It's bound to end the war!"

"Wow! That's great. I don't know what an atomic bomb is exactly, but if it will end this damn war, I like it!"

Both men had been wounded during action in the war and received Purple Hearts. Sean was wounded in France and sent to recover in a British hospital before being sent home. Ricky was a marine and had been injured by a land mine on a Pacific Island beach during its invasion. He was sent to a hospital in Hawaii and, after several surgeries, was honorably discharged from the service. His injuries left him with a pronounced limp. He had argued that he was still fit for duty and wanted to fight, but the doctors disagreed. The idea that the war might be over was thrilling news.

Sean had been so excited when he got to the bar that, at first, he didn't notice Ricky's black eye and swollen face in the bar's dim light. Then he looked closer at his friend and said, "What happened to you, Ricky? You look like hell!"

"It's what I need to talk to you about, amigo. I need your help."

"Anything, amigo! What do you need?"

"There's a new gang operating, forcing Mexican businesses to pay them protection money. They came into my parent's store and threatened them. My father told them to go to hell, and they roughed him up some. My mother tried to stop them, and they shoved her onto the floor. I was working in the back room when I heard her scream. I ran out front, and two of them jumped me. They said they would return in a week, and the store would owe them fifty dollars. Then they left, laughing, and pointing at us as they went out the door."

"Are your parents all right?"

"Yeah, I took them both to the hospital. Dad just needed a few stitches. Mom had a big bump on her head, but they said she didn't have a concussion. They are both scared to death. Nothing like this has ever happened before."

Sean was furious. Ricky's parents were like Sean's own family. He and Ricky had been best friends since high school when Sean saved him from a beating by a gang of young hoodlums at a football game. He had often stayed with his family, and they treated him like another son. He wasn't going to sit still for a gang beating them up.

"Do you know who they are?"

"Nope. They showed up recently and started demanding protection money. The rumor is they are out of Mexico, maybe connected to a gang down there."

"Find out anything you can, Ricky. I'll contact a friend in the Phoenix Police Department who deals with gang problems. Let's get together in a couple of days and compare notes. Then we can plan how to get rid of that bunch."

"Sounds good, Sean. Thank you. I didn't know what else to do."

They finished their beers and left. Sean thought about how Ricky had helped him crack a human sex trafficking ring a few months earlier and then had traveled with him deep into Mexico to find a kidnapper known as the Weighmaster. He would do anything to help his friend.

CHAPTER 15

The bomb was still all anyone could talk about the following day in the district office. A lot of questions were directed to Sean because of his wartime experience. His only response was that Japan should surrender if the damage from the bomb was as tremendous as it sounded. He said it was far beyond anything he had experienced.

The commander said, "All right. We don't know what will happen next, but we can't stand around here jawing about it all day. You all have work to do—get to it."

Sean headed out on patrol. He would stop off in Buckeye later to see if the local police had more information about the mystery car with its windows shot out. Suddenly, his radio erupted in an all-points alert—there had been a robbery at the Valley National Bank in west Phoenix. All available cars were advised: Three robbers had held up the bank and made a getaway in a black Chevrolet sedan, last seen heading west on Van Buren Street. Consider armed and dangerous. Report any sightings immediately.

The first sighting was called in by a deputy on patrol in Tolleson, a few miles west of Phoenix. The deputy was in pursuit on Van Buren Street. Sean was near that location and headed north, hoping to cut them off west of the town. Maybe the two deputies could box them in. He stopped at the intersection with Van Buren. He heard the siren before he saw the cars, and then he saw them about a quarter mile away, coming fast. He waited until they were about a hundred yards away and pulled across the intersection in front of the robber's car. They swerved to miss him, ran off into an irrigation ditch paralleling the road, and the vehicle came to rest on its side in the ditch.

Sean grabbed the twelve-gauge shotgun from its mount by the front seat and took up a position behind the front of his cruiser. The pursuing cruiser squealed to a stop, then pulled over sideways behind the robber's car. Sean recognized Charlie Murphy, the other deputy. The robbers were boxed in and caught in a crossfire if they chose to shoot it out with the deputies. The front and back doors of the robber's car swung open, and two men stuck their heads up to see where the deputies were.

Murphy yelled, "Come out of there, nice and slow, and put your hands in the air!"

The robber in the back seat leaned out with a Thompson submachine gun and opened fire on Murphy's position. The deputy ducked behind the patrol car, shielded by the engine's block, as the .45 caliber slugs slammed into the metal. Sean fired a round from his shotgun, but the door shielded the robber. The blast shattered the glass in the door, and the robber ducked back inside the car. Sean laid the shotgun on his hood, then unholstered his Colt .45 auto. The car's driver managed to boost himself up and fired a shot at Sean with a revolver. The robber's aim was off, and Sean fired two shots in return through the car door's open window. The robber jerked backward and fell back into the car.

Sirens sounded as more police closed in on the scene. The robbers were in an untenable position—their car was on its side, and their only escape was through the two free doors. Soon, two more Sheriff's deputies were covering them, and there was nowhere to go. One of them yelled, "Hold your fire! We're comin' out."

"Hands first!" Sean yelled back. "We will shoot you if we see a gun!"

The robber in the back was the first to come out. He showed his hands, then braced himself to crawl out of the vehicle. Murphy yelled, "On the ground! Hands behind your head! Don't make a move!" The man did as he was told.

The second robber, who was in the front seat, called out, "My partner's dead! I have to crawl over into the back seat to get out. Don't shoot me!"

"Show me your hands, then come out of there nice and slow," Murphy yelled. The man did as he was told and followed instructions to lie on the ground with his hands behind his head.

Sean approached the car slowly and cautiously. He eased around the open front door, following the barrel of his pistol. The robber he had shot lay slumped over on the seat in a pool of blood. He had taken Sean's first shot in the head, the second in his chest. He had been dead before he hit the seat. Sean was rated an expert marksman with a pistol during his time in the Army. He rarely missed his target.

The district commander showed up and took charge of the scene. The two surviving robbers were placed in the back of two deputies' cruisers to be transported to the county jail in Phoenix for booking. He called an ambulance to retrieve the dead man from the car and transport him to the county morgue. Then he called for a tow truck to retrieve the car and take it to the county's impound lot. The loot from the holdup was in a canvas bag in the car. Murphy got it out and gave it to the commander for safekeeping. It would serve as evidence in a trial for the robbers and then be returned to the bank.

Several private vehicles had stopped, and their drivers were milling around, asking questions, and trying to get a look at the robber's car. Then, a couple of news reporters showed up. Sean and Murphy kept them away. It was noon by the time the scene had been cleared. Sean and Murphy had to return to the office to make reports and be interviewed by an after-action team. The interviewers' report indicated that both officers were justified in discharging their firearms.

It wasn't how Sean wanted to spend his day, but he was glad to have been in the right place at the right time. He was anxious to try to find Harley.

CHAPTER 16

The three men from Mexico arrived late on Tuesday night. Rossi had arranged rooms for them at his motel; they agreed to meet the next morning for breakfast. The leader of the Mexican team was named Diego Alvarez, but his associates knew him as El Puma. The nickname came from his almost uncanny ability to track and find his prey, like his namesake.

He grew up in Caborca in northern Sonora, Mexico, and knew the desert well. His parents eked out a meager existence working on the farms in the area, but Diego left home as a teenager rather than face that kind of life. He fell in with a local gang connected with the Gulf Cartel and began helping smuggle drugs across the border. He proved himself to be very capable of navigating and traversing the harsh desert and soon became the leader of the local operation.

His fame and value to the cartel grew after he had tracked down and killed one of the gang who had stolen a shipment of drugs and disappeared into the desert. The man was familiar with the country, having worked with El Puma's gang on several operations. He thought no one could find him if he stayed away from known roads and trails.

It only took El Puma two days to track him through the harsh desert landscape. He had a kind of sixth sense for tracking. A broken branch on a creosote bush, a rock kicked out of place, a footprint in a sandy wash, and other minor details painted a clear path for him to follow. The man was caught completely unaware when El Puma came upon him at daylight on the second day. The thief had leaned against a mesquite tree to sleep; he woke up to someone kicking the sole of his boot. El Puma shot him in the head, gathered the backpack filled with drugs, and walked away. He left the man lying there for the vultures and coyotes to enjoy.

The cartel's bosses recognized his value and began to use him as their go-to man for finding and eliminating those who chose to steal from the outfit or those who thought they could walk away from their connection to the gang. Diego's set of skills reminded them of how the big cats of the mountains stalked and killed their prey. The nickname of El Puma became known and feared throughout the organization.

Rossi outlined his problem for the men. "This man we're after just killed two of my best men and almost killed me, too. He laid a trap and ambushed us in front of his house. He's a hunter and at home in the desert. I think he went into hiding somewhere in the desert country west of Buckeye. He stole some very valuable bonds from my employer in Las Vegas, and I think he has them stashed wherever he hides out in the desert."

El Puma said, "I know that area well; I've tracked two men through it in the heat of summer. There's very little water out there, not many places a man could hole up for a long time. Do you know anything more about where he might be?"

"The men who stole the bonds from my employer also stole an airplane to get away from Las Vegas a little over two weeks ago. The dumbasses got caught in a storm and flew into a mountain called Woolsey Peak. The man we're after was the first one to get to it after the crash. He took the bonds and left before anyone else arrived. I think he was probably huntin' somewhere around there and just happened to find the wreck right after it happened. So, maybe he has a camp somewhere in that area."

"Are police also looking for this man?"

"I believe they are. They are probably lookin' for me, too. They captured two of my men who were trying to question a deputy sheriff we thought had information. I gotta assume they now know who I am. That's why I need you—I gotta stay outta sight until this is over."

El Puma nodded and said, "We need time to gather more information about this man you seek. I will let you know when we are ready to find him."

"Very good. You can reach me or leave a message for me here."

The meeting broke up, and the Mexicans gathered their gear and headed out.

🌵

Sean and Ricky met up at their favorite watering hole that night. Sean said, "I spoke to a guy in the Phoenix Police Department who works on gang activity. He told me he'd been hearing recent reports of a spike in Mexican gangs operating in the area. They're mostly into drugs, but some of them have other rackets, like protection money. He did say one group, in particular, is big in the protection scheme, and the department had been getting a lot of calls.

"Did he have any details? Where are they based?"

"He said they're working on it but haven't identified where they operate from, only that it's somewhere in south Phoenix. What've you found out?"

Ricky took a long pull on his Coors. "I think I have the name of the leader and maybe the street his house is on. A guy I know who left Mexico, because he didn't want to join a gang, told me that word on the street was that the leader of this bunch was the same guy who was pressuring him before he left. His name is Hector Lopez. Apparently, he brought three or four of his buddies with him from Mexico. He lives in a house on South Seventh Avenue near Baseline Road in Phoenix."

"We should be able to find the house," Sean said. "Did your contact have any description of the guy, what he drives, or anything to help us identify him?"

"He said he thinks they drive a blue, late-model Chevy sedan."

"Well, that narrows it down to a few hundred cars around Phoenix that could fit."

"It's all I have, amigo."

"You have a lot more than I found. Good work!"

"Yeah, but what can we do with it?"

99

"Let's finish our beers and go cruise that neighborhood, see what we can see. Let's take your car; my truck might stand out too much in that area."

"Yeah, my car looks like something a Mexican would drive, all right."

That got a laugh from both of them. They paid their tabs and headed out into the night in Ricky's beat-up 1935 Plymouth. It had one front fender painted white. Ricky had to replace it and never got around to painting it green like the rest of the car. It had plenty of dents and scratches to go along with it. They started north on Seventh Avenue from Baseline, driving slow, looking for a blue Chevy sedan. They saw some kids playing basketball in a driveway and stopped. Ricky hung out the window and said, "Hola! Como estas. Do any of you know where Hector Lopez lives?"

One of the boys appeared to be the oldest, and he stepped next to the car and said, "¿Por que lo buscas? Why do you want him?"

"A friend in Juarez told me to look him up. Said he might have work for me."

The kid was suspicious. He pointed at Sean and said, "Who's the gringo?"

"He's my sister's husband."

After a pause, the kid said, "You can usually find him down there." He pointed back south the way they had come. "It's the second house from the next corner on the east side. But I don't think he'll be there this early."

"Muchas gracias, amigo. I'll come back later. Without this gringo."

The boy laughed and said, "Adios!"

They left and drove slowly past the house the kid had pointed out. It was dark, and there was no car in the driveway. Ricky said, "What do you think, amigo?"

"Maybe if we hit the place around two in the morning, we can catch whoever's there sleeping. We don't want to go in there if three or four gunmen are sitting around drinking tequila."

Ricky chuckled and said, "Yeah, we wouldn't want them to spill a perfectly good bottle of tequila!"

They drove back to the bar to retrieve Sean's truck. He said, "Maybe tomorrow night, Ricky. We'll need some time to prepare."

"Whatever you think. Let me know."

"Hasta luego, amigo."

"Hasta luego, Sean."

CHAPTER 17

Sean left the district office at eight a.m. to start his day's patrol. He was waiting to turn onto Highway 80, which was also the main street through Avondale. He waited for a white Dodge pickup truck to pass by. It caught his attention—that type of truck was uncommon outside the military. He noticed three Mexican men in the cab and a Sonora, Mexico, license plate on the back. Maybe those trucks were available in Mexico. He didn't give it any more thought—cars and trucks from Mexico were a common sight.

He planned to spend as much time as possible trying to get more information about Harley and the mysterious car at the motel with its windows shot out. He made the rounds of the three gas stations in town. The third was the Texaco station, where the department maintained an account. The owner filled his gas tank while Sean asked if he knew where Harley was. The man replied, "Well, Sean, it seems like everyone wants to know that. He stopped in here and filled up his truck's tanks…and boy is that a thirsty truck…right after his brother was beaten to death in their machine shop. I ain't seen him since. Rumors are floatin' around he may have had somethin' to do with that car at the motel with its windows shot out. But I don't know nothin' for sure 'bout that."

"Okay. Thanks, Chester." He handed the owner his card and said, "Let me know if you see him or hear anything about where I could find him."

"Sure thing, Sean. Thanks for your business!"

Sean stopped off at the coffee shop next to the bank. He figured a piece of homemade apple pie and a cup of coffee would give him a chance to listen to whatever gossip was floating around town. Several people asked him if he knew anything about

Harry's death or the mystery car at the motel. Sean said it was all under investigation, and he didn't have any information.

He heard Betty, one of the waitresses, say to Ruby that she should be careful about what she says about Harley from now on. She might get him in trouble. Sean knew both women and when Ruby passed by his table, he said, "Mornin', Miss Ruby. Got a minute?"

She had that deer-in-the-headlights look in her eyes. "I'm pretty busy right now, Sean."

"I only need a minute. I want to talk to you about Harley."

Her face changed instantly, and Sean could sense her unease. He said, "It's really important that I find him. I think his life might be in danger."

She studied him for a few seconds, seemed to make a decision, and then said, "I can't talk here. We close at three. Meet me in the rear parking lot then." She moved on, bustling around the other customers' tables.

Sean finished his pie and coffee, left a nice tip on the table, and went back to canvassing the various businesses in town. He returned to the brothers' machine shop to look around, hoping to find something useful that might have been missed. He had the lock's key and let himself in. Nothing appeared any different at first. But then he found a freshly sawn piece of plywood with sawdust still on the floor. That hadn't been there after the murder. Then he noticed several bent ten-penny nails scattered around in the sawdust, as if someone had been hammering the nails and discarded the occasional bent ones. Someone had definitely been doing something in here after the murder. Nobody but him and Harley had keys to the lock. There was a spare in the file in the district office, but that was all. He needed to add a question to his interviews with the locals about seeing anyone here since the murder.

At three p.m., he parked in the lot behind the coffee shop. Everyone left, and the only cars left were his and Ruby's. She came out about fifteen minutes later and said, "I don't want to talk here, Sean. Follow me to my house."

They drove to her rented farmhouse north of town. "C'mon in, Sean. Let's talk inside." She motioned him to an armchair in the living room, and she sat on the couch. "I've known you since you were in high school here, Sean. I knew your father, too, when he was a deputy. He was a good and honest man; people say you are just like him. I feel like I can trust you. At least I hope I can..."

"Thanks, Ruby. I'm trying to live up to my father's legacy, but his were some big shoes to fill."

"You said you are concerned about Harley's safety. I am, too. Tell me what's going on and how I can help."

"I think Harley has gotten himself into a very dangerous situation. Have you heard about the airplane crash on Woolsey Peak?"

She nodded and said, "Hell, everybody's heard about it. It's pretty much all anyone talked about for a week."

"Did you know Harley was the first one there after the crash?"

Ruby's eyes got big, and she said, "He didn't tell me that!"

"We found his fingerprints on a pickaxe he left by the wreck. We think he stole money from the dead passengers. But, more importantly, we think he took something else from the plane that was very valuable. That plane belonged to a Las Vegas casino organization, and they sent men to find whatever he took. It might have been a large amount of cash."

"I think he would have turned it in if he found something like that!"

"Well, Ruby, all I can say is another deputy, and I were there the next day, and there was nothing of value in the wreck. Harley had to have taken whatever it was, and now he is in danger. These are some very bad people looking for it. We think it's likely they were the ones who murdered Harry at the shop; they probably tried to beat information out of him to find Harley. I also think Harley may have shot some of those men when they

104

came to his house. The car left at the motel with the windows shot out last Sunday was possibly part of that."

Ruby put her head in her hands and started sobbing. Sean waited until she regained her composure, then she said, "Harley did seem to have a lot more cash than usual. He told me it was from a big sale of a bighorn sheep ram's head. I've always told him he was going to get in trouble for killing those sheep because it's against the law, but he kept doing it. I had no reason to think the money came from anything else. Tell me what you need to know."

"I need to know how to find him before the casino's people do. They've been asking a lot of questions around town; it's just a matter of time before they find him. I know he has a hunting camp somewhere in the Gila Bend Mountains, but I don't know where. I think I can help him if I can find him before the casino people do."

She was quiet for a minute, then said, "He took me out there once. Said I and his brother were the only ones he had ever shown it to. Swore me to secrecy." She paused, then continued, "It's way off out there on the other side of Woolsey Peak. It's a terrible road and hard to get out there. That's why he built the truck he calls the Beast. It has the clearance and four-wheel drive he needed to get around out there. His camp is up a big wash, maybe a half mile from the road. He has a bunker there with supplies where he can hole up for a long time if he needs to."

"Why would he need to do that, Ruby?"

"He became sort of paranoid about Nazis or communists or some such taking over the country, and he wanted to be prepared. He told me he would take me out there with him if that ever happened, and we would live off the land and his supplies until the country got straightened out. I told him I didn't think anything like that would happen, but I couldn't change his mind. From what you've told me, I would guess that's where he is now."

105

"Thank you, Ruby. I'll keep this between us; no one will know where I got the information. You may have saved his life."

"Find him, Sean, and talk some sense into him!"

"I'll do the best I can, Ruby." He gave her one of his cards and told her to call him if she had new information. Then, he returned to the district office.

✤

El Puma had dropped his men on Main Street in Buckeye that morning. He told them to work their way through town, speak to any Mexicans they encountered, and see if they could get any information about this gringo Harley Henderson they were looking for. He was going south to the town of Gila Bend to try and find an old contact he knew; he would meet his men in the town park when he returned.

It was about ten in the morning when he parked in front of Bob's Bar in Gila Bend. It was a seedy, bucket-of-blood kind of joint just south of the railroad tracks. A Coors beer sign proclaiming, "It's The Water!" was on one window, and a Budweiser beer sign that said, "The King Of Beers" hung on the other. A late model Buick was parked beside the building; he assumed it was the owner's. The only vehicle in front was a worn and rusty old Ford pickup. El Puma smiled to himself. Some things never change, he thought. This is my lucky day.

He parked and went inside. The place was dim and smoky, even at this hour of the morning. One customer sat on a bar stool while the bartender washed glasses from the previous night. El Puma sat on a barstool next to the lone customer. The old man looked as leathery and ancient as the last time he had seen him. El Puma said, "Hola, Antone!"

The old man didn't look at him and took a sip from his Coors. "Hola, Diego. I knew it was you when you walked in the door. What are you doing way up here in Arizona?" He had a raspy voice from a lifetime of smoking cigarettes and drinking too much booze.

El Puma chuckled and said, "It's good to see you too, old friend. I need your help."

"Why else would you come all this way to see an old man?"

"I'm looking for a man you might know something about. He's a big man, a hunter named Harley Henderson. I'm told he spends a lot of time in the Gila Bend Mountains."

Antone was a member of the Tohono O'Odham tribe of Indians, also known as the Papagos. He lived on a small branch of the main reservation located a short way north of town. He was a little stooped from age and had the grizzled look of a man who had spent a lifetime in the hot Arizona sun. But his mind was sharp, and his brown eyes held a mischievous look. He had hunted the range of mountains north of the Gila River for his whole life and claimed he knew more about them than any other living man. He had helped El Puma find someone in the area a couple of times in the past. It was always profitable for both men.

Antone looked at El Puma, tilted his cheap western straw hat back on his forehead, and said, "Yes, I know of this man." Antone sipped another beer. It was his habit to come to the bar at opening time and have his first beer of the day. El Puma had known him to drink beer all day and into the night and never show the effects of the alcohol.

"Do you know where I can find him? I will make it worth your while."

"How worthwhile? An old man has to eat."

El Puma was ready for this and laid a U.S. fifty-dollar bill on the counter next to Antone's beer can. The old man smiled and smoothly pocketed the bill.

Antone began, "This man you seek is a dangerous man in the desert."

"All men I seek are dangerous."

"But this man is different. He lives in the desert most of the time. He maybe knows almost as much about it as me. He kills the bighorn sheep that live in the mountains and sells their heads. To me, this is evil. The bighorns are sacred to my people—

guardian sky spirits. It is wrong to kill them the way this man does. It is illegal for white men to kill them, too, but the game wardens have never been able to catch this man you seek with a ram's head in his truck. I'm told he sometimes guides other white men to find them, and they pay him a lot of money. More than you are paying me today." He looked expectantly at El Puma.

"You old dog. How much is it going to cost me for you to get to the point?" He laid another fifty-dollar bill on the counter, which disappeared as quickly as the first.

The Indian winked and said, "You should know nothing worthwhile comes cheap. So here is how to find this man. Go back toward Buckeye on the highway. You will cross a dam on the river, then go through some low hills. A few miles past the dam, a dirt road leads to the west, toward the place they call Agua Caliente. That road is a bad one after all the rains we have had. You will need a strong pickup truck." He drained his beer and pushed the empty over toward El Puma. Diego laid two dollars on the counter and signaled the bartender for another beer for Antone and one for himself.

Antone took a long pull on the cold beer and said, "On this road, you will see the place white men call Woolsey Peak. An airplane ran into it a few days ago; I heard a couple of men died. Watch for another little track that goes toward the mountain. It will be hard to see after all the rains—it's mostly just tire tracks." He paused and looked at his friend, then continued, "I also heard somebody might have taken some things from it—maybe some things with great value, eh?" He waited for a reply, but El Puma's face was passive, and he said nothing. Antone continued, "A canyon leads up in the direction of the peak somewhere on the west side of that mountain; there is a small spring there. The man you seek has a hunting camp nearby." He took another drink of beer and said, "That's where I would look if I was you."

"Muchas gracias my old friend. I'll see you." He left his change on the bar and left. Driving back the way he had come on US 80, he crossed the Gila River on the bridge below Gillespie

108

Dam, then continued on the winding road that climbed through the hills. The dirt road the Indian described came up a few miles later; it wasn't much of a road and was very muddy from the rains. He stopped and looked at the country in the distance. The mostly flat summit of Woolsey Peak dominated the view. It had been several years since he pursued a man through this piece of desert between two mountain ranges. It was every bit as rough and remote as he remembered.

He was thoughtful on his way to Buckeye. He needed to do some careful planning to find this big gringo. Those desert roads would be treacherous after the recent heavy rains. He was fortunate to have a vehicle with four-wheel drive. His friends in the cartel had somehow gotten their hands on some Dodge three-quarter ton four-wheel drive trucks made for the US military. They had painted over the Army green color with white paint and given one to El Puma for his use. He would need it to find the place the old Indian described. He found his men at the park, and they returned to their motel to discuss a plan.

CHAPTER 18

Harley had picked up a few more supplies at the market, topped off both his truck's gas tanks, and then headed for the desert. It was mid-morning, and monsoon thunderheads were already building to the southeast. He meant to be settled in at Site One before the rains made the road too sloppy or flooded the wash below his camp. He unloaded and stored the new supplies and additional guns in his bunker.

He had put many long hours of hard work into building the bunker. Working by himself, with a pick and shovel, was tedious work. He used dynamite to blast a hole into the side of the canyon, then shaped it to an opening about twenty feet deep, six feet wide, and six feet high. Ironwood and mesquite timbers were strategically placed to shore up the ceiling and sides. He brought in three railroad ties and built a secure entrance. His brother made a steel door and had helped Harley mount it. It had two hinged portals he could open for ventilation and the bolt closed for security. The finishing touch was the heaviest Squire padlock available. The brothers admired their work when it was done; Harry figured it would take a couple of sticks of dynamite to blow it open. He had an Army surplus cot, four wool blankets, a couple of metal mess kits, various kitchen utensils, and two Primus single burner kerosene stoves to give him all the comforts he needed. His firearms were wrapped in oilcloth and stored in metal waterproof boxes along with enough ammunition to hold off a small army. He had also acquired some black market military ordnance through his survivalist friends.

Harley stocked the bunker with canned goods he could open and eat without a fire if he had to: canned hams, Vienna sausages, pork and beans, and canned fruits. He also had an ample supply of saltine crackers, hard tack, and salt pork. He made his own venison jerky and kept plenty in storage. Ten five-gallon jerry cans were filled with water. He rotated them regularly with water from the nearby spring to keep them fresh. He reckoned he could last several months on his stash.

When the weather was good, he slept outside under a brush ramada he had built using thick mesquite limbs for uprights and framing. Staves from dead saguaro cactuses laid across the framing made a good covering for shade during the day. He ate and slept outdoors when the weather allowed.

He had chosen this site strategically with an eye to the day that the government, communists, or some other crazies might come for him. His father had taught his sons never to trust the government and be suspicious of any new ideas. He worried the US would lose the war, and Nazis would take over, or the Japanese would overrun the country. He was unaware of the recent atomic bomb dropped on Japan—it would have made no difference to him.

Harley was convinced his father was right. Who knew what could happen next if this crazy war ever ended? All he could do was be prepared for whatever might come. Now he knew the Las Vegas people, the cops, or both, would be looking for him. It was only a matter of time until they located him. He was prepared to defend himself against all comers.

Site One was up a narrow canyon that descended from the mountains. The wash in the bottom was passable with four-wheel drive, so long as it wasn't flooding. The canyon got narrower and steeper as it went higher. A small spring feeding into the wash had water for several months of the year, which was one reason Harley chose the site. It was also remote and difficult to access— a perfect hideout. There was room on the bank to park his truck where the wash flattened slightly. He had made a rough exit ramp lined with rocks to get in and out of the wash with his truck. He could see clearly down the wash to where it exited the canyon and flattened on the valley floor. Anyone coming up the wash would be visible from his vantage point. The rough sides of the canyon provided natural cover, and he had built several concealed shooting platforms just downstream of his camp. He could take out anyone who tried to come up before they knew he was there. He doubted anyone would come for him over the mountains because it was rugged and dangerous terrain; he would deal with it if it happened.

He built Site Two in the low hills below Signal Mountain, a few miles northwest. He could pull back to it if all else failed. It was not as elaborate as Site One, but he could survive there and defend himself effectively. He could hike to it if his exit from Site One were blocked at the bottom of the canyon,

A thunderstorm had passed north of him, and he decided to sleep outside. He shot a cottontail rabbit with his .22 rifle, skinned it, and put it on a spit over a small campfire. Then he opened a can of pork and beans, put it in a small pot, and set it on the side of the coals. Fresh rabbit was one of his favorite foods, and they were plentiful there because of the nearby water source.

He sat in his camp chair and took his time with dinner. There was no rush, and he thought he deserved a little relaxation after the past days' events. He considered what the casino people's next move would be. They would no doubt be more cautious and better prepared after he killed two of their men in Buckeye. But those guys were city types—they wouldn't know anything about the desert. He thought about what he would do in their place: First, he'd hire someone who knew the desert, preferably someone familiar with this part of it and how to track game or people. Where would he find someone like that? No one around here fit that bill. He'd have to import someone. Second, he'd need to take his target alive. He was no good to them dead. They could search forever and not find where he hid the bonds.

He figured a casino would have plenty of money, and they could no doubt find someone who could find him. He made a plan to make that very difficult for them. He lay down on his cot and stared up through the canyon's walls at the blanket of stars in the Milky Way above him. There were no lights for miles around to spoil the view. Two shooting stars briefly lit the sky before he drifted off to sleep and dreamed of Ruby lying there beside him.

The next morning, he sat about placing surprises for anyone who ventured up the canyon. Yesterday, before he left town, he found a four-by-eight foot three-quarter-inch piece of plywood in the shop. He had used the table saw and cut off two pieces, each two feet wide. Then he drove ten-penny nails in two alternating rows the length of each board. The nails went through the board and stuck out a little over two inches on the other side. He looked over his handiwork and smiled. These things ought to shred some tires, he said to himself. Hey! That's what I'll call 'em—tire shredders! The boards went into the bed of the Beast, and he drove down near the mouth of the canyon.

He placed the first one a hundred yards up the canyon in the wash. He dug a shallow depression for it to set in, then dug a little deeper trench on the upstream side. He put the board in place and then lined the upstream side with rocks to keep water from washing out the board. Then he dug another deeper trench about three feet in front of the first. The tire shredder board was covered with sand, so the makeshift spikes stuck up about two inches above the covering. He placed the second one another hundred yards up the wash, buried the same way. A small stack of rocks to the side of his tire shredders gave him markers to tell where they were. He had just enough room to drive around them.

He went back to his camp and began to lay out his arsenal. The first rifle was a Springfield .30-06 with a sniper scope. Second was his lever action .30-30 Winchester. It was his favorite for closer work. Then he got his two favorite pistols, a Smith and Wesson .357 magnum and a Colt Model 1911 .45 automatic. He had over-shoulder bandoliers with ammunition for each rifle and a waist gun belt and holster for the .357. The .45 auto would go into his waistband in the back. He had two extra clips for it in his pants pockets. Lastly, he sharpened and oiled his Buck knife with a five-inch blade. It went into his other pants pocket.

113

He thought he would probably look like pictures he had seen of Pancho Villa's raiders when he strapped it all on. All he lacked was a big sombrero with the brim turned up in front. There was nothing left to do but wait.

CHAPTER 19

Ricky met Sean at his house in Goodyear, and they prepared to go after the leader of the gang that had been terrorizing Mexican businesses for protection money. It was two o'clock in the morning when people were most vulnerable. Sean handed Ricky a black ski mask and said, "I picked up two of these at a sporting goods store. Thought they might come in handy someday. These guys have seen you; you don't want them to recognize you tonight."

"Gracias, amigo. I had that same thought."

"You should do the talking. The less they know about me, the better. Did you bring your pistol?

"Yeah, and my old baseball bat. And I brought a couple of rolls of duct tape that might come in handy."

"Let's hope we don't need our guns. We should be able to pull this off without waking the whole neighborhood."

They put their gear in Ricky's old car and drove to Phoenix. South Seventh Avenue was dark and quiet. Ricky parked a couple of houses away from the gang leader's place. There were no lights in the house, but they sat for a few minutes watching to be sure there were no signs of activity. Ricky took the bulb out of the car's dome light before they opened the doors, then they gathered their gear, put on the ski masks, and walked up to the house. It was dark and silent. Two cars were in the driveway; they figured at least two men would be inside.

Sean whispered, "I hope they don't have any women inside. Be ready for anything." He gently turned the doorknob. It was unlocked, and the door opened easily. "Listo?" he whispered.

"Listo!" Ricky breathed, and they stepped into the house.

Sean had taped some red tissue paper over the lens of his flashlight so they wouldn't have their night vision blurred by a bright light. They crept through the house and saw no one. A mess of empty beer cans and tequila bottles was scattered on a coffee table in the living room. All the better, Sean thought. The booze will have dulled their senses even more.

There were two bedrooms. The dim red light from Sean's flashlight revealed a man and woman in bed in the larger bedroom room and a lone man in the next. Sean indicated the lone man and nodded. They walked up to the bed, and Sean grabbed the man by his shoulders to hold him down as Ricky put a piece of tape over his mouth. Ricky whispered, "Silencio," and put the barrel of his .357 magnum against the side of his head. The man's eyes bulged in the red glow from the flashlight. They quickly taped the man's ankles together and his hands behind his back. Then they moved to the other bedroom.

The couple was naked and uncovered on the bed. It was stiflingly hot in the room; the evaporative cooler in the window was only blowing muggy, warm air due to the monsoon humidity outside. The cooler's motor hummed, and the belt that turned the blower made a soft slapping sound. Sean unholstered his .45 auto and nodded to Ricky. He nodded back, and Sean switched on the overhead light. The woman didn't stir, but the man woke up, blinking and disoriented in the harsh light. Ricky had said he would do all the talking because it would all be in Spanish. The man saw Sean standing at the foot of the bed with the big pistol aimed at his head and Ricky pointing a big revolver at him. He was suddenly very awake and shouted in Spanish, "Who the hell are you? What do you want?" The woman just moaned.

Ricky said, "Wake your woman and tell her not to scream. Do as we say, and you might live."

The man spluttered, "Do you know who I am?"

"Yeah," Ricky said, "we do."

Ricky covered the man while Sean moved to the bedside and quickly put a piece of duct tape over the woman's mouth. Her eyes opened wide, and she started to move; Sean shook his head, showed her his pistol, and she was still. Sean quickly taped the woman's hands and ankles. A chair was in one corner, and Ricky told the man to sit on it. Then Sean taped the man's arms behind it and taped his ankles together. The man began cursing loudly in Spanish; Sean walloped him on the side of his head, and he was quiet. Then he put a piece of tape over his mouth.

Ricky continued in Spanish, "We know very well who you are, Hector. You are the sonofabitch who's been terrorizing people with your friends, forcing them to pay you for your so-called protection. We're here to show you what happens to people like you around here." He picked up his baseball bat and smacked it on his palm while he studied the man as if deciding where to place the first blow. Hector's eyes grew wide, and he struggled futilely against his restraints. Then Ricky hit him. A rib gave a satisfying crack, and he swung the bat from the opposite side with the same result.

"Do you understand our message, Hector?"

Hector nodded vigorously.

"I don't think you do," Ricky said, then he hit him again. Twice. Hector moaned in pain as two more ribs cracked. Ricky continued, "Here's what's going to happen now. You can go to the hospital and get your ribs bound up. Then you and your friends are gonna pack up and go back to Mexico. Today. And never come back. Do you understand?"

Hector's eyes blazed hatred at his tormentor, but he nodded that he understood.

"That's good, Hector. Because if you come back here we will pay you another visit and I will let my big friend here explain it to you again. He is not as gentle as me. You might not survive the conversation. Do you understand?"

Hector nodded rapidly again.

"That's good, Hector. We'll leave you and your friends now. I'm sure your other friends will show up sometime and cut you loose. You can tell them what happened to you will happen to them, too, if they stick around."

They left them there, Hector and his girlfriend naked to the world, bound with duct tape. Ricky said, "The sight of Hector's scrawny ass and his girl's big tits should give the other gang members something to talk about when they find them." They had a good laugh, and Ricky said, "You know, this turned out a lot better than I thought it would." They laughed again and headed back to Sean's house.

By then, it was after four a.m. Dawn was a couple of hours away; Sean saw no reason to go to bed. He was too keyed up to sleep, anyway. He made a pot of coffee and turned on the big Philco radio in his living room. It was tuned to KOY radio in Phoenix to catch the news. The excited announcer was yammering about a bomb. He finally slowed down enough to give a recap of the news bulletins: President Truman had announced that another much more powerful atomic bomb had been dropped in Japan—on a city named Nagasaki. There were not many details, only that the bomb had caused widespread destruction and likely killed several thousand people. The newscaster went on, repeating what little information was known and speculating whether it would finally end the war.

Sean turned the radio off and sat sipping his coffee in silence. He wondered if it could truly mean the war would end. He sometimes felt like it would go on forever. The Japanese had shown no signs of surrender when the first bomb was dropped three days earlier. Would they now? He knew the horrors of war and had seen it firsthand. The news reports described death and destruction on an unimaginable scale. Surely, this would bring Japan to its knees and end this horrible war.

He made toast and scrambled some eggs for breakfast, then took a hot shower and got ready for work. It would be a long day after a long night.

CHAPTER 20

The commander, the detectives, Brad, and Sean met in the commander's conference room. The talk was all about the latest atomic bomb dropped on Japan. Everyone had an opinion and speculated on what it meant for the war. The consensus was that Japan would have to surrender or face the total destruction of their country.

The commander said, "We'll no doubt know more in a few days. In the meantime, crime never sleeps. Let's start with an update from the detectives." Surprisingly, Detective Harper took the lead. He generally stayed in the background while his partner did all the talking. His hawkish features and a pencil-thin mustache gave him a predatory appearance.

Harper said, "First, the results on the prints from the motel room and the shot-up Chevy in Buckeye came back from the FBI. They were for two known east-coast muscle men for the Jersey mob. They both had long rap sheets. We think they were brought in to replace the two thugs who were arrested after the break-in at Sean's house. The two motel rooms had been booked under the name Thomas Train." He waited until the chuckles over the name died down, then continued, "The second room had been wiped clean. It's not a big leap to connect those two guys with Jimmy Rossi, the guy the Vegas casino sent to find whatever they lost in the plane crash." Harper paused to light a Camel, then went on, "The blood found around the front door of the Henderson brothers' house may have belonged to the missing mob goombahs. All we know about it for sure is that it was human. There were some traces around the front step that indicated one or more bodies may have been moved and put into a vehicle—a vehicle with oversized tires similar to what Sean found near the plane crash scene. The empty .30-30 shells found at the scene would be consistent with one or more people being shot as they stood on the porch." He paused for effect and said, "All that leads us to conclude that Harley Henderson killed those two guys, then dumped their bodies somewhere. The rented Chevy from the motel was likely what they had arrived in, and Harley must have tried to take out the driver, too. Thus, the broken glass."

The commander said, "That's certainly a lot of information. Thank you, Detective Harper."

His partner, Detective Johnson, said, "My partner is nothing if not thorough." He sat back with a Cheshire cat's grin on his face.

The commander said, "Sean, you have something new?"

"Yes, sir. I believe I know where to find Harley. I spoke to a source who had actually been to his camp in the mountains near Woolsey Peak. I also learned that he is paranoid about the country being taken over by Nazis or the Japanese or the total collapse of the government. He has a bunker stocked with enough supplies to last until things return to normal."

"Great," Detective Johnson snorted. "Another wacko. Just what we need."

Sean continued, "I've known this guy since high school. He's always been a little sideways in his thinking. And he's always been a gun nut. My guess is that he would have a sizeable arsenal in that bunker if he thinks he might have to shoot his way out or repel invaders."

"You think he's holed up there now, Sean?" the commander asked.

"It seems likely, sir. He hasn't been seen recently anywhere around Buckeye. He knows the casino's people are looking for him. But my guess is he probably has whatever he removed from the crash site stashed at or near his camp."

The commander said, "Brad, anything to add?"

"No sir, not at this time. I've spoken to many people around Buckeye but don't have any new information."

"There's a lot here to digest. We need to try and bring it all to a head before more people mysteriously disappear."

Sean said, "Sir, one thing I believe would help. We could hire a plane to take us up and scout the area before we try to move on Harley. He's a hell of a shot with a rifle. It would be risky to go in there until we have a better picture of where he's hiding."

"Good idea, Sean. It's too bad our volunteer Air Posse was put on hold for the war. This would have been right up their alley. Go ahead and make the arrangements. The department will cover it."

Detective Johnson said, "We will try to run down this Rossi guy. He dropped out of sight after he interviewed Sean. He's bound to be holed up in some motel nearby, calling the shots. He may be getting desperate—I'd bet his bosses in Vegas are starting to lose patience, especially if they're losing men. Desperate people make mistakes, and he's bound to make one. We'll be there when he does."

The commander said, "Stay in touch with your counterparts with the Las Vegas police, too. Find out all you can about Rossi's activities there." The meeting broke up, and the men went about their assignments.

Sean and Brad discussed their next moves. Sean said, "One thing for sure—I don't want one of us or someone else to be shot getting too close to Harley. I think he's under a lot of pressure and likely to be trigger-happy."

"No kidding, Sean. That run-in we had with him when we arrested him was enough for me. That's one dangerous man."

"I'll go to the Buckeye airport and see if we can hire a plane and pilot to take us on a scouting trip. Tomorrow's Sunday, so I'll try to set it up for first thing Monday morning."

"Sounds good, Sean. I'll let you know if I pick up anything new today. There's still a couple of folks I need to talk to."

They headed out to their patrol cruisers. Sean was driving on Highway 80 toward Buckeye when he encountered a wreck involving two cars. It was at a dangerous intersection called Tamarack Corner. Visibility wasn't good for cars entering US 80, and cars tended to drive too fast on the highway. Several other cars were stopped on the road. Sean kicked on his red lights and

121

drove up next to the wrecked cars. Two men were down on the ground, going at it. They rolled around on the pavement, cursing and punching at each other. Sean grabbed his nightstick, approached the men, and yelled, "Hey! That's enough. Break it up, or I'll haul both of you off to jail!"

The men started to get up when one of them grabbed the other by the collar and punched him in the face. He drew back to hit him again, and Sean gave him a good rap on the knuckles with his nightstick.

"Ow!" the man said. "You broke my knuckles!"

"I didn't hit you hard enough to break anything, sir. But I might if you don't settle down." The man looked like all the air had gone out of him. Then the other driver started cursing and yelling about how it was the other driver's fault, and Sean could see they were about to go at it again. He stepped between them, put a hand on each man's chest, and pushed them apart. "All right, all right! Enough! One of you sit over there on the side of the road, and the other on the opposite side. I need to clean up this mess, and then we'll sort out who's at fault here."

The men grudgingly complied. Neither of them wanted a whack from Sean's nightstick. Sean got on his radio and called for two wreckers and another deputy to help with traffic. By the time they arrived, Sean had determined the man who had turned onto the highway was at fault. "You men are both lucky you weren't hurt. This is a bad intersection; if you're in too much of a hurry pulling out, you're likely to get hit. Now, you guys act civilized and exchange your insurance information. No more fighting. It's over. You can get a ride into town with the wreckers." He wrote the driver who caused the accident a ticket for failure to yield.

Sean stuck around helping the other deputy direct traffic until the wrecks were cleared. When it was done, he said, "Thanks for the help, Robbie. Those two guys were a handful."

He drove through Buckeye to the airport on the west side of town. He found a pilot he knew working on his Stinson and said, "Hi, Tom! Long time no see!"

"Hey! Hi Sean! How ya been?"

They exchanged pleasantries for a while, and Sean told him he needed to hire a plane at the department's expense.

"I'm your man, Sean! When do you need it?"

"Monday morning, if you're available. It would only be for an hour or so, all nearby. We are looking for something out near Woolsey Peak."

"Something to do with that plane that crashed out there?"

"Not directly. We just need a better look at the area from the air."

"No problem. I'll be ready. Say 9 o'clock?"

"That's perfect, Tom. It will be me and another deputy. We'll see you then.

🌵

Sean decided to take a different route back to the district office. He'd seen enough of Highway 80 for the day. He passed through the little community of Perryville; his memories of the investigation of the Weighmaster there seemed longer than just a few months ago. He came upon a dog lying beside the road a couple of miles east of the village. He could see it was injured but alive; he pulled over to see what he could do for it.

It was a young male with beautiful tan hair around his eyes, muzzle, and floppy ears. His chest and forelegs were the same tan; the rest of his body was black. His tail had been bobbed, giving him a stout look. He didn't recognize the breed. The dog whimpered and looked at him with pleading brown eyes. Sean squatted beside him and said, "Hey, buddy. Take it easy. Let's see what's wrong." The dog continued a low whimper, and Sean could see his front leg was misshapen and bleeding. Probably hit by a car, he thought, and the bastard just drove on and left him to suffer.

The dog gave a low growl and showed a menacing set of teeth when Sean gingerly touched his leg. "It's okay, buddy. I'm gonna help you out." He reached out slowly and stroked the dog's head, continuing to speak to him in a low, soothing voice. The dog relaxed a little. Sean opened the trunk of his patrol car and took out a wool emergency blanket. He wrapped the blanket around his right arm several times to avoid becoming acquainted with the dog's teeth. He opened the car's passenger door and returned to the dog. "It's okay, buddy," he said again. "You're gonna be okay." He reached under the dog's back and gently lifted him. The dog cried loudly and nipped at Sean's arm covered by the blanket. "It's okay, buddy. It's okay." Sean kept soothing the dog as he laid him on the car seat. "Let's go for a ride."

He took him to a veterinarian near his district office. He opened the vet's door and went back for the dog. He lifted him gently off the seat and carried him inside. The vet said, "Bring him into the exam room and lay him on the table." The dog seemed to know they were trying to help him and lay still on the table, whining softly.

"Is this your dog, Sean?"

Sean explained about finding him beside the road, and then he said, "Fix him up, doc. I'll pay whatever it costs."

The examination revealed the dog's leg was broken, and the bone had pierced the skin. It was still oozing a little blood. The vet said, "I can set it and bandage the wound, but I'll have to sedate him to do it. It'll take about an hour for the sedative to wear off."

"I'll come back for him then. What breed of dog is he? I don't recall seeing one like him."

"He looks to be a Rottweiler mixed with a German Shepherd. See how his hindquarters have that elongated look that Shepherds have? The head and front quarters look like a Rottweiler. The black body with tan markings is also a Rottweiler trait. I'd say he's a little less than a year old; he's going to be a big boy. He's

124

probably sixty or seventy pounds now. He'll go well over a hundred pounds when he's fully grown. You gonna keep him?"

"I don't know. Maybe. I just found him, and I couldn't leave him there to die beside the road. I'll let you know when I come back for him. He reached over, scratched the dog's ears again, and said, "It's okay, buddy." Then he left for his office.

By the time he finished his report for the day, it was five o'clock. A little over an hour had passed, and he drove his pickup to the veterinarian's office. The dog was coming out of the sedation and was still a little glassy-eyed. The vet said, "He's going to be fine. It was a clean break and set nicely. He can walk on it, but it will be sore for a while. The flesh wound was minor and will heal quickly. He's going to lick and tear at the bandages. I'll give you some extra so you can keep his wound covered. Bring him back in two weeks, and we'll check the break."

Sean paid the bill and said, "I think I'll keep him, doc. My last dog was killed, and I could use a friend around the house."

"Yeah, I heard about that, Sean. Sarge was a great dog; I remember when you brought him in for his shots. There's no way to know if this guy has been vaccinated. We should probably do that pretty soon."

"I'll bring him in for it when he recuperates."

"One more thing, Sean—a dog like this will have a lot of energy and a bite that can do serious damage. I'd recommend you find a trainer to work with and get him off on the right foot…so to speak." He snickered at his off-the-cuff joke.

"That's a good idea, doc. Thanks. I think I know someone who can help me with that."

Sean gathered the dog in his arms, took him out to his truck, and gently laid him on the seat, "Let's go home, buddy," he said. He took him to his house and let him hobble around while he put food and water in Sarge's old dishes. He still had lots of canned dog food in the cupboard. The dog wolfed it down and looked expectantly at Sean. "That's all for now, buddy. Don't wanna overdo it." The dog followed him around the house, watching as he changed into jeans and a t-shirt and walked barefoot back to the kitchen. Sean made himself a bologna and tomato sandwich and stood watching the dog. He tore off a little piece of the meat and tossed it to the dog; he caught it handily and was ready for more. Sean gave him another small piece and said, "No more, buddy. Gotta save some for me." He studied the dog while he ate his sandwich. "Buddy. I guess that's gonna be your name from now on, pal." He could have sworn the dog smiled at him. Then he licked his foot, followed him into the living room, and lay down beside the chair where Sean sat. An old Martin guitar leaned against the arm of the chair, and the dog watched with interest when Sean picked it up. The dog's ears stood up when he strummed a chord, and Sean laughed. He played a little bit of Wildwood Flower, and the dog lay listening and watching.

Afterward, Sean laid Sarge's old bedding on the floor beside his bed. Buddy seemed to know instinctively it was for him, stood on it, turned around three or four times, then curled up and watched Sean. He scratched his ears and said, "Good dog, Buddy. You're a good dog." They were both sound asleep in a few minutes, and Buddy snored contentedly beside his new master.

Sean spent Sunday getting acquainted with Buddy and teaching him about his new home. First, the dog got a bath, and then Sean showed him how to use the dog door he had installed for Sarge. It only took a little show-and-tell encouragement for the dog to understand how it worked. Buddy walked around the backyard, checking out the high cedar fence, sniffing at the traces of Sarge, and marking the territory as his own.

Sean's next-door neighbor agreed to come in a couple of times a day to check on the dog when Sean was at work. She spent a little time with Buddy that day so he would be comfortable with her when Sean was away.

CHAPTER 21

Brad and Sean met at the district office Monday morning, then headed for the Buckeye airport. Sean drove the Jeep, and Brad followed with his patrol car. The Jeep would be needed if they saw something they needed to follow up on from their airplane surveillance.

Tom, the pilot, was ready for them when they arrived. Sean said, "Tom, I think this plane is the same model as the one that crashed on the mountain."

He replied, "Yep. Same one. These Stinson Reliants are workhorses. They're the most trustworthy thing in the air, so long as you maintain and treat them right. But they ain't gonna hold up if you fly one of 'em into the side of a mountain!" He opened the aircraft's door and said, "I'll get in first, then you guys climb aboard."

The three of them had plenty of room in the spacious cabin designed for four passengers. The plane's wings, tail, and upper fuselage were painted bright yellow, set off against the underside of the body's olive green. Sean slid under the steering yoke in the co-pilot's seat and studied the array of instruments set into the walnut wood dash. He had been in enough airplanes to have some familiarity with the basic instrument functions: altimeter, fuel, airspeed, and attitude. There were several others he didn't recognize. Brad sat in the passenger seat behind the pilot; the men would be able to scan opposite sides with their binoculars.

Tom said, "You guys ready?" Both deputies gave him a thumbs up. He fired up the big Pratt and Whitney radial engine, checked all his gauges, and then taxied out to the runway. It was a perfectly clear day without a monsoon thunderhead in sight. The men could see a hundred miles in either direction when they gained cruising altitude. It was only a few minutes until Tom steered the plane to follow the Agua Caliente Road and make their first pass over the foreboding desert wilderness.

Sean had briefed the pilot on what they were looking for. They would maintain an altitude of around two thousand feet and make their first pass along the Signal Mountain area northwest of Woolsey Peak on the opposite side of the valley; Ruby had told Sean that Harley had a second camp somewhere in that area. Then, they made a one-hundred-eighty-degree turn and followed the edge of the Gila Bend mountains back toward Woolsey Peak. Sean thought he had spotted the canyon Ruby had described from her visit to Harley's main camp. Then they repeated the one-eighty, descended to five hundred feet, and followed the same pattern as the first pass.

Sean told the pilot they had seen enough and to return to the airport. They flew over a white pickup truck making its way along the primitive track below them. Something about it looked vaguely familiar to Sean, but he couldn't place it. Probably hunters, he thought. They landed and thanked the pilot; Sean told him to bill the Sheriff's Department. The two deputies went into town to discuss what to do next.

Harley heard the roar of the plane's engine before he saw it pass far across the valley to the north. He watched it skim the area around Sentinel Peak, then turn around and come back along the Gila Bend Mountains to the west. Then, it circled and repeated the pattern at a lower altitude. He was certain now they were looking for him. There's only one thing this could mean, he thought. Somebody tipped them off! Ruby! No one else knew where he was. He'd make her pay when this was over!

Something snapped in Harley's mind. He went into a rage, storming around his campsite, kicking his coffee pot over, banging his fists on the hood of the Beast, and cursing everyone he thought he needed to take revenge on: that guy from the casino who murdered his brother, his lawyer, Ruby, and even that deputy sheriff that arrested him. They had all turned on him. He was only trying to better himself. None of them could understand that.

The canyon was still in shadow around his camp. It was doubtful they could see his dark grey truck. The distinctive colors of the plane were familiar to him; its owner kept it at the Buckeye airport. He had seen it come and go from there many times. His instincts told him this was a scouting party, and they would be coming for him soon. He didn't want to have a last-stand shootout with the cops—at least not yet. That would be a last resort. It was time for a new plan. He packed some of his weapons in the beast, then gathered his gear and stored it in the bunker. When he was ready, he waited another half hour to make sure the plane didn't come back, and then he left Site One. He went down the canyon and carefully maneuvered around his hidden tire shredders in the sandy wash bottom. He drove along the track to where it joined the main road, then turned west toward Agua Caliente. He would take a long way to the west around the mountains and circle back through Gila Bend.

Sean and Brad settled in at a table in the local café for coffee and to compare notes. Sean had acquired a recently published topographic map from the U.S. Geological Survey and spread it on their table. It had excellent data; it even showed the small spring up the canyon where they believed Harley had his camp. Sean put his finger on that spot and said, "I'm about ninety percent certain this is where Harley is. From the air, it looked like a pretty easy place to defend. He could set up a little way up the canyon mouth and pick off anyone who tried to approach. He's been a hunter all his life—it would be a regular duck shoot for him."

Brad whistled softly. "Yeah, I see that. Judging from our past experience with the guy, I wouldn't want to give him that opportunity."

"I wouldn't have taken him for a killer before all these recent events. His brother being murdered may have sent him over the edge. And if he's got a bunch of money from that casino, it might make him a little crazy wanting to hang on to it. He and his brother had a pretty tough life after their father died. He may be planning to make a run for Mexico. There's no telling what he might do— a lot of men have killed for less."

"Do you have any ideas we could try?"

Sean studied the map. "Well, the canyon comes down along the west side of Woolsey Peak. We might be able to go over the mountain from the east and come down on him from above. I doubt Harley would expect anyone to come at him from that direction, so we'd have the element of surprise working for us. But it would be tough. I've hiked that country hunting deer with my father, and it's very difficult. The top of Woolsey Peak is fairly flat, but it's like a forest of teddy bear cholla cactus. It's slow going; you have to pick your way through them and watch every step on loose rocks. If you trip and fall, you'll be digging out cactus thorns for days. There's plenty of cactus on the slopes, too. Remember how tough the climb was when you and I went up to the wreck?"

Brad nodded.

"It's even tougher going down the other side to reach that canyon. It would take the best part of a day. We might have to stay overnight and take him in the morning."

They sat sipping their coffee in silence for a few minutes. Brad blew out a breath and said, "And then there's the snakes— I don't want to end up like poor Steve. But, if you're in, I'm in. I'm tired of goin' around in circles lookin' for this guy."

"Let's go back to the office and talk it over with the commander. We'll need some support to bring him in if we're able to capture him. Then we'll have to prepare for the hike and possibly sleep overnight on the mountain."

El Puma and his men had left their motel before dawn that morning. "We should have this gringo and be back here by nightfall," he told his men on the road. "Remember—we have to take him alive. Shoot to wound him only. If you can't do that, then hold your shot." They talked about various ways they might approach him without being wounded— or killed.

El Puma said, "We will go in on foot. One of you take each side of the canyon, and I'll go up the wash. Keep an eye out for someplace to take cover if he starts shooting." They reached the turnoff and headed west.

The Army-issue Dodge truck rode like a buckboard over the rutted road, but it easily climbed in and out of the washes. It was one of the few vehicles available with four-wheel drive, and they felt lucky to have it. El Puma and his men had often used it to pursue their prey across the trackless desert. This road was nothing compared to that. They just had to take it slow and easy and let the four-wheel drive do the work.

El Puma saw the plane flying across the plain to the north of them. He began to be suspicious of what it was doing when it circled back. It passed over them, made a wide sweeping turn, and went back in the opposite direction, this time at a lower altitude. He knew he had competition for his prey when it circled back at a lower altitude.

"We have company, muchachos," he told his men. "I think it may be la policia in that airplane buzzing around. We need to move fast." The driver sped up, jarring their teeth and bouncing them against each other on the desert track. They stopped when they neared where the wash coming out of the canyon cut across the road. El Puma studied the entrance to the canyon with his binoculars. He could see nothing from that spot; they would have to move closer. They eased along the wash's east side into the canyon's mouth. He said, "See those tracks in the sand along the bottom of the wash? Drop us down there and move slowly up the canyon." The driver did as instructed when suddenly there were two loud bangs. The truck moved a few more feet, and the vehicle's front end dropped into a trench with a jarring thud. "Que paso?" the driver yelled. "What's happened?"

131

The men bailed out of the truck to find the problem. El Puma studied what had happened and started cursing. The damn gringo had set a trap, and they drove right into it. He studied their position and said, "We may be lucky to be alive, amigos. It would be a simple thing for him to have picked us off when we got out of the truck. Look up there." He pointed at the rock formations higher up the canyon. "It would have been easy for a skilled hunter to take us out. He may not be in position, or he may not even be here. But he surely would have heard the bangs from our tires being punctured. We have to move with great caution." They spread out along the wash according to their earlier plan, keeping to any sparse cover available as they moved up the canyon.

It was obvious their quarry wasn't there when they reached the campsite. El Puma felt the coals in the small campfire. They were still warm. "He has not been gone long. And he left in a hurry. You can see how things are scattered around." They examined the bunker door, and El Puma whistled softly. "It would take dynamite to budge this door. We need to be sure and bring some if we have to come back here." He thought briefly and said, "The bonds we are after might be inside. We will discuss it with Señor Rossi tonight. Let's get out of here!"

They always carried two spare tires for the tuck. But first, they had to get the truck out of the trench the front wheels were in. The driver put it in reverse, and the other two men pushed for all they were worth on the front to get the truck back on level sand. They changed the tires and headed back on the long drive to Phoenix to report what they had found.

CHAPTER 22

Harley turned off the dirt desert road onto U.S. Highway 80, about thirty miles west of Gila Bend. He drove into the town, filled the Beast's gas tank, and bought a couple of bags of stale potato chips at the gas station. He continued north on the highway until he reached the Gila River bridge at Gillespie Dam. He pulled off the highway onto the dam's access road and parked out of sight from the highway. Then he laid down on the seat for a nap; he had a long night ahead.

He woke up as the sun dropped behind the mountains to the west. He waited until full dark, got back on the highway, and headed north toward Buckeye. He slipped into town the back way; he didn't want to take a chance on someone seeing him when it was light. He drove around behind the machine shop and parked. Knowing that he now owned the building and its contents felt weird. He doubted he'd ever make much use of them— except for now. He unlocked the back door and slid it open wide enough to drive the Beast in. Then he locked the door and started walking toward the house, which was also his now. He stayed out of sight of the few passing cars and made sure no one was nearby before he approached his house. He had parked his brother's old Ford truck beside the house after the cops finished their investigation. It started as soon as the engine turned over, and he headed toward Phoenix. Then he checked into a cheap motel on Van Buren under a fake name, ate dinner at a nearby greasy spoon diner, and called it a night.

The following day, he called Fishburn, his attorney, from the pay phone in the motel lobby. Harley said, "I need to see you about the bonds. When can you meet me?"

"Can't we do it over the phone?" Fishburn was cautious, but he smelled money to be made if he handled things right.

133

"Naw, there's too much to talk about. I'm staying in town and need to talk to you now."

"Where do you want to meet?"

Harley gave him the address of the diner next door and said, "Meet me in an hour." The attorney agreed, even though he'd have to juggle several appointments. The lure of those bonds was worth a lot more than a couple of small clients.

Harley could see the diner from the motel's lobby. He watched Fishburn arrive and go inside, then gave him ten minutes to be sure no one else showed up. The sonofabitch sold him out once; he might try it again. He didn't see anyone else enter the diner and walked over and joined the lawyer at a table.

They ordered coffee, and Fishburn said, "I'm a busy man. What do you want to talk about?"

"Yeah, yeah, don't get yer panties in a bunch. You know what I've got, and it's worth a hell of a lot more than whatever business you're missing." He paused and took a sip of coffee before continuing, "I wanna make a deal with the casino people for the bonds."

The lawyer nearly dropped his coffee cup. "What? What kind of deal? These people aren't looking for a deal. They want those bonds and will stop at nothing to get them."

"Well, that's all good, but I've got their damn bonds, and they're gonna have to deal with me to get 'em back."

"Harley, listen to me. You don't know these people. They'll take the bonds, then they'll kill you."

"Yeah. Like they did my brother."

The attorney was silent for a moment and said, "What do you want me to do?"

"I want you to set up a meeting. Here's the deal: I'll keep twenty-five percent of the bonds and give them the rest."

"They'll never go for that, Harley. Hell, you're talking about a quarter million dollars!"

"That's better than losing all of it, ain't it? Tell 'em I'm tired of killin' off their people. They can deal, or more of their guys will get dead. Maybe that guy Rossi hisself."

Fishburn sucked in a breath. He couldn't believe what he was hearing. This hair-brained scheme was hazardous for Harley and for him. "What's in it for me?" he asked.

Harley smiled and said, "I thought you'd never ask. I'll give you five percent for setting it up. All you gotta do is make a few phone calls."

"Five percent! Five percent! I'll be risking my neck here. I won't do it for less than twenty percent."

"Ten percent, or I'll find another lawyer to help me."

"All right, all right. Ten percent, then. How do you want to do it?"

"You make contact with Rossi tomorrow and see if they'll deal. I'll call you in the afternoon, and if they agree, I'll give you the details to set up the meeting."

"It's your funeral, but I'll do the best I can."

Harley checked out of the motel and headed for Buckeye. He was seething inside, banging on the steering wheel, cursing everyone he thought he could trust. His big plan had gone to hell, all because someone ratted out his location at Site One. Ruby! It had to be Ruby. No one but his brother had known that location until he took her there. Now he realized his mistake—what a fool he had been. She would pay for what she had done to him.

He rolled into her driveway as she was getting home from work. As he pulled in, she was starting into her house with a double armload of groceries. She heard a car come into her driveway and turned to see who it was. At first, she didn't recognize the truck. Then she saw Harley and realized it was his brother's pickup.

Harley climbed out of the truck, his face like a roiling thunderhead. Ruby knew she was in trouble instantly but had nowhere to run.

He growled, "Let me help you with those groceries, baby. Then we need to talk." She handed him one of the bags, and he followed her into the house. They sat the bags on the kitchen table, but he backhanded her across her face before she could say anything. She reeled backward and caught herself against the kitchen counter.

"What did you do?" He yelled. "Who did you tell?"

Ruby sobbed and said, "I only wanted to help you."

"You bitch! Some help! I'll only ask one more time—who did you tell?"

"Sean! It was Sean, the deputy sheriff. He said you were in trouble and wanted to keep you from getting hurt!"

"I told you to never, ever, tell anyone about my place. You've ruined everything!"

"I'm sorry, I'm sorry! Sean said..."

He hit her again with his fist, square in the face this time. Blood gushed from her broken nose, and he hit her again. "You bitch!" he screamed in a blind rage, repeating it over and over as he beat her. He had her pinned against the counter, and she couldn't run. Then he wrapped his ham-sized hands around her neck and squeezed until the terror went out of her eyes, and she slumped against him. She crumpled into a lifeless form on the kitchen tile when he shoved her away.

He stood there looking at her, still in a mindless rage, and yelled, "You bitch!" again and kicked her motionless body. Then he went into her living room, collapsed into an armchair, and sat trying to calm his breath until his crazed fury began to pass. He returned to the kitchen after he calmed down and found a can of Coors in the refrigerator. The church key hung on its string by the fridge, and he used it to open the beer. He kicked Ruby's body again as he walked by, mumbling "bitch" to himself, then flopped down in the easy chair and tried to think.

🌵

The commander had agreed with his deputies' plan and authorized them to borrow the equipment they would need from another district— a Jeep with a recently acquired military-style two-way radio system used in rescue operations. John Snyder, A Mesa district deputy, was trained to operate the unit and assigned to the operation along with Robbie Fuller, another deputy from the Avondale office. The Mesa deputy brought the Jeep and radio. It had a long willowy antenna curving over the passenger compartment and tied off at the front.

The men gathered around the conference room table to go over the plan. Sean spread his map and said, "Brad and I will leave early tomorrow morning. We'll drop the first Jeep at our jump-off point for the hike. Robbie, you, and John will pick up our Jeep and then take both vehicles up to the rendezvous point at the mouth of the canyon here." He showed them where the wash came out of the canyon's mouth on the map, then continued, "We'll stay in touch with the two-way radio and let you know our progress. I expect it will be mid-afternoon when we reach Harley's camp. Hopefully, we'll take him by surprise, then walk him out of the canyon to you. He'll have to be thoroughly tied up in a Jeep to take him out of here. We can transfer him into one of our patrol cars when we get back to the highway."

Robbie said, "Show us how the radio works, John. I've never seen one."

They went out in the parking lot, and John demonstrated the system. "I'll operate this unit as a base station while Sean or Brad operate the handset. Its pack weighs 35 pounds, so you guys will need to pack light."

"We used these in my Army unit," Sean said. "I'm familiar with how it works."

"Great!" John said. "I'll meet up here with Robbie in the morning and establish contact with you on the mountain. The radio has a range of about five miles if there aren't any obstructions."

They tested the radios and were satisfied it was working. Then, they went over the rest of the details and packed the Jeeps with the supplies they would need.

Sean and Brad left at four a.m. the next day. They wanted to be at their starting point at first light. Sean carried the radio pack, while Brad had a small pack of food, a first aid kit, and extra ammunition. Both carried two canteens of water on their belts. They planned to trade off the packs every couple of hours. At noon, they made their first radio contact with the other deputies. They had climbed Woolsey Peak and were preparing to start down the canyon. Sean told the men they would make one more contact before approaching the camp.

They passed some strange rings of rocks on top of the peak. They were arranged in concentric circles and looked totally foreign in such a desolate place. "What are these circles for, Sean? They look like they've been here forever."

"I asked an Indian guy I know who said he had been up here many times. He said the ancient ones made them because they considered this mountain sacred. They had some kind of rituals involving the circles. There are several of them up here."

"It's a strange place. But a helluva view!"

They had views of the Gila Bend Mountains to the west, Signal Mountain to the north, and the Eagletail Mountains beyond. It was a wild and rugged country.

The deputies reached a position in the late afternoon where they could scan the campsite with binoculars. Sean said, "I don't see any sign of movement. And there's no vehicle in sight. We may have missed him, but let's proceed slowly and quietly." He checked in with the others on the radio and told them to maintain radio silence until he next contacted them. The two deputies picked their way over rocks and boulders along the canyon until they reached the camp. They approached with weapons ready, but the camp was deserted. There were signs of recent use, but Harley was gone.

Brad ran his hand over the bunker's steel door and said, "Wow. It would take dynamite to get this thing open. How the hell did he build something like this way out here?"

"I don't know, Brad. He's a resourceful man. But there's nothing we can do here now. Let's contact the others and tell them the bad news, then get out of here."

Sean hated having to report their failure. But there was no other way to find out if Harley was there. A frontal approach would have resulted in a firefight if he had been. They would have to keep looking elsewhere.

✤

Harley had spent the night in the bed he had shared with Ruby so many times in the past. He had no remorse for killing her. She deserved it so far as he was concerned. He told himself that a friend you couldn't trust didn't deserve to live.

He awoke at dawn as he always had. He felt strangely refreshed after a better night's sleep than he'd had in a while. He went into the kitchen and made a pot of coffee, stepping around and sometimes over Ruby's body. The refrigerator had bacon and eggs, and he fried up all the bacon and three eggs. He had a few hours before the lawyer would be in his office—plenty of time to set up the plan he had devised.

A large stack of haybales was directly across the road on the farm across from Ruby's place. The stack was eight rows wide and six bales high. It would make a fine shooter's hide; no one would give a second glance to a haystack in the middle of farm country. He judged it to be about a hundred yards from the house's front porch—an easy shot for him. The top of the haystack was about fifteen feet above the ground. One end was conveniently stair-stepped where the farmer had removed bales for his cattle; getting up and down the stack would be easy. The elevation would be a great advantage when the shooting started, and he could see a long distance each way down the road in front of the house. Perfect, he thought.

He made sure no one was around, and there was no traffic on the road. Then he crossed the road and climbed up the end of the haystack. The top row of bales was stacked perpendicular to the highway and house across the road. He slid two bales out of the second row from the end and tossed them down where others had been removed. It left enough of a gap to allow him to lie down in the gap between the bales in the adjoining rows. He couldn't be seen from across the road or by passing cars. The bales made a perfect barrier should anyone be lucky enough to get off a shot at him. He had a clear view of Ruby's house in front of him and the roadway for a hundred yards or so in either direction.

His .30-06 Remington with a sniper scope was behind the seat in his brother's truck. He took it and extra cartridges on a bandolier back to his hide on the haystack. When the time came, his .357 would go into its belt holster at his waist. There were extra rounds for the pistol in slots on the belt, but he doubted he would need them. He was satisfied with his plan and went back to Ruby's house to call the attorney.

Fishburn's secretary answered the phone and said, "Oh yes, Mr. Henderson. Mr. Fishburn is waiting for your call."

Fishburn picked up the phone and said without preamble, "I got hold of Rossi. I had to call the Lucky Joker casino in Vegas and get bounced around til I could finally talk to the owner. He sounded pissed off but agreed to relay a message to Rossi to call me. He was madder than a hornet that I had talked to his boss; sounds like things aren't going well between them."

"Yeah, yeah. What'd he say?"

"He said there was no way he would agree to your terms. I told him it was the only way he would get any of the bonds back. Then he slammed down the phone."

"Was that it? All he said?"

"He called back about fifteen minutes later and said he would accept your terms, but he said he needed to know where you want to meet so he can check it out."

Harley chuckled. "Yeah, the last time he came lookin' for me didn't go so well. So, here's the deal. You tell him I'll meet him at exactly noon tomorrow." He gave the lawyer directions on how to get to Ruby's house, then added, "Tell him he'll see my brother's blue Ford truck parked in front of the house…and you tell that bastard to come alone, too. No more of his goons."

"I'll tell him. How can I reach you to confirm it?"

"I'll call you back in an hour. Set it up." Then he hung up the phone. He smiled to himself. No way a guy like that would come alone. He called Fishburn back an hour later, and the lawyer confirmed the plan.

That night, Harley drove Ruby's car a half-mile east of her house, where a copse of salt cedar bushes ringed a small pond. He parked the car on the side, away from Ruby's house, where it wouldn't be seen from the road. Then he moved his brother's old Ford pickup into the driveway, where it was in plain sight. His preparations were done. All he could do was wait.

CHAPTER 23

Buddy woke Sean up at daylight, scratching and sniffing around the bedroom, and then Sean heard the dog door in the back open and close on its hinges. The dog returned a few minutes later as Sean got up. He looked at his new master expectantly.

"You hungry, boy? Need somethin' to eat?" The dog would have wagged his tail if he had one. Instead, he stood shaking his backside and panting with his long tongue hanging out. "Let's go see what we can find," and Buddy led the way into the kitchen. Sean opened a can of food, put it in the dog's bowl, and sat it beside the water dish, and Buddy dove in with a passion.

Sean put on a pot of coffee and switched on the big Philco radio in the living room. As always, it was tuned to KOY's early morning news program. But this morning was different—the announcer was chattering so fast it was almost difficult to sort out what he was saying. Something about Japan… the announcer finally slowed down and said, "Ladies and Gentlemen! Great news! We have just received word that Japan surrendered at seven p.m. our time last night. Emperor Hirohito made the declaration at noon Japan time. This is breaking news, and we'll update you as soon as we have more. Again, Japan has surrendered! The war is over!"

Sean stood for a full minute, dumbfounded by this news. The world was about to change in ways he couldn't imagine. It was a hard thing to wrap his brain around. It seemed like the war would go on forever despite two atomic bombs being dropped on Japan's homeland.

His next thought was that he wished Annaleigh could have been there with him to celebrate. They would have hugged each other and danced around the room like giddy teenagers. He was reminded how much he missed her at times like this.

He returned to the kitchen, cracked three eggs in a skillet, and scrambled them up. "It's just you and me, Buddy, but it's a great day anyway." He toasted two slices of bread and sat down to eat his breakfast. The radio droned on in the living room, repeating the same news over and over.

When he got to the district office, it was buzzing with news of the Japanese surrender. Everyone wondered what would happen next: When would the soldiers come home? Where would they work? How would they act...the speculation went on and on. Sean left on patrol.

Harley was up early, pacing the floor, anxious to get on with his plan. The news that was electrifying most of the country was unknown to him; he cared nothing about news and seldom listened to the radio. The only thing on his mind was revenge for his brother's murder.

He rolled the plan over and over in his mind. He was sure Rossi wouldn't come alone. The coward would be afraid to face him by himself. Harley figured he would do something like he tried at the house belonging to him and his brother. Rossi sent his men to the door while he stayed in the car. Harley had narrowly missed him then—he wouldn't miss this time.

The clock on Ruby's kitchen wall ticked along mercilessly slow. Finally, at eleven o'clock, he stepped outside and looked around carefully. There was no one around, no cars on the road. He crossed the road and took up his position on the haystack. The scouting party would no doubt be along soon. It was humid tucked into the alfalfa hay, and the hot August sun beat down on him. He was quickly drenched with sweat, tied his handkerchief around his forehead to keep it out of his eyes, and pulled his grey Case farm equipment cap down to shade his view from the sun's glare. He was ready.

A white Dodge pickup truck drove by the house a half hour later. It looked like the ones he'd seen pictures of the Army using in the war, except for the color. Harley could see three men inside. They cruised by very slowly, going east, then turned around and made another pass. They parked beside the road about a hundred yards west of his position. A few minutes later, a black Cadillac showed up. It stopped beside the pickup, and the drivers of both vehicles had a conversation. Then the pickup turned around, drove slowly back, and parked beside the road in front of Ruby's house; the Cadillac eased forward about fifty yards and parked beside the road.

Harley was sure it was Rossi in the Cadillac. That coward is pulling the same trick as before, Harley thought. Stay out of sight while someone else does his dirty work.

The three men got out of the pickup truck and cautiously moved toward the house. Harley could see they were Mexican. Two of them carried shotguns, and the other, who appeared to be the leader, drew a large revolver from a waist holster. The two with shotguns were moving to take a position on either side of the house while the leader approached the front.

"This ain't gonna work this time," Harley whispered. "You won't get away from me again." He swung the rifle barrel to his left; there was just enough room to place the Cadillac in his scope's sight. He had never seen Rossi, but the man behind the car's steering wheel had to be him. Who else would have shown up in a Caddy? he thought. A slight adjustment on the scope framed the man's head dead center in its crosshairs. Harley took a breath, eased it out, and slowly squeezed the trigger. There was an explosion of blood inside the car; the driver's head snapped back, and then his body slumped over the steering wheel. Harley could see that the top half of the man's head was gone.

The sharp crack of the rifle's shot froze the three Mexicans advancing on the house. It was loud and very close, but they didn't have a sense of where it came from. There was another crack, and the man on Harley's left collapsed in the yard. The bullet had passed through his back and likely severed his spine before passing through his heart. El Puma instinctively dropped to the ground and shouted for his other man to take cover. But the

144

warning was too late—the second man had spun around toward the sound of the shot, and the next round took him in the chest. The impact of the round flung him backward against the wall of the house. He was dead before his body finished sliding down onto the ground. El Puma took off in a crouching, zig-zagging run toward his truck. Another shot barely missed him—he felt the sting of dirt and gravel hit his leg before he dived behind the truck bed. Another shot slammed into the back bumper just behind where he landed.

El Puma had a brief glimpse of the shooter's position as he ran for cover. The stack of hay bales made an excellent and well-protected shooter's hide, nestled between the hay bales. The distance was too great for accuracy with his handgun, but maybe it could buy him some time—he might even get in a lucky shot. He reached over his head and opened the door on the truck's driver's side. He might live through this if he timed it right and was blessed by the Virgin Mary. He slowly raised up at the back of the cab and fired three quick shots at where he thought the shooter was. Then he dived inside, slammed the door, and leaned to the side on the seat. A bullet immediately crashed through the rear window and passed through the window on the driver's side. Glass shards sprayed above him inside the cab. In the time it took the shooter to reload, he reached with his left leg to depress the clutch and engage a gear, and then he stomped on the truck's foot starter. It roared into life, and then he hit the gas pedal. The truck was in second gear and lurched ahead as he sat up. Another round came through the rear window. It grazed his forehead, dazed him slightly, and went through the front windshield, leaving a spiderweb of cracks in front of him. He kept the engine revved high and sped down the road, swerving from side to side. He was soon too far away for the shooter to get another shot.

"Damn! Missed him!" Harley said out loud. "Nothin' I can do about it now." He grabbed his rifle, climbed off the haystack, and ran across the road to Ruby's house. He had to hurry to carry out the rest of his plan before someone called the cops about the gunshots. He leaned his rifle against the house, grabbed the first dead man to his right, and dragged him up the porch and inside the house. Then he went to the other side and dragged the second man inside. He had placed a five-gallon can of gasoline in the house that morning and spread it liberally around the rooms. He took one last look at Ruby, walked to the front door, and threw a lighted match into the living room. The gas burst into flames that quickly raced through the house. The wooden frame structure was entirely engulfed in minutes.

He grabbed his rifle and ran back toward the Cadillac. He stopped and looked inside at the dead man sitting in a pool of blood on the seat. The engine was still running. Harley thought it was a great scene; it would give the cops a lot to talk about when they showed up. Then he ran the quarter mile further east where Ruby's car was hidden.

CHAPTER 24

El Puma drove a few miles away from the blazing house and pulled over into the shade of a cottonwood tree beside the road. His scalp was bleeding freely from the grazing wound the bullet made. He got out and washed the blood off his face in clean water flowing in an irrigation ditch beside the tree. He dunked his head in the water to try and remove drying blood from his scalp and hair, then took off his shirt and used it to dry his head as best he could. A first aid kit under the truck seat had some basic supplies. Using the rearview mirror, he sprinkled a packet of sulfanilamide in the wound, then applied a gauze dressing and taped it down as best he could. He'd find a hospital to treat it later.

He sat in the truck for a few minutes, trying to calm his nerves and think what to do next. Rossi had led him and his men into an ambush, which he had only survived by the grace of God. Rossi died, too, and good riddance. Such a man should not have been in charge.

That damned gringo. This was the second time he had set a trap for him. The more he thought about it, the more his rage and thirst for vengeance grew. He would find him, and he would avenge his men's death. His honor required it. He would not be able to face his employers in the cartel in Mexico if he failed. And he would never work again.

But first, he had to get proper treatment for his wound. An infection could slow him down, and he might need stitches. Then he would find and kill this gringo.

🌵

The volunteer fire department arrived at Ruby's house just in time to put water on the remaining embers. A Buckeye Police patrolman arrived despite the house being outside the city limits.

He looked at the body in the Cadillac and got on his radio to call for help. The call was relayed to the Sheriff's Department, which dispatched a patrol and ambulance. Sean was only a few miles away and was the first to respond to the call.

He stopped behind the Cadillac and put his emergency lights on. Ruby's house, he thought. What's happened here? He first noted that the car's engine was still running, but the car was out of gear. A body was slumped over the wheel with pieces of shattered glass stuck in the blood on his body and the seat. That meant the driver had stopped before he was shot. A shot had come through the windshield and nearly decapitated the man. It took him a minute to recognize Rossi. What was he doing here by Ruby's house? He got on his radio and called for more backup and a crime scene crew.

One of the firefighters was waving Sean over to the burned house. The fireman said, "It looks like there are at least three bodies in the ashes. Can't tell much about 'em, but one might be a woman. We don't want to disturb 'em. Figured that's your guys' job."

"Okay. I've called for a crime scene crew and more men to help here."

"We're gonna take off. We doused the hot coals; there's not much else we can do here."

"Okay. Thanks for your help." He gave the volunteer his card and said to call him if he thought of anything that might be important. The firefighters loaded their gear and were leaving when the coroner's ambulance and two more deputies arrived. The district commander arrived shortly after that.

The commander stood in the street surveying the scene and said, "Damn, Sean! What happened here?"

"I don't exactly know, sir. It's pretty complicated. The firemen said there were three bodies in the ashes of the house. I knew the woman who lived here. Her name was Ruby Reynolds. The firemen said they thought one of the bodies was a woman; it was likely her. And here's the wild card, sir—she was Harley Henderson's girlfriend."

The commander's jaw dropped. "What! Good grief! What's that crazy sonofabitch done now?"

"There's more, commander. See that Cadillac parked off the road down there?"

The commander looked where he pointed.

"There's another body in it. I'm almost positive it's that guy Rossi from the Vegas casino."

The commander stood in shocked silence for a minute, shaking his head. "We need to get the detectives out here, too. It sounds like we may have a solid murder case shaping up against Henderson. I'll put out an all-points alert to stop him on sight. Get me a description of his truck, and we'll get it out immediately."

The crime scene crew arrived, and the commander told them to process the shooting in the Cadillac first. He stood by watching for a couple of minutes, shaking his head at the gruesome sight in the car. Then he called for a specialist in investigating arson to help with the scene at the burned-out house. He told everyone it would be a long day, but they would stay here until the investigation was finished.

A large crowd formed, asking each other questions and speculating on what had happened. Most of them knew Ruby, and the rumor was that she died in the fire since she didn't show up for work at the coffee shop that day. The deputies had their hands full, keeping everyone back and directing traffic around the site. The crime scene crew finished with Rossi's Cadillac; the detectives arrived and had a look. Then, the body was removed and placed in an ambulance to take it to the county morgue. A wrecker towed the Cadillac away, finally clearing the road and making traffic control easier.

Sean began walking around the perimeter of the scene when things quieted down. He found tire tracks in the dirt beside the road in front of the house. There was shattered glass along the

149

edge of the pavement nearby. Another vehicle had been parked there, and one of its windows appeared to have been shot out. The tires spun grooves in the dirt when they left, indicating they left quickly. He looked from there to where Rossi's car had been parked, trying to connect the two vehicles. But it made no sense. He waved one of the crime scene technicians over and pointed out the tracks in the dirt and glass on the pavement. Then he stepped into the middle of the road and slowly turned in a complete circle, trying to put the pieces together. One thing that looked a little out of place caught his eye—some hay bales were out of place on the haystack across the road. He walked over to the end of the stack where bales had been removed and created a kind of stairstep at the end of the stack. There were fresh footprints around the area that looked to have been made by large boots. He stepped carefully around them, then made his way up the bales to the top. Two bales were out of place. He kneeled to look closer and found several rifle cartridges barely visible in the deepening shadow between the bales. He left them where they were and climbed down to get a crime scene technician to process what he had found.

It was getting dark when the crime scene crew wrapped up their work, and the burned bodies had been transported to the morgue. The commander told the detectives, Sean, the leader of the crime scene crew, and the arson specialist to meet in his office at eight the following day. So far there had been no reported sightings of Harley Henderson.

❧

Sean had a message to call his friend Ricky. "Hola, amigo," Ricky said when he picked up the phone.

"Hi, Ricky. What's up?"

"You heard the news about Japan's surrender, right?"

"Yeah, it's pretty much all anyone was talking about this morning."

"Well, it's a good reason for a couple of old war dogs like us to celebrate. We're having a big party at my parents' place tonight.

It would be great if you could come. All my family, lots of friends, maybe some pretty señoritas will be there. We'll have mariachis, dancing, and all the beer and tequila you want to drink."

"Sounds great, Ricky. I'll have to go easy on the booze. I have a big day at work tomorrow. What time does it start?"

"Eight o'clock. See you there!"

Sean had a lot of work to do on reports for the day; it was seven o'clock when he got home. He barely had time to feed Buddy, shower, and shave before he left for the party. He had been to Ricky's parents' home many times. There was always good food, and Ricky's parents treated him like one of their own.

There was a large crowd on the big backyard patio when he arrived. The mariachis had already started, and people were helping themselves to food from large platters of tamales, enchiladas, and a big steaming pot of red chili. When Sean arrived, everyone started applauding, much to his embarrassment. He was a war hero, but he was also a local hero. Word had gotten around how he and Ricky had chased off the gang stealing from Mexican merchants in the area.

Ricky's mother hugged Sean, his father shook his hand, and then Mama Martinez took him by the arm and said, "Come! There are many new people to meet and many old friends to see." She steered him through the crowd, telling everyone of his accomplishments. He felt like his face was permanently red. Many people had questions about his time in the war, and he tried to skim over it without being rude.

He finally broke away from Mama's guidance and found Ricky by a big tub of Coors on ice. Ricky opened one, handed it to him, and said, "Some party, huh? I got the same treatment as you before you got here. You'd think the two of us won the war!"

They had a good laugh, and Sean said, "Yeah, I get that impression. Thanks for doing this."

"It was my folks' idea. They wanted to celebrate the war's end. But mostly, they wanted to celebrate us." Ricky discretely pointed to a beautiful raven-haired girl off to the side. "I'm sure my mother introduced you to my cousin Elena."

Sean nodded.

"You should ask her to dance. She told me earlier she wanted to meet you. She's a sweet girl—you'll like her." The band struck up a slow waltz, and Ricky said, "Go have some fun, amigo, and dance with that beautiful girl!"

Sean wasn't much of a dancer, but he knew how to waltz. Elena accepted his offer of a dance, and they moved into the crowd on the patio. It was the first time he had danced with a woman since Annaleigh's death. It felt a little strange; he wasn't sure what to say. But she did enough talking for both of them and peppered him with questions about the war and being a deputy sheriff. She was a strikingly beautiful young woman. Ricky had told him she was nineteen years old, but she looked younger. Her black hair accentuated her flashing black eyes, and her smile outshone the lights around the patio. She had a laugh that sounded like music to Sean's ears. He felt a long absent beginning of a spark between them. She showed him how to dance the traditional zapateado. He felt clumsy and like he was all feet, but he finally got the hang of it. He was soon flexing his knees, stomping, and moving around the floor to the fast rhythm of the mariachi's music. They danced another waltz, and he told her it was time for him to leave because he had an early start at work the next day. He asked her if he could see her again sometime, and she said he would have to speak to her father. It was a Mexican custom for a man to ask the father's permission to court his daughter. Sean didn't think he was ready to take a step like that. He said goodbye to Elena, Ricky, and his other friends and left.

He was glad to get home. It had been a long day. He could hear Buddy barking as soon as he got out of his pickup in the driveway. The dog jumped up and licked his face when he opened the door. He laughed and pushed the dog away, saying, "Get down, Buddy, get down. I'm glad to see you, too." He could have sworn the dog was laughing. He wasn't sure if it was because he was glad to see him or because he thought Sean might feed him again. Either way, he was glad to have the dog's company. Buddy's limp was a little less, and he seemed to have settled into his new home.

Sean switched on the radio to see if there was anything new about Japan's surrender. Most of what was discussed was speculation and interviews with so-called experts. He switched it off and thought they might have some real news tomorrow.

He got another cold Coors from his refrigerator. He knew he'd regret the extra alcohol in the morning, but he needed to unwind from all the events of the day. His head was still spinning from his encounter with Elena as he settled into his easy chair in the living room. He hadn't realized how much he missed a woman's touch. Buddy lay down at his feet, and his ears pricked up when Sean grabbed his guitar and strummed a chord. It was the best way Sean knew to relax; Buddy seemed to relax too and snored contentedly at his feet. He noodled around on the guitar, thoughts of the day's activities floating around in his mind. One thing was sure—tomorrow, the pursuit of Harley would be the number one priority for him and the rest of his division. He put the instrument down and headed for bed with Buddy close behind.

CHAPTER 25

The district commander's small conference room was crowded as the deputies, detectives, and crime scene investigators squeezed into chairs. The air was thick with cigarette smoke, and one small window wasn't up to clearing it out. Over the years, the walls had taken on a distinct patina of nicotine stain. Sean tapped a Lucky Strike out of a freshly opened pack and lit it with his lighter emblazoned with the insignia of the Screaming Eagles, his paratroop division in the Army.

The commander opened the meeting. "Let's hear first from Larry. What did your team find?"

Larry, the lead crime scene investigator, referred to his notes and said, "First, the Cadillac with a dead body parked on the road a short way from the house. It is registered to a Nevada company, possibly connected to a casino there. The dead man's driver's license identified him as James Rossi, address Las Vegas, Nevada. The glass in the front windshield was shattered, likely from a bullet fired from a .30-06 rifle. Empty shell casings were found to confirm this. The bullet's impact blew the top of the man's head off. Other fingerprints that we have not yet matched were found in the car. Are there any questions about the car?"

Hearing none, he continued, "The bodies in the house were badly burned. We determined one of them was female, possibly Ruby Reynolds, who rented the house from a local farmer. We haven't yet determined her cause of death. The other two appeared to have been shot in the upper body. We are waiting on autopsy results to confirm all of this. There were signs that a vehicle had been parked nearby and then accelerated rapidly away. We found a couple of good tire tracks and made castings of them for future identification. The men were likely killed by the same rifle as Mr. Rossi. Sean found evidence of spent .30-06 shell casings in what appeared to be a shooter's perch arranged on top of the haystack across the road. There were also footprints around the base of the haystack, and we made castings of them. That's about it for now. Any questions?"

The commander said, "Thank you, Larry. That was very thorough. We may have questions later. I'd like to hear from Charles Owens about the arson investigation."

Owens said, "The fire was definitely arson. Gasoline had been used throughout the house as an accelerant. The gas can the arsonist used was left inside the living room of the burned house. We are working with the lab to find any fingerprints that may be on it, but that's a long shot. As Larry said, the two men in the fire were likely killed elsewhere and placed in the house's living room. We are waiting on the autopsy of the woman's body to determine the cause of death. That's all I have for now, commander."

"Thank you, Charles. What do you detectives have to report?" he asked, looking at Detective Johnson.

Johnson cleared his throat and lit another Pall Mall. "Well, it's clear that all this ties into Harley Henderson as the chief suspect. Sean pointed out that Miss Reynolds was Henderson's girlfriend, and they had a long-term relationship. The fact that Rossi was at the scene points to a connection with the plane crash last July. He had been trying to find Henderson, as confirmed by numerous people we have interviewed. I believe he had also interviewed you and Sean, commander." Both men nodded, and he continued, "We don't know what specifically he was looking for, only that it was something valuable that had been stolen from his employer, the Lucky Joker Casino in Las Vegas. The murder of Harry Henderson, Harley's twin brother, is almost certainly the work of Rossi and his henchmen from Las Vegas. People we have spoken to who knew the twins told us they were very close and owned a machine shop business together. Our working theory, as of now, is that Harley found out who had killed his brother and was out for revenge. He somehow orchestrated this ambush at his girlfriend's house, possibly using himself as bait to kill those responsible for his brother's death. We also think the shooting connected to a car left at a motel in Buckeye may have been Harley's first attempt to take out his brother's killer. That's all we have for now, commander."

The room was quiet while the men smoked and digested all that had been said. The commander said, "Sean and Brad, can you add anything to what we've heard?"

Brad looked at Sean, who said, "It all adds up, sir. I agree that Harley's likely on a revenge-killing spree. Ruby Reynold's death might be partly my fault. I believe Harley saw our plane when Brad and I did reconnaissance flights over his camp area. He could probably tell by the pattern of our search we were looking for him, and he hightailed it out of there. That's why the camp was abandoned when Brad and I hiked into it. Ruby told me when I interviewed her that Harley had said she was the only person other than his brother who had ever been to his camp. I think Harley must have figured out she told me where he was hiding, and he killed her for it."

The others sat in stunned silence. Sean went on, "I knew Harley in high school at Buckeye. He always had a foul temper and was a mean bully. Most people gave him a wide berth. I would say he was capable of doing all this stuff, and he may not be done. We don't know who else could be involved in this. It's possible he could come after Brad or me, too. We arrested him just before all this killing started." He paused, then continued, "If he's done taking his revenge, he'll probably try to run to Mexico. He will know now that we will be looking everywhere for him and will likely take a long route through the desert to get there. He could avoid all the highways and checkpoints. Maybe we should have some air surveillance in case he tries that. That's all I have. Maybe Brad can add more."

Brad shook his head and said, "I have nothing to add."

A lengthy discussion followed, and the commander laid out everyone's assignments. He said, "That's a great idea about air surveillance, Sean. I'll ask the sheriff if we can activate our volunteer air posse. They might be able to help now that the war has ended. This would be a perfect job for them. And we'll put out a statewide alert for Henderson. We'll find him if he comes out of the desert. Sean and Brad, I want you to focus on the area around Buckeye. See if there have been any sightings of him or if anyone might have an idea where he might hole up."

Detective Johnson said, "We'll follow up with the Las Vegas police. Maybe they can find out something about why that plane crash was such a big deal. I'd also recommend everyone be on their toes—with Rossi dead, the casino owners are likely to send someone to replace him, possibly with a bunch of mob types to help. Things could get even more ugly."

The meeting broke up at ten o'clock, and everyone went about their assigned tasks.

🌵

Michael Fishburn, III, sat in his office with the morning's Arizona Republic lying on his desk. The color had drained out of his face when he read about the fire and shootings north of Buckeye. The article said at least four people were dead. What could it mean? Either Harley had ambushed Rossi and his men, or something happened that resulted in a gunfight. With Rossi dead, the casino would undoubtedly send a replacement, possibly someone far worse than Rossi. He had to assume that whoever they sent would want information from him since he was the go-between for communications with the casino. He could wind up like Harley's brother if they don't like what he can tell them.

His wife and two children were oblivious to what he was involved in. Now, he feared they might be at risk, too. He could send them out of town, but it wouldn't do any good for him to leave. They would never stop looking for him. He picked up the phone and made airline reservations to Chicago for his family. They could stay there with her parents. Then he called his wife and told her what he needed her to do.

She said, "Michael, I'm frightened. Are we in danger? Are you in danger? What's going on?"

"Elizabeth, you could be in danger. That's why I want you far away from here. Don't tell anyone where you are going, and don't call any of your friends after you get there. I don't want anyone to know where you are."

She started sobbing into the phone, and he continued, "It will be all right. I will get all this straightened out soon, and we will all be safe. Just pack what you need and be at the airport on time. I'll call you at your parent's house after you get there. I love you and tell the children I love them. We'll talk soon."

He hung up the phone, found the Maricopa County Sheriff's Department's number in his telephone directory, and called. He told the receptionist that he had information about yesterday's shootings at Buckeye. She put him on hold, and a minute later, the Sheriff came on the phone.

"Mr. Fishburn, this is Sheriff Roach. How can I help you?"

"Sheriff, I'm mixed up with the people involved in the shootings near Buckeye yesterday. I fear for my life, Sheriff. I'll tell you everything I know, but you will need to protect me."

"Can you come into my office now? I'll put you with my detectives handling that case. They will help you with what you need."

"Thank you, sheriff. I can be there in an hour."

The sheriff said he would have his detectives ready when he arrived.

The lawyer gathered what information he had that might be useful and put it in his briefcase. Then he walked out to his receptionist's desk and said, "Shirley, I need you to cancel my appointments for today and any others we have on the calendar. Then I want you to close up the office and leave. Consider yourself on paid vacation until I call you and tell you to come back in."

"Mr. Fishburn! What is it? What's going on?"

"I don't have time to explain, Shirley. Just do as I ask, and I will be in touch later." He walked out the door, got in his new Lincoln, and headed downtown to the sheriff's office. The Lincoln had been paid for with his fee for cashing Harley's bonds.

The receptionist at the front desk showed him to a conference room on the second floor. "Someone will be with you shortly," she said.

Five minutes later, two detectives introduced themselves as detectives Johnson and Harper. Johnson began, "We are handling the shooting incident at Buckeye. We understand you have information about the parties involved. What can you tell us?"

Fishburn said, "I need assurances from the department that you can protect me before I tell you what I know. I fear for my life, especially if these people find out I've talked to you."

"What people would that be?" Johnson asked.

"Can you help me or not?" the lawyer asked. "If you can't, I will have to leave the country. Right now. Today!"

"Take it easy, Mr. Fishburn. Yes, we can help you. But you will have to help us understand what kind of help you need."

"Protection!" Fishburn yelled. "Those men will kill me!"

"We will arrange protection for you based on what you tell us. Why don't you start at the beginning?"

The lawyer took a deep breath and exhaled. Then he told them everything.

🌵

Harley had called his taxidermist partner in Cashion and made arrangements to stay at his shop after the shooting at Ruby's house. He pulled around the back of the shop, and Snuffy opened the door and said, "Hey, Harley, what's goin' on? What'd you get yourself into?"

"You don't wanna know, Snuffy. It's a big can of worms. I need a place to stay, maybe a couple of nights."

"No problem, pal. Mi casa su casa and all that. Stay as long as you want. You want something to eat?"

"Yeah, if it's no trouble."

"I've got bologna and sandwich stuff in the refrigerator up front. Help yourself. And the cot you've used a few times before is over in the corner. This is great timing, too. Our mutual friend just delivered the stuff you asked for. I'll help you load it up before you leave." Snuffy paused a few seconds and continued, "And Harley…I ain't seen you in months and don't know where you went."

"Thanks, Snuffy. You're a good friend."

He was up early and made a pot of coffee in the taxidermist's little kitchen at the front of the shop. Snuffy came in and showed him the merchandise that had been delivered. Harley looked it over and gave a low whistle. "Man, this is great stuff. I can't wait to try it out." The two men loaded it in the trunk of Ruby's car.

Harley had one more bone to pick before disappearing for good—Fishburn. The damn lawyer had sold him out to the Las Vegas bunch. He would head for his office when it opened and pay him an unannounced visit.

Fishburn's office was closed when he got there. There was no sign on the door to indicate when it would be open. Harley thought that was strange; Shirley, the secretary, was always there during business hours. He began to feel uneasy in the pit of his stomach—something didn't smell right. He parked a little way down the street where he could watch for the lawyer or his receptionist to show up. He wanted this visit to be a surprise.

Fishburn's Lincoln slid into his parking space a little after noon. He jumped out with his large briefcase, unlocked the door, and rushed inside. The detectives had arranged a safe house for him to stay, but he needed a few other records from his office before he went into hiding. He was busy pulling files from a cabinet drawer when a deep voice said, "Goin' somewhere?"

He instantly recognized Harley's voice, spun around, and said, "Wha… What are you doing here? What do you want?" Then he noticed the large pistol in Harley's right hand, pointed straight at his chest. He threw his hands up and backed up against the wall.

160

The color had drained from his face for the second time that day. "What are you doing, Harley? Why the gun?"

"You just couldn't help yerself, could ya? Couldn't just do what I asked you to. You cut a deal with that Rossi guy, didn't ya!"

"No, Harley! You've got it all wrong! All I did was relay the instructions you gave me. There was no deal!

"Sure. That's why Rossi showed up with three thugs for a friendly little business transaction. I suppose you'd get yer payoff when that was all done."

"No! No! It wasn't like that!"

Harley shot him through the heart. The roar of the .357 magnum was deafening in the small room. Then he shot him in the head for good measure. It should give a clear message to any more of that Vegas bunch that came looking for him. The attorney lay in a pool of blood in front of his file cabinet as Harley walked out. He left the front door standing open.

Sean had spent the morning interviewing people around Buckeye, hoping to get some idea of where Harley might be. So far, he was coming up empty-handed. After noon, he got a dispatch call to respond to a burglary in the little settlement of Liberty, a few miles east of Buckeye. It was a sleepy village with an elementary school, a Methodist church, and a scattering of homes. The school had been built in 1910 and served the surrounding farm area.

The reported burglary was a few houses down the street from the church. A woman came out of the front door when Sean pulled into the driveway. She had strikingly beautiful, wavy copper-red hair and a smattering of freckles across her nose. Sean had to force himself to keep his mind on business.

The woman said, "I am Sandra Preston. I called the police because someone broke into my house while I was away this morning."

Sean introduced himself, and she led him inside the house to the back door. She said, "They broke in this door. I guess they didn't want to be seen at the front.

"You said they, Mrs. Preston. Why do you think there was more than one person?"

"Oh, it's just a figure of speech. I don't really know." She paused, looked him in the eye, and said, "And it's Miss Preston. That's what my students call me. I teach fourth grade." She had a disarming smile, and Sean had to force himself to pay attention to business again.

"Do you know what's missing?" he asked.

"That's the thing—I can't find anything missing. It looks like he or they went through my chest of drawers and dresser and just scattered stuff all over." She led him into the bedroom, showed him the mess scattered all over the room, and continued, "It looks like they were in my closet, too. My good dresses are all on the floor."

"Why would they have done this? Is there something of value missing? Did you have jewelry or money in a shoebox or anything that might have drawn them here?"

"No, nothing. I'm a school teacher and barely make enough money to get by. I've never owned anything I'd consider valuable, and I certainly don't hide money in a shoebox, a mattress, or anywhere else. I keep my money in the bank."

"Can you think of any reason for this break-in?"

"Maybe. It could be a man who's been watching me for the last few weeks. I've noticed him around when I am outside, and he leers at me when I pass him in my car. He's been hanging around a lot more lately. I don't know who he is. I have never spoken to him, but he's making me quite nervous." She looked around and said, "Strangely, the only things disturbed were my clothing and personal things." Suddenly, she exclaimed, "My underwear. It looks like some of my underwear may be gone. Oh, my god! What should I do?"

"Can you describe this man?"

162

"Well, let me think…Khaki. He always wears rumpled khaki pants and a faded blue denim work shirt. He has sort of wild-looking blonde hair sticking out in different directions. I've noticed him walking down the road past the other houses. I don't think he lives around here."

"We'll put him on our watch list. In the meantime, I'm going to drive around the area. Maybe I'll get lucky and find him. Do you have someone who can fix the lock on the door?"

She nodded and said, "My landlord is two doors down. I'm sure he'll fix it."

He prepared to leave, but she touched his arm to stop him and said, "Now I know where I've seen you. You were in that rodeo parade in Buckeye a few months ago. The Grand Marshall!"

Sean blushed. "Yep. That was me."

"I remember you were sitting in the back of a convertible at the head of the parade…and a beautiful woman was sitting beside you." She caught herself, put her hand over her mouth for a few seconds, and continued, "Oh my god! Was that the girl who was killed by a bomb about that same time?"

Sean nodded, and she said, "I'm so sorry. I didn't know. What an awful thing that must have been for you."

"It was awful for her family and me. We were engaged to be married, and her death turned everything upside down for a while."

She reached out, took his hand, and looked him in the eye. "I'm so sorry," she repeated. Her eyes were green emeralds under her stunning red hair.

Sean was momentarily mesmerized. After a few seconds of awkward silence, he said, "Thank you." She squeezed his hand and smiled that disarming smile again. Sean fumbled for words and finally said, "I'm going to try and find your burglar now. Here's my card—call me if you think of anything else. If you give me your phone number, I'll check back in with you later to make sure everything's all right." He gave her another card, and she wrote her name and number on the back. Sean went out to his

163

patrol car, feeling a little dazed. He got in the car and started backing out to the street. When he looked back, she was standing on her front step, waving at him. Then he noticed he was sweating as if he'd been working in the sun.

He drove slowly down the street north of her house. The school's athletic field was on his right, and no one was in sight. He continued down the lane past the houses and started to turn around when a flash of color caught his eye. There were some cottonwoods along an irrigation ditch west of the road, and it looked like an old, faded blue tent was pitched between them. He turned up the farm road alongside the ditch and stopped by the tent. A man was sitting cross-legged on the ground in front of it.

Sean got out and approached the man. He didn't seem to be aware of the deputy's presence. He sat there mumbling unintelligible words; his eyes looked distant, vacant. He was wearing khaki pants and a threadbare blue denim work shirt. His blonde hair looked like it hadn't seen a comb in months.

Sean said, "Excuse me, sir. Can I speak with you?" The man continued mumbling to himself. Sean spoke to him again and tapped the bottom of his shoe with the toe of his boot. The man's eyes went wild, and he came up off the ground like he was spring-loaded and plowed into Sean with his arms windmilling and flailing at Sean's face.

It was so sudden that Sean was momentarily stunned, then his training and reflexes kicked in. He grabbed one of the man's arms, twisted it behind his back, and forced him to his knees. The man struggled like a wild animal, yelling gibberish and trying to break Sean's hold. Sean finally forced him down on the ground and managed to get handcuffs on him. Then he marched him, kicking and struggling, to his patrol car and shoved him into the back. He bounced around in the seat like a bobcat in a cage, banging his body against the doors and hitting his head against the protective barrier on the front seat.

Sean heaved a sigh of relief and leaned against the car for a minute. Then he searched the man's tent. The inside of the tent

164

had a sour odor that made his eyes water. The floor was littered with a pitiful collection of odds and ends: glass soda pop bottles, beer cans, a half-eaten apple, a yard gnome with bright colors, candy wrappers, and assorted garbage. There were no clothes except two pairs of white women's underwear clipped with a wooden clothes peg to a seam on the side of the tent's wall.

Sean took down the garments and put them on the seat of his car. Then, he drove back to Miss Preston's house. She came out when he pulled into the drive and parked behind her old Chevy coupe. He gathered the two pairs of panties, embarrassed to hand them to the woman. His face was bright red, and he said, "I believe these are yours, ma'am."

She couldn't help laughing at his embarrassment. Then she looked the garments over and said, "Well, they certainly look like mine!" Both of them burst out laughing.

Sean was relieved the tension was lifted and said, "I'd like you to take a look at the man in the back of my car." He walked her over, and the man plastered his face onto the car window when he saw her, staring with a crazed look in his eyes. He continued yelling senseless stuff punctuated with an occasional curse word.

She moved to the side to get a better look and said, "That's him. Where did you find him?"

"He was camped in a tent about a half-mile north of here. He seems to have serious mental problems. I'll have to take him to the county hospital. They can secure him and figure out what's going on. I'll also book him for burglary and theft. Hopefully, we can keep him off the streets."

Miss Preston was visibly relieved and started shaking. Sean instinctively reached an arm around her and pulled her close, telling her softly it was all over, and everything was all right. She put her arm around him, and they stood there for a little while until she stopped shaking. Then she pulled away and said, "I'm sorry for acting like a little girl. Please don't think me forward. I was scared to death before you caught him. I was afraid he'd come back at night."

165

"No apology needed. I'm glad I could help. Hopefully, you'll rest well tonight."

"I will," she said, "and I hope you will stop by again. I'd love to talk to you under different circumstances."

Sean felt tongue-tied and finally blurted out, "I'd like that too, Miss Preston. I mean, I'd be happy to check on you, make sure you are all right."

She smiled that smile again, took his hand in a gentle shake, and said, "Call me Sandy. Until then." Then she turned and walked into her house. Sean watched her walk away and up the step to the porch. She was beautiful even in a loose-fitting, plain white summer dress. It couldn't entirely conceal the very feminine shape underneath.

Sean drove to Phoenix to drop his prisoner at the county hospital. The man continued yelling and banging himself against the front seat barrier and the car doors. Sean was anxious to be rid of him. He had radioed ahead that he was bringing a mentally disturbed man who would need restraint. Two burly orderlies came out of the hospital and wrestled the man out of the patrol car. Sean's mind was far away from the deranged man in the back seat. He couldn't stop thinking about Miss Preston. The way she smiled, her unpretentious beauty, and even the faint scent of her perfume lingered in his awareness. Maybe, he thought, I'm starting to move past Annaleigh's death.

⚜

El Puma had gone to the emergency room at the county hospital. They cleaned and dressed his scalp wound, put in a few stitches, gave him some more sulfanilamide, and told him to change the dressing every day. He stopped at a hardware store, bought a brush, and then cleaned up the broken glass in his truck. Window replacements would have to wait. It was annoying to drive looking through the gunshot spider web on his windshield—but, he thought, at least I'm alive. He bought a bottle of tequila and spent the night in a cheap motel sipping the liquor. The tequila took his mind off the sting of his scalp wound as he plotted what

166

to do next. But the sting of being caught in an ambush was worse than the wound on his head.

He figured the gringo had Rossi's bonds stashed at the campsite in the desert, most likely in the bunker with the iron door. It would take a huge pair of bolt cutters to remove the lock on the door, and even that might not work. Dynamite would do the trick, he thought, and be easier to carry. He knew a place that sold it, no questions asked. If he were very lucky, he would catch the gringo there with the bunker open. Either way, he would retrieve the bonds. His more important task was to exact vengeance on the gringo for killing his two men. Getting the bonds would be a side benefit.

CHAPTER 26

The commander called an emergency meeting the next morning
with the two detectives, Sean, Brad, and several other deputies.
The conference room was packed and quickly filled with
cigarette smoke. The commander said, "We have important news
about Harley Henderson. Detective Johnson will fill us in on the
latest events."

The detective lit a Pall Mall and settled himself more
comfortably on the chair. He looked like a comic book version of
a detective: His large belly hung on his lap halfway to his knees,
his nose looked like it had been broken several times, and it was
now red and laced with tiny veins from long-term alcohol use.
But his eyes were clear as he looked at the men around him. He
took a long drag on his cigarette and cleared his throat before he
began. "Yesterday, an attorney named Michael Fishburn
contacted our office and said he had important information about
the Henderson case. He asked us to provide protection for him in
exchange for what he could tell us. We agreed. Turns out he had
been Henderson's lawyer for years. Harley contacted him shortly
after the plane crash on Woolsey Peak and asked for help—he
had taken a bunch of bearer bonds from the plane and didn't
know what to do with them. He showed Fishburn four of the
bonds valued at ten thousand dollars each." He paused to let that
sink in before continuing, "The lawyer got them cashed for a fee,
of course, and Henderson told him there were more he would
bring him later. Somehow, the Lucky Joker Casino organization
in Vegas found out he had cashed them and sent Jimmy Rossi to
find out where he got them. He scared the crap out of the
attorney, and he spilled the beans about Henderson." He stopped
and asked if there were questions before going further.

One of the deputies asked, "What's a bearer bond?"

Johnson explained they were a kind of investment certificate used for financing in business. "The term "bearer bond" means what it sounds like…whoever has possession of one can cash it. According to Fishburn, the ones from the plane were issued by a mining company in Nevada. Any other questions before I move on?" There were none, and he continued, "Fishburn pointed the casino's people at the machine shop in Buckeye to find Harley. They found his brother instead and beat him to death trying to get information to find Harley. We believe that triggered Harley to go after them and led to the shooting at the Henderson's house in Buckeye. That incident was likely responsible for the so-called mystery car with the windows shot out at the Buckeye motel. Harley evidently killed two of Rossi's henchmen that night and dumped their bodies somewhere, probably in the desert. We think he narrowly missed Rossi as he escaped in the car."

The group sat in stunned silence. Johnson lit another cigarette and went on, "Sean interviewed Harley's girlfriend, Ruby Reynolds, and she told him about Harley's hideout in the desert. We think Henderson somehow learned about it and killed her for betraying him. The preliminary autopsy results indicate Miss Reynolds died by strangulation." He paused, took two more drags off his cigarette, and crushed it out in the ashtray in the middle of the table. It was now overflowing with cigarette butts, and the room was cloudy with smoke. The commander opened the one small window, but it didn't help. Johnson continued, "The lawyer said Harley contacted him to set up a meeting with Rossi because he wanted to split the bonds and stop them looking for him. The attorney obliged and sent Rossi to the Reynolds' house per Harley's instructions. That resulted in the shooting there that killed Rossi and two other men. Harley put the two dead men inside the house with Miss Reynolds' body and set the house on fire."

This information was nearly unbelievable for the gathered officers. They had never heard of or seen anything like what the detective described. They started asking questions, and Johnson held up his hand to quiet them and said, "That wasn't the end of it. We arranged for Fishburn to use a safe house after our interview. He said he needed to get some files from his office before he went there, but after a couple of hours, he didn't show up at the safe house. We went to his office and found the front door standing open. The lawyer was lying dead on his office floor with two gunshot wounds, one to the chest and one to the head. They appeared to be from a large caliber weapon. We think that either Harley or the Vegas mob was waiting for him. That's all we have for now."

Everyone started talking at the same time, and the commander held up his hand for silence. He said, "Well, gentlemen, we have our work cut out for us now. I've already spoken to the sheriff, who agreed to make finding Henderson the department's top priority. Here's the plan: First, we are putting out a statewide alert for any information about him. It will be in the newspapers as well as on wanted posters. Second, we will set up checkpoints on the main roads around Buckeye. Third, the sheriff has activated the air posse; they will start flying surveillance over the Buckeye and desert areas where we think Harley has his camp. Lastly, we will maintain twenty-four-hour patrols around the Buckeye area. The sheriff has made any extra help we need available. I will develop a roster of deputies for the patrol assignments. It sounds as if Henderson has degenerated into a cold-blooded killer—all of us will have to be very careful. We have to find this man before someone else gets killed. Any questions?"

Sean raised his hand and said, "We don't know what happened to Miss Reynold's car. She had an older blue Chevy sedan when I met her. Harley may be using that instead of his truck—that thing stands out like a sore thumb."

"Good point, Sean," the commander said. "We'll add that to the bulletins and our patrols' watch list."

The rest of the meeting was spent working out patrol logistics. The commander assigned Sean to focus on following up with his contacts around Buckeye.

Rudy Bianco called Joe Leone, aka Joe the Fish, into his penthouse office at the Lucky Joker Casino. Joe was the casino's head of security. He had the unfortunate nickname because his eyes were set very wide in his face and reminded people of fish eyes. "We just got a call from the Vegas cops. They said Jimmy Rossi had been killed in Arizona, and the cops down there wanted to know what to do with his body. I want you to go down there to take care of that and then stay there to bird dog whatever's goin' on with the cops' investigation. Rossi screwed the pooch on the deal and got himself killed. I want you to pick up wherever he left off. We've got a million bucks worth of bonds floatin' around the desert somewhere, and we need 'em back. Call in whatever backup you need."

"Damn, boss. Rossi's dead? He was one of the best! What's goin' on down there?"

Bianco growled, "I don't know what the hell's goin' on. That's what I'm sendin' you to find out. Get on it!"

El Puma was at the construction and mining supply shop in Phoenix when it opened. He bought four sticks of dynamite and fuse material—better to have too much than not enough. Then he stopped at a market and bought some food to carry with him: beef jerky, some tortillas, a hunk of cheese. It would be enough for what he planned to do. He stopped at a gas station, filled his gas tank and water cans, and headed for Woolsey Peak. He passed three sheriff's department patrol cars along the way; one was parked a short way from the turnoff to Agua Caliente Road. They are looking for my gringo, he thought. They must want him pretty badly. But not as much as me. This gringo is slippery like a snake...I don't think el policia will catch him. He turned off onto the dirt track that led to Harley's hideout.

171

He wouldn't make the mistake of approaching the gringo's camp directly again. The man was a tricky one— who knew what other sly traps he might have had on the obvious approach? He left the dirt track a couple of miles east of the wash that led to the camp and drove toward the base of the mountain. It was rough going with rocks and boulders everywhere, giant saguaro cacti, patches of teddy bear cholla and other cactuses, mesquite, and palo verde trees. He found a spot among several palo verde trees where he could hide his truck from the view of any passersby.

It was late morning, blazing hot and humid. He saw thunderheads starting to form to the south-east. The monsoon had been bringing a lot of rain to southern Arizona; now, it looked to be pushing further north. He didn't mind the rain, but it would make the hike ahead of him more treacherous with slippery rocks. He couldn't afford to break a leg out here. He stuffed an old poncho, his other supplies, and a canteen of water into a canvas knapsack. A second canteen was hooked onto his belt. He put on his bandolier with extra ammunition for his Smith and Wesson .38 special revolver and his Winchester .30-30 rifle. The rifle was the last thing he slung over his shoulder, and then he set off for the mountain.

He planned to climb up the eastern face, then work around to the canyon on the other side, much as Sean and Brad had done a few days earlier. He would come down on the gringo's camp from above. It was doubtful the man had lain any traps along that route.

A thunderstorm moved in just as El Puma found a position with a good view of the camp. There was no sign of the gringo, and he pulled the poncho over his head and hunkered down under an overhanging rock outcrop to stay out of the rain. It was getting toward dusk and raining very hard. Frequent lightning lit the landscape, giving it an otherworldly appearance. Thunder shook the ground and reverberated off the canyon walls, dislodging a few loose stones. The storm hammered the canyon for about half an hour, then moved on, rumbling across the narrow valley to the north. El Puma lay down on the wet ground; he used his knapsack for a pillow and was instantly asleep. He would see what tomorrow brings.

CHAPTER 27

Harley holed up in the West Phoenix motel for three nights after killing the lawyer. He figured the cops would start getting tired of looking for him; maybe they'd think he ran to Mexico. But he knew they were still out there and had spread his picture all over the state. He bought a Phoenix newspaper in the motel lobby and saw his mug shot photo staring back at him above an article about the fire and murders near Buckeye. The article said the Maricopa County Sheriff's Department had notified all police agencies in the state to be on the lookout for him. He would need to be extra cautious now.

He wasn't willing to leave the country without the bonds. It would be worth the risk to retrieve them; they were his ticket to an easy life south of the border. He stewed over the problem in his dingy motel room until he devised a plan. The only way he would be able to pull it off was by moving at night. The road to his camp would be treacherous at night, but he was confident the Beast would be up to the task.

On the fourth night, he left the motel in Ruby's car and drove to Buckeye. He parked it and walked the few blocks to the machine shop. He quietly opened the sliding door in the back and pulled the Beast out of the building. Then he locked the door so no one would know he had been there.

He drove slowly out of town and stayed on back roads until he was a couple of miles west of Buckeye, then got onto Highway 80 and headed south. No traffic was on the highway at that late hour, and no sign of cops watching for him. He turned off on the Agua Caliente Road and drove slowly so he could see the track leading to his camp. Driving carefully, he eased into and out of the numerous washes. He couldn't afford to make a mistake and get stuck. Even the Beast had its limits.

Harley knew that piece of the desert better than anyone. He had spent much of his life camping and hunting in the area; his eyes were attuned to every nuance of the landscape. His headlights picked up something unusual a couple of miles before the wash leading to his camp. He stopped and looked closely—someone had turned off the track here in the fresh mud, heading toward the mountain. He grabbed his flashlight and followed the track a short way. A heavy vehicle, like a pickup truck, made the tire tracks. They were easy to follow in the disturbed soil. He thought it might have been made by cops or someone looking to come up behind him at his camp.

He laid his Smith and Wesson .357 magnum revolver on the seat, then took his .30-30 rifle out of the window rack and leaned it against the seat beside him. He eased the Beast off the road and slowly followed the muddy tracks. The recent rains had washed the tracks out in places, but there were still enough signs for him to follow. He came upon the vehicle in about a mile. It was clearly illuminated in his headlights, and he instantly recognized it as the pickup he had shot the back window out of in front of Ruby's house. He got out and searched the vehicle with his flashlight. There was nothing in the front or back. He remembered the Mexican who had survived the gunfight; he must be the driver of this truck, he thought. It could mean only one thing—he had come for him.

Well, he said to himself, two can play this game. Hell, it might even be fun. Sunrise was a couple of hours away, and he took a nap in the seat of the Beast. First light woke him, and he gathered his gear: the .357 in his gun belt with extra bullets, the rifle, a bandolier with ammunition for the rifle, his backpack with binoculars, a couple of pieces of venison jerky, and his army-issue canteen clipped onto his belt. Then he set off for the mountain. He could follow his pursuer's signs, even though the rains had washed away most of his boot prints. A broken branch on a creosote bush here and there, a rock kicked aside, and an occasional disturbed area where the man had slipped and regained his footing told Harley's experienced eye where his prey had gone.

He heard the snake before he saw it. It was a Mojave rattlesnake, sunning itself in the sun's rays on a flat rock just ahead of him. It was a beautiful pale green color, coiled to strike with its beady eyes tracking Harley's every move. The snake continued its warning rattle. "Boy, you're a fat one, ain't ya," he said to the snake. "If I had more time, I'd add your skin to my collection and have rattlesnake roasted over my fire tonight. Guess it's your lucky day," he chuckled and gave the snake a wide berth.

The black rocks on the mountain were still wet from yesterday's rain, sparkling in the growing sunlight. They were slippery, too, and he had to watch his footing. This ain't no time to slip and fall on my ass, he told himself. Don't want a commotion to alert my friend, either. Don't know how far off he is. He made it to the top of the peak and had to pick his way carefully through the teddy bear cholla cactuses. They grew like a miniature forest up here. He could see for miles over the surrounding mountains. He always admired the view, but he had no time to enjoy it this time.

His prey left many tell-tale signs of his passage. He thought it was the mark of an amateur. The edge of the mountain above the canyon where his camp was hidden provided a clear view of the area leading to his camp. He crawled to the rim and carefully scanned both sides of the canyon with his binoculars, looking for anything out of place. Nothing moved, but Harley knew how to be patient when stalking game. Stalking a man was no different. He settled himself in a comfortable position where he could see any activity in the canyon.

4

That damn gringo! El Puma thought. Where the hell is he? Did I get it wrong? Maybe he didn't have to come back here, and those bonds are somewhere else. Well, I'll give it today. What's one more day in this miserable place?

176

The sun's warming rays came late in the deep canyon shadow and had now burned off the damp overnight chill. The damp chill changed to stiflingly hot humidity as the sun climbed higher in the sky. He stood up to stretch and took a few steps away from the protective overhang to relieve himself. His canteens were almost out of water, too—another reason to leave his hiding place today. He could refill them at the spring in the canyon below before hiking back to his truck. The gringo would have to wait for another day.

🌵

Harley perked up at the first sign of movement. Something was stirring in the deep shadow under an overhanging rock ledge. He focused his binoculars on the spot and saw the Mexican emerge. The man scratched his ass, relieved himself, and had a long look around. He was too far away for Harley to get a good shot before he crawled back under the outcrop. Harley studied the area between his position and the outcrop. He would have to move further along the mountain's edge and try to come down on the man from behind. It was the only way he could approach him and keep from showing himself.

He moved stealthily as a cat, picking his way carefully along the mountain's rim. He sat and studied a way down toward his prey, then started easing himself down the slope, testing his footing for each step. When he was about two-thirds of the way down, he spooked a covey of quail in the brush. They took off in a furious beating of wings, then glided down the canyon past the rock outcrop. Harley froze, then slipped his rifle off his shoulder. He braced himself on a large boulder and waited. The quail called to each other down the canyon; otherwise, it was quiet as a tomb.

There! Harley saw just a hint of movement at the edge of the rock outcrop. He focused the sight of his rifle on the spot. A man's head slowly materialized from behind the rock, swiveling around, searching for what had disturbed the quail. Then he froze, looking directly at Harley. Harley squeezed the trigger but saw the bullet raise dirt just below where the target had been. The report of the rifle's shot echoed around the canyon. A pair of cactus wrens fluttered out of a small palo verde tree, and then all was silent.

❧

El Puma waited for his heartbeat to slow and tried to think of a way out of this predicament. It hadn't occurred to him that someone might come down on him from above. It was the third time he had underestimated this gringo. How did he know I was here? How the hell did he find me? I have to find a way to even the odds. Several large boulders were about a hundred feet down the slope from him. If he could get to them, he'd have some cover, and maybe he could pick off the gringo. There was no sound of movement behind him. All was still. He said two hail Marys, crossed himself, and made a dash for the boulders below. A bullet hit right behind him and went whining out across the canyon. He dove for the ground behind one of the boulders as another bullet ricocheted off the rock behind him and showered him with fragments.

He thought he'd try another tack and yelled, "Hey, gringo! It don't have to be this way. Let's you and me talk. We split up those bonds you got hid down there, eh? Both walk away with nobody gettin' hurt. What you say?"

A bullet ricocheted off a boulder in answer, showering him with more rock shards. The sun's rays beat down in the canyon, baking the black rocks and making it nearly unbearable. El Puma was drenched with sweat; he knew his adversary was in the same situation. Neither one could move without exposing himself to the other's gunfire.

❧

Harley picked out a path leading downward toward his right side. There were several big rocks he could duck behind for cover. He might have a clean shot at the Mexican if he could move far enough. This ain't gettin' me anywhere, he thought. Got to change the game! He took a deep breath, held his rifle against his

178

chest, and ran slip-sliding down to his first goal. A shot struck the ground right behind his feet. He caught his breath and then made a run for the next boulder. He hit the ground and slid behind it just as a bullet ricocheted off the rock. Two down, one to go, he thought. Got to run like hell! He ran as hard as he could and slid onto the ground behind the rock. He leaned around the side of the boulder and got off a quick shot at the Mexican. It looked like it hit him in the shoulder and knocked him down. Harley quickly moved a little further down the slope, and the Mexican got off a shot with a pistol, which grazed Harley's arm. He dropped into a crouch and shot the Mexican in the chest. El Puma fell backward with his arms and legs splayed at odd angles to his body. Harley walked over to him and poked him a couple of times with the barrel of his rifle. The man's eyes stared at nothing in the bright morning sky.

The wound in Harley's shoulder hurt like hell. He hadn't even noticed it until the adrenaline began to wear off. He rolled the Mexican on his side and pulled out his wallet. The name on the Mexican driver's license was Diego Alvarez. It meant nothing to Harley. There was a hundred dollars in cash, which he shoved in his pocket. He examined the dead man's guns—they were identical to the ones he was carrying. "Well, at least you had good taste in guns," he said to the dead man. "I'll just add these to my own collection if you don't mind." He laughed at his little joke, strapped both rifles over his shoulder, tucked the extra pistol in his belt, and set off down the canyon to his campsite. He opened the bunker and put the additional firearms inside. Then he opened his big first aid kit and went to work on his wound. He used a hand mirror in the kit to look at it; it was superficial and should heal quickly. He opened a packet of sulfanilamide, sprinkled it over the wound, and carefully bandaged it. It hurt, but not the worst he had ever had—he was good to go. The big Squire padlock gave a reassuring click when he closed it on the door, and he headed down the canyon. It was a couple of miles to hike back to his truck.

Massive thunderheads billowed to the south and east, and they appeared to be heading toward the area. That was a good thing, he thought. It should keep the air patrols grounded for a while. That would give him a little breathing room to carry out his plan.

He reached the Beast and headed back toward Site One. The wash had flowed after the last rains, and the water exposed his tire puncture boards. It also filled the trenches he had dug with sand. He didn't have time to spend on reworking the traps now. He had another, more deadly scheme to put in place. He parked the Beast near the bunker and started taking out supplies and putting them in the truck's bed. He took out all his extra firearms—you could never have too many, to his way of thinking. Canned foods, extra ammunition, bedding, water, and gasoline would add to his stock at Site Two. It would be his home for at least a few weeks, maybe longer.

He thought he might never come back to Site One. It's where they would continue to watch for him. He had a little surprise in mind for any searchers that came snooping around. He took an Army M-2 antipersonnel mine out of the box of a half dozen he had acquired at the taxidermist's shop. Then he dug a cylindrical hole about ten inches deep right in front of the bunker's door, where he figured someone would step to examine the lock. He carefully placed the mine's housing with an attached tripwire stand in the hole, filled the hole around the device, and removed the fuse's safety pins. All that remained slightly above ground were the prongs that would activate the fuse when someone stepped on it. When the mine was triggered, it would launch its sixty-millimeter mortar shell about eight feet in the air before it exploded. According to what Harley had been told, it would kill anyone within thirty feet of it. He smoothed the area around the site and scattered a few rocks to make it appear undisturbed. He smiled to himself and wished he could be there to see it in action.

The bearer bonds were hidden in a small alcove between two massive black boulders about twenty-five yards from the camp. He had carefully wrapped their case to keep moisture out, then stacked rocks around the opening to conceal it. It was exactly as he had left it, and he quickly tossed the concealing rocks aside and grabbed the case. He would find another hiding place for it at Site Two.

The storms were closing in; they looked like they would bring heavy rains. He had to try to reach Site Two before the big wash between Woolsey and Signal Mountains flooded. It was rough going, and he pushed the Beast hard, bouncing over rocks and climbing in and out of small washes. He had to be careful to take a circuitous route to avoid leaving any clear trail where he had gone. Hopefully, the coming rains would wipe out most traces of the truck's passage.

The first storm hit just as he arrived at Site Two. He sat in the Beast and waited for the hail and rain to subside. Thunder from nearby lightning strikes shook the truck and rattled the glass in the windows. The site was well situated to avoid flooding, and the water drained off quickly. The rain dwindled to a sprinkle, and he transferred his extra supplies to the bunker. He had built an identical bunker at this camp; it was just as impregnable as the other one.

Site Two had one distinct advantage over its sister site—it afforded a panoramic view of the rough country between it and Woolsey Peak. He would see anyone coming long before they reached him—and he had some surprises for anyone who came too close.

He finished unloading the Beast and organizing his supplies in the bunker. He had a specially made tarp stored in the bunker with a grey and black desert camouflage pattern that fit well with the landscape. It would be virtually invisible from a distance when it was staked down over the beast. He doubted a spotter in an airplane would pick it out among all the rocks around the camp. He was satisfied with his preparations and ready to call it a night. A campfire at night could give away his position, so he used his camp stove to heat a can of stew for dinner. The storm had passed, and he moved his cot outside. Then he stretched out and was instantly asleep.

CHAPTER 28

Sean was back on his regular patrol duties. Harley had eluded roadblocks, increased patrols, and aerial surveillance. He had disappeared. Today, the department would post a one thousand dollar reward for information leading to his capture. Sean doubted it would amount to anything, but it was worth a try.

He got a dispatch call to investigate a domestic disturbance at a farmhouse outside Buckeye. Sean pulled up next to a dilapidated old house that hadn't seen a coat of paint in the thirty or forty years since it had been built. Four mongrel dogs came racing out to meet him. They were mostly interested in peeing on his patrol car's tires, but they set up a racket to let the owners know he was there. A screen door flew open, and a teenage girl burst out onto the porch. She had a terrified look in her eyes as she ran up to Sean.

She yelled, "You've got to stop him! He's gonna kill her! Please! Stop him!" Then she started sobbing and slid down onto the ground beside Sean's car. She caught her breath and said, "He's got a knife, and he's trying to kill Momma! He already cut her bad! Please stop him!"

Sean grabbed his nightstick and ran up to the house. He could hear a woman screaming inside, and he stepped through the open screen door and yelled, "Police! Stop what you are doing. This is the police!"

A woman yelled, "Up here!" and started screaming again. Sean heard things being thrown around and a lot of stomping from upstairs. He went up the stair steps two at a time and was nearly knocked off the landing by a woman who exploded out of a room to his left.

"Help me! My god, he wants to kill me!" the woman screamed.

Just then, the man ran out of the room, and Sean stepped between him and the woman. He had a crazed look in his eyes and brandished a large, bloody butcher knife. It took him a couple of seconds to register who Sean was, and then he lunged at him with the knife. Sean sidestepped the blow, bringing his nightstick down hard across the man's wrist. There was a loud crack, the man yelped, and the knife clattered on the floor. The man tried to grab Sean with his good hand, but Sean caught his wrist and twisted his arm behind him. He forced him to the floor and put his knee on his back while he handcuffed him. The man screamed a chain of obscenities and writhed around on the stair landing.

Sean kept his knee on the man's back and spoke softly, trying to calm him down. He finally quit struggling after a few minutes and said, "The bitch! I shoulda killed her. I still might!"

"Settle down, sir. It's over. You're not going to kill anyone. Here's what's going to happen. I'm going to let you up, and you and I are going to walk slowly down the stairs. I will crack your head with my nightstick if you try to run. Do you understand?"

"Yeah, I understand. You broke my wrist with that damn club! Hurts like hell, too!"

"All right. Stand up and move down the stairs, slowly, one step at a time."

Sean kept a tight grip on the cuffs behind the man's back as he followed him down. The man bolted when he touched the bottom. Sean gave a hard jerk on the cuffs, and the man stumbled backward and fell on the floor. Sean said, "Last chance, buddy. You come along peacefully, or you'll have more broken bones to whine about. Get up!" He hauled the man onto his feet by his shirt collar, grabbed the cuffs behind his back again, and pushed him stumbling out of the house and down the porch steps to his patrol car. He opened the back door and shoved the man inside. Then he went back to the woman.

She was bleeding freely from two deep wounds on her arms and several more minor gashes. She had obviously held off her husband's knife blows with her arms. He got a first aid kit from the trunk of his car, sat the woman down on her porch, and dressed her wounds. Her daughter was sitting beside her with her head in her hands, sobbing.

Sean said, "Stay here, ma'am. I'll call an ambulance for you and your daughter." He made the radio call, returned to the woman and her daughter, and told them to explain what had happened. The woman said her husband had been agitated since he lost his job two weeks earlier. He had started drinking and accusing her of being unfaithful. Then he started beating her. When her daughter tried to stop him, he had beaten her too. Then he had come at her with the kitchen butcher knife.

"Thank god you got here when you did, deputy!" the woman said through her sobs. "He would have killed me. Maybe my daughter, too."

"You're okay now, ma'am. He'll be charged with assault with a deadly weapon and resisting arrest. I'll book him into the county jail."

The ambulance arrived a half hour later. He told the medics the woman had been stabbed with a butcher knife and that both women were in shock. They put them in the ambulance and headed for Phoenix.

Sean walked to his car, followed by the pack of dogs. They sniffed at him, intrigued by Buddy's scent on his clothes. The dogs thoroughly watered all four tires again before he left. Sean took his prisoner to the district office's holding cell and booked him for assault with a deadly weapon, resisting arrest, and assaulting an officer.

The incident reminded him that he had promised to check in on the pretty school teacher in Liberty. It was on his patrol beat, anyway. He pulled into the woman's driveway, and she came out on the front step. She was dressed in a green checkered pattern gingham dress, and her red hair was pulled back into a girlish ponytail. She took Sean's breath away. He waited a few seconds to compose himself before getting out of the car.

"Morning, Miss Preston," he said. It felt like he had a mouth full of cotton.

"Good morning, Deputy O'Conner. What a nice surprise!"

"I wanted to check on you. Have you had any more trouble with strange men?"

She started giggling.

Sean turned red and blurted, "I didn't mean that the way it sounded!" Then they both started laughing. He said, "I just arrested a man who was trying to hurt his wife, and it made me wonder if you were safe. I wanted to check to be sure the lock on your back door had been repaired."

She smiled at him and said, "That's very kind. My landlord fixed the door the same day of the break-in. Won't you come in? I'll make a fresh pot of coffee if you'd like some."

"Yes, ma'am. That sounds nice."

"It's Sandy...Remember?"

"Yes ma...Sandy. I'm sorry. It's a force of habit for me."

She had a lilting, musical laugh—he could listen to it all day. They sat and drank hot coffee while they told each other a little about themselves. The more they talked, the more it seemed they were a perfect fit. Sean asked her if she'd like to have dinner with him, his friend Ricky, and his girlfriend on Saturday night. She readily accepted. Then she walked him out to his car and took both his hands in hers, and Sean felt that same electric jolt he had felt when she took his hands the first time.

She said, "Thanks for stopping by to check on me. It was very kind of you."

He knew he was falling hard for her and couldn't help himself.

He drove into Buckeye and used a pay phone at the Texaco station to call Ricky. He was good to meet for dinner on Saturday. He said, "By the way, my cousin Elena asked about you, amigo. She said you didn't ask her father if you could see her again."

"Well, I was a little embarrassed. I didn't know I'd have to talk to her father if I wanted to see her again. So, I just let it slide."

Ricky laughed into the phone. "I get it, amigo. It's a scary thing to ask a girl's father if you can date his daughter."

"Embarrassing, Ricky, not scary."

Ricky laughed again, saying, "Yeah, yeah…see you on Saturday. I'm anxious to meet this new girl in your life."

Joe "The Fish" Leone sat reading the newspaper in the coffee shop of the Hotel San Carlos in downtown Phoenix. He was very interested in an article detailing a search for the wanted murderer. The article described several crimes the wanted man had committed and, almost as a postscript, that he was rumored to have stolen something from an airplane crash site in the desert far west of Phoenix. It was the first hint he had seen of anything associated with the plane crash. The man must be the same one Rossi had been looking for. And this guy was wanted for the murder of a lawyer named Fishburn. That was the contact Rossi had used to get information about the bonds.

He also noted that the Sheriff's Department was offering a one thousand dollar reward for information leading to the man's capture. It gave him an idea, a way he might get ahead of the cops to find the guy. He went back to his room and called the boss at the Casino. Bianco readily agreed with his plan and had ten thousand dollars wired to a bank in Phoenix. He authorized Joe to spend the money and bring in any help he needed. It would be a small investment to recover their bonds.

The hotel concierge directed him to a messaging service and a printing shop a couple of blocks away. He made the necessary arrangements with the messaging service and paid them in cash for one month's service. Then he went to the nearby printing shop and told the owner what he wanted; the man said he would have it done by five o'clock that day.

Then he went into a nearby bar to have a few beers and wait for his project to be done.

The two detectives, Johnson, and Harper, traveled to Las Vegas to confer with their counterparts in the police department. Johnson said, "We got some information we think will be useful to you from a Lawyer named Fishburn in Phoenix. He was murdered the same day we talked to him, presumably by our chief suspect in other murders. He's also the chief suspect in taking your casino friends' property from the plane crash.

"Do tell," Detective Black said.

"The main thing," Johnson continued, "is we now know what the casino folks are so keen to recover. It was a million dollars in bearer bonds, apparently stolen from the casino."

Both the Las Vegas detectives sat in shocked silence for a minute. Black said, "Well, that explains a lot. Those guys will be wanting that back in the worst kind of way. It probably explains the mystery of the body found beside a road and the bloody car we found at the airport after the casino's plane went missing. Do they know who the guy is that has their bonds?"

"We have to assume they do. They sent that guy, Rossi, to find out about it from the lawyer. Our suspect ambushed and killed him, along with several other people."

Detective Flowers said, "Yeah, we heard. He had a reputation for being a real badass and enforcer for the mob. Your boy must be a tough cookie!"

"He seems to be," Johnson replied. "He's a hunter and some kind of survivalist. And he's a hell of a shot."

Flowers said, "We've had some contact from the feds about this bearer bond business. They think the casino is using them to launder cash from their operation. Word is a mining company here in Nevada is known to have made several issues of those kinds of bonds."

Johnson said, "We'd like to know if the casino sent a replacement for Rossi. We suspected Rossi was involved with murdering our suspect's brother when he or his goombahs tried to beat information out of him. That led to another ambush by our suspect. We think he killed two of Rossi's men and dumped their bodies in the desert. It looks like he narrowly missed killing Rossi that time. We don't want any more people getting killed by overzealous mobsters trying to beat information out of people."

"Holy crap!" Flowers said. "It sounds like the wild west down there. We'll see what we can find out about who the casino sent to replace Rossi." He waited a few seconds and continued, "And one more thing…it seems Rossi had a tidy side business going importing drugs from Mexico and selling them through several casinos in town. Maybe your guy did us a big favor!"

The detectives chewed on the details of all that had happened and agreed to talk daily by phone to keep each other updated. Johnson and Harper checked into the Golden Gate Casino and Hotel. They couldn't pass up a chance for a bit of R&R on the company's dime.

Joe the Fish picked up two hundred flyers and looked them over. They said:

$5,000 REWARD

FOR ANY INFORMATION LEADING TO THE WHEREABOUTS OF HARLEY HENDERSON. LAST SEEN NEAR BUCKEYE, AZ.

REWARD PAID ON CONFIRMATION OF INFORMATION.

CALL WESTPORT 6-9951 DAY OR NIGHT AND LEAVE MESSAGE

The following morning, he picked up several rolls of tape, then drove west of Phoenix through Tolleson and Avondale and on to Buckeye. In each town, he found a couple of teenage kids hanging around on the streets and offered twenty dollars in cash for each of them to go around town hanging up the posters. Then he went back to his hotel in Phoenix and called his boss. "I'll need some help to follow up on the contacts that flyer will bring. I'd like to bring Jimmy and Tony down here. They're two of my best men from the casino. They are good at wading through bullshit from people, and I expect there will be a lot of those kinds of tips with this thing."

Bianco said, "I'll send them to you today."

"One more thing, boss—tell them to bring clothes suitable for the desert. And boots."

"Keep me posted."

The phone line went dead; Joe hung up the receiver and headed for the hotel bar. He figured he was going to be very busy the next few days.

CHAPTER 29

Sean walked into the district commander's office early the next morning. He laid one of Joe's flyers on the commander's desk and said, "Looks like we have competition to find Harley. It must be the casino people trying to get ahead of us. They're likely to get a big reaction for that kind of reward."

The commander studied the flyer. "Yep. Five grand will generate a lot of interest. Where'd you find this flyer?"

"I saw it on a light pole on the corner of Main Street. They're plastered all over the place."

"Somebody's gonna get hurt if they go after Harley directly. And the Vegas mob being involved makes it even more dangerous. We've got to try to get ahead of this." He called Gloria, the district clerk, into his office and said, "I want you to bring all our deputies in for a meeting at nine this morning. Any of them on patrol need to come in immediately." She left and spoke with the deputies who were still in the office, then got on the radio and messaged the others on patrol.

It was standing room only in the commander's conference room when all the men gathered for the meeting. There was a lot of excited chatter about what was happening—it was unusual for everyone to be called into a meeting on such short notice.

The commander stood up and said, "Men, we have a potentially explosive situation on our hands." He passed around the flyer and continued, "We believe this flyer is something the people from the Vegas casino have hatched to try and get ahead of us to find our suspect. They are looking to recover a lot of valuable bonds that were taken from their airplane that crashed by Buckeye. This kind of reward money will bring all kinds of crackpots out of the woodwork, along with regular folks who see the possibility of making some money. I want you all to be aware of this. You may

191

be contacted by people looking for any information we have. Do not say anything. We don't need a bunch of armed citizens roaming around the desert looking to get their heads blown off. And we don't want to be tripping over Vega mobsters. If you hear any rumors about our suspect's whereabouts, you are to report it directly to me. Questions?"

The room erupted in questions, but they only led to rehashing what was already known. The only new things were the flyer and the fact that the mob was again actively trying to find Harley.

🌵

Joe the Fish's telephone started ringing at 7 o'clock that morning. The woman at the answering service said calls had swamped them. He told her to keep a log of all the calls and the times they called, and he would collect the information later. He expected his reinforcements from Vegas to arrive by noon, and they would start working through the calls and weeding out the useless information.

When his men arrived, they had lunch at the hotel's restaurant while Joe filled them in on what was needed. He had booked two more rooms for them. While they were getting settled, he went to the answering service office to collect the call logs they had received that morning. There were over fifty of them, and they were still coming in. He told them to continue the log and that he would return before they closed that evening to pick up the next batch.

Back at the hotel, they split the calls between them, and the men took their share to their rooms and went to work. Joe told them to meet back at his room once an hour to go over what they found. The answering service called Joe in the afternoon and asked him to pick up the additional calls they had received; they said they were having difficulty keeping up with the volume. By the end of the day, they had received over two hundred tips. They worked into the night and narrowed the calls down to ten that sounded legitimate, which they would follow up on the next day. Only two of those ten sounded worth pursuing. One man claimed

192

to be Harley's uncle and knew where he would be hiding. The other was a man who said he had actually been to Harley's hunting camp and could lead them there.

Joe took Tony with him to interview their two prospects. Jimmy would continue to follow up on contacts from the answering service. Both of the contacts were in Buckeye. The man claiming to be Harley's uncle met them at the coffee shop on Main Street. He reeked of beer, and his eyes were bloodshot, but he seemed to be sober.

"Yessir," the man said, "I knowed Harley and his brother Harry all their lives. Harry's dead now; somebody killed him in his shop."

Joe said, "Sorry to hear that, Mr. Henderson. What can you tell us about Harley?"

"Walll, Harley was always a loner, ya know. He spent all his time foolin' around in the desert, huntin' and stuff. That's why he made himself a permanent camp out in the mountains. He'd druther be there than around folks in town."

"Can you take us to that camp?" Joe asked.

"Walll…I never was exactly there, ya know. Harley liked to keep it secret. But I kinda know where it ought to be."

"Do you think he's there now?"

"That there's a good question. I don't know if he's there. He might be. Only way to know is to go have a look."

"But you can't take us there?"

"Nope. All's I can do is tell you where to start lookin'."

"Thank you, Mr. Henderson. We'll be in touch if we need more information from you."

"When do I get the money?"

"If you can lead us to him, we will pay you. Call us if you think you can do that."

The two casino men walked out and left Henderson fuming at the table.

The next man they wanted to talk to was named Jones. He lived in the oldest part of town. The original paint had peeled off the house long ago, and the wood was cracked and splitting from years in the dry air. A half-dead mulberry tree grew in the yard, surrounded by scraggly Bermuda grass that had gone to seed. They had to knock twice on the door until an elderly man finally answered. He wore threadbare khaki pants and an armless undershirt with brown stains around the armpits. He was also barefoot. Grey hair stood in unruly shocks above a grey, scruffy beard.

"You the guys lookin' for Harley?" he wheezed. Joe nodded, and the man said, "Well, come on in and sit a spell. I'll tell you what I know."

Joe and Tony looked around the room. There was only a faded green couch and a rickety-looking old armchair with its original floral pattern completely worn off the seat and arms. The men sat down on the couch, raising a small dust cloud and sinking below the front of the cushions—there was no padding left in them. The only decoration in the room was a faded painting of a cowboy roping a steer.

Joe said, "Thank you for contacting us, Mr. Jones. Tell us how to find Mr. Henderson."

"I can tell you, but I doubt you'd ever be able to find him on your own," he replied. "The country that boy likes to hang out in is some of the roughest in the state, and there ain't no street signs." He let that sink in, then continued, "I can take you to his camp, but I 'spect it'll be dangerous. I've heard he don't like visitors," the old man chuckled then broke into a phlegm-filled coughing spasm.

"How did you come by being there if he doesn't like visitors?" Joe asked.

"I've hunted deer in that country since I was a boy. The last time I was out there, maybe three or four years ago, I chased a big muley buck up a canyon on the other side of Woolsey Peak. When I got up the canyon a ways I come on a permanent lookin' camp. It had a bunker dug into the side of the canyon with a steel door and a big-ass padlock on it. I knowed it was Harley's

194

because his brother Harry told me about it once when we were drinkin' beer and talkin' about huntin' out there." He fished a can of Prince Albert tobacco from his pants pocket and a packet of Zig-Zag cigarette wrappers from his shirt pocket. He took his time shaking a little tobacco onto the paper and carefully rolled it. Then he gave it a lick, struck a match, and lit it. He started coughing when he took his first drag but inhaled more smoke anyway. Then he continued, "I can take you there. But I want half the money upfront and the other half when we get back…if we get back."

"What do you mean if we get back?" Joe asked.

"Well, in case you ain't heard, Harley is a mean sonofabitch. The cops say he's already killed a bunch of people. I don't 'spect he'd hesitate to add you to that list of dead folks. He knows the desert like he was born in it, and he's a damn good shot. So, you go out there, you're takin' a chance."

Joe said, "All right, old man. I'll agree to your terms. But if you're jerking us around, you might not come back from that little outing."

Jones gave a cackling laugh and slapped his leg, then started coughing again. When it was done, he said, "That's a good one. None of us may come back anyways!"

"Let's go, then," Joe said, his impatience showing.

"You boys happen to have a four-wheel drive truck?"

"What?" Joe snapped. "No, we don't!"

"Well, me neither." He puffed on his cigarette and continued, "Only two ways to get out there—in a four-wheel drive rig or horseback. Horseback is how I done it. But you boys don't look like horse people to me."

Joe was obviously at the end of his rope. He blew out a breath and said, "Okay, do you know where we can get a four-wheel drive rig?"

"They ain't many around, cuz they all went to the military for the war, ya know. But now the war's over, ya might be able to rent or buy one from a dealer. The best one is a Dodge Truck. If you cain't get one of them, a Jeep will do. They's a Dodge dealer in Phoenix that might be able to help ya out. Let me know when you get one, and I'll be ready."

Joe wanted to shake the scruffy man til his frail bones rattled, but he seemed to be telling the truth. He said, "Okay, old man. We'll find one. But you better not be messin' with us. That wouldn't go very good for you."

"One more thing," the old man said. "Better not be wearin' those city duds. Gonna need some good boots, too. We may have to walk a ways. And I'll be wantin' the first half 'a that reward money before we go."

"We'll be ready. You be ready, too," Joe snarled. Then he and Tony stormed out of the house. They could hear Jones' cackling laugh all the way back to their car.

When they arrived back at the motel, Jimmy had another stack of messages he was working through. "Not as many as yesterday, boss. I think there's sixty or so."

Joe said, "Tony can help you get through them. I have to try to find a four-wheel drive rig." He returned to his room and found the Dodge dealer in the phone book.

A salesman said they just got a new truck in stock. "It's the first one we've had since the war started."

Joe asked if he could rent it, but the salesman said they didn't do rentals.

The dealer was on the other side of town, and he left his two men to wade through the latest responses to his reward offer. He told them to be ready to go early the next morning and dress for a hike in the desert. He stopped at a bank to withdraw cash, then drove his 1944 Plymouth onto the dealer's lot. A salesman immediately approached him, offering him a great trade on a new Dodge.

"I'm not looking to trade. I called earlier and talked to a man named Fred about a truck."

"Yes, sir! I'm Fred. Pleased to meet you, Mr...."

"Leone. Show me the truck."

196

The salesman led him to the back side of the lot and showed him a hulking green vehicle with black fenders. He said, "It's your lucky day. We just got this truck in two days ago. It's still painted Army green. We were gonna paint it a different color, but we can give you a little discount to take it as is. It's brand new, only has ten miles on it. I can make you a great deal!"

Joe looked it over while the salesman prattled on about the upgrades on the truck: a driver armrest, a sun visor, dual vacuum windshield wipers, a dome light, a little extra padding on the seat, and a heater. It was also equipped with a winch on the front and standard four-wheel drive. The thing sat high off the ground and looked like a holdover from the war. "How much?" he asked the salesman.

Fred rubbed his chin, sizing up his mark. "Well, for you, we can offer a special price of three thousand dollars if you take it today."

"Hell, I could buy a new Cadillac for less than that!"

"Yes, sir. I'm sure you could. But this is the only one of these around. I don't know when or if we'll get another one. Remember, this rig has all those options I told you about, too."

"I'll give you twenty-five hundred dollars cash right now. Take it or leave it."

"Let me speak to my manager, Mr. Leone. I'll be right back."

Typical car dealer song and dance, Joe thought.

The salesman returned in five minutes and said, "We can do twenty-seven fifty if that works for you."

"Twenty-seven," Joe said.

Fred wrung his hands as if he were making a life-and-death decision. Finally, he said, "Sold. Let me get the paperwork ready."

They spent forty-five minutes getting all the paperwork done; then Joe used the office phone to call Tony. He told him to get a cab to the dealer and bring the truck back to their motel. "Get the salesman to show you how all the stuff on it works, too. You're gonna be drivin' the damn thing."

197

None of the new calls sounded promising. At least old man Jones promised to take them to Henderson's camp. They called him that night and told him to be ready the next morning.

❡

Cars and pickup trucks of every description were prowling the desert's dirt tracks, looking for some sign of Harley. The five thousand dollar reward had ignited a firestorm of interest. Some people even got into fistfights, arguing about where he might be holed up. They were all racing each other to be the first to get a lead on Harley's whereabouts. Rumors grew and flew around the small towns west of Phoenix: The Beast had been seen west of the White Tank Mountains north of Buckeye, Harley had bought gas in Cashion and headed for the Estrella Mountains south of there, a waitress at Stout's Hotel coffee shop in Gila Bend swore he had breakfast there, he had been seen in Agua Caliente west of Gila Bend, and on and on.

The few people who knew Harley focused on the area around Woolsey Peak. He talked about it all the time to his few friends in high school; now, most of them were wandering around the area of the peak, looking for any sign. None of them really knew the area, and they weren't prepared for the conditions they faced once they left the highway. A couple of them had their cars stuck in washes with sand up to the bottom of the car's doors; one had ripped open his car's oil pan trying to get over some large rocks, and his engine froze up. Another had run out of gas and walked back to the highway, nearly exhausted from dehydration.

Harley watched with amusement through his binoculars. He could see for miles east of his position and tracked the various vehicles' movements. It was obvious they were looking for him. So far, no one had shown up in a vehicle capable of even getting close to Site One, much less Site Two. But it was only a matter of time until others who knew what they were doing showed up. He had to be prepared.

Various kinds of military hardware and ordnance in the United States had been diverted to the Pacific theatre when the war in

198

Europe ended. As in all wars, a substantial amount was lost in transit or stolen outright. If you knew the right people, much of it could be had in the black market. Harley knew the right people. His taxidermist partner was, like Harley, a survivalist with many connections among like-minded people. Some of those people were actively engaged in selling black-market military goods to people like Harley. He had arranged to purchase several items before he went into hiding, including land mines, hand grenades, a Browning automatic rifle, and a Thompson submachine gun. All that was in addition to the civilian firearms he had stockpiled over the years. He was prepared to use all of it if he were cornered. He hoped it didn't come to that. He simply wanted to take his bearer bonds and live the good life in Mexico or South America.

🌵

Joe the Fish and his two men drove up in front of Jones' house at about eight a.m. He was waiting for them and came out to look at the truck. "Hot damn!" he said. "Where'd you find this baby?"

Joe replied, "I bought the damn thing. Get in, and let's go."

Jones looked in the truck's bed and said, "Where's your gear?"

"What gear? You didn't say anything about any gear."

"Well, hell, boy. Don't you city folk know anything? We're goin' out into some wild desert country, and it's damn hot. You'll be wantin' some water before we even get off the highway. He looked around and said, "I don't see any hats. You ever been out in the desert sun on a hot August day?"

Joe's patience was growing very thin. He again wanted to shake the old man til his teeth rattled. But he said, "All right, old man. You made your point. Where can we get what we need?"

"They's a Western Auto store downtown. They oughta have canteens and hats, at least. They're prob'ly open now, and ya can buy what you want. Then we can stop at a gas station, put water in the canteens, and fill the gas tank."

"We filled the tank before we left Phoenix."

"Yeah, but I promise you the one thing ya don't wanna do out there is run out of gas. It's a long, hot walk back to civilization."

"All right, all right. Let's load up and get it done. Jimmy, you'll have to ride in back 'cause we need Jones up front to give us directions."

"One more thing," Jones said. "I'll be wantin' my money afore we go."

Joe pulled an envelope out of his pants pocket and handed it to him. "Now, find this bastard!" he snarled.

Jimmy climbed into the truck's bed, grumbling about what a pain in the ass this day was going to be. They bought canteens, hats, and a five-gallon jerry can at the store. Jones insisted they buy the can for extra gas because he sure as hell didn't want to walk out of the desert. Jimmy bought a couple of wool blankets he folded up to make a cushion to sit on. He figured it would be a long day. They stopped at the Texaco station, filled the canteens, the jerry can, and the truck's gas tank, and were finally on their way.

They passed a deputy sheriff's car parked near the turn-off for Agua Caliente. Then they hit the rough dirt road and followed Jones' directions to a turnoff on a faint road that was nothing more than rutted tire tracks. The truck's stout suspension made for a rough ride as they bounced over rocks and ruts in the little-used track. They came to the first difficult wash crossing and put the truck into four-wheel drive. It was a new experience for Tony, and he crept cautiously into the sand. The truck barely spun a tire before they climbed up the other bank. They crossed several more similar drainages, and the country got rougher. Then, they came to a large, deep arroyo with steep banks. Tony saw that other vehicles had gone up and down the banks at an angle and eased the truck over the bank. The truck leaned to one side as they crept down the steep bank, then tilted abruptly before they got to the bottom. Jimmy jumped out and walked the rest of the way up the opposite bank. He didn't want to be thrown out if

200

the truck tipped over. Tony nursed the rig along at a crawl, and they made it out of the wash.

Jones directed them past a couple of other tracks that branched off, and they continued along the peak's north side. Jones said, "Look up there. That's prob'ly yer wrecked airplane." Sun glinted off the wreckage of the Stinson high up the slope. Joe had Tony stop so they could look; he and his men crossed themselves before they continued. It was late morning when Jones directed them to turn up the wash that led to Harley's camp. He said, "The place is about three-quarters of a mile up this wash. Go slow and be ready to bail out of this rig in case he starts shooting at us."

They came to the first of Harley's tire shredders. Tony could see where Harley had driven around it up next to the bank and followed the tracks. He did the same at the next one. They continued slowly up the canyon, watching carefully for any signs of additional traps. The camp came into sight and appeared to be deserted. They eased up to the flat area in front of the brush ramada and the bunker.

"Well, where is he?" Joe demanded.

"Damned if I know!" the old man replied.

They got out and looked around. "What's that god-awful smell?" Jimmy said. "Smells like somethin' dead."

Jones said, "Yup. Prob'ly a dead coyote or somethin. Could be our man got off up there and died. The stink's on the breeze comin' down the canyon. I'll go have a look. You boys see if there's any sign of what yer lookin' for."

Joe and his men looked around, and Marco said, "If it's here, it's in that bunker. That's a serious steel door and lock." The three men gathered in front of the bunker door. Tony stepped closer to have a look at the padlock. He took another step and felt something give under his foot. There was a loud bang as the land mine's mortar round launched out of the ground and exploded. There was no warning, no time to run—just a terrific explosion that left the men sprawled on the ground in bloody tatters.

Jones had just found El Puma's decomposing body when the deafening explosion echoed off the canyon walls. He saw the three men on the ground and rushed to see if he could help them. He quickly saw there was nothing he could do. They were all dead. He saw where the mine had come out of the ground and started nervously looking around himself. He had heard about those kinds of mines being used in the war, and he didn't want to step on another one. "Damn," he said out loud. "That Harley's sure as hell a tricky one!" He walked carefully, one slow step at a time, looking closely before he put a foot down. He got back to the truck and exhaled the breath he had been holding. The truck had some shrapnel damage to the body, and the glass was blown out of the passenger side window. It otherwise looked okay. He got in, started it up, then turned around and drove slowly away from the camp. Well, hell, he thought to himself. I didn't get all the money, but at least I got half and this truck. He returned the way they had come and parked the truck in the rickety garage beside his house. Then he went inside, poured himself a tall glass of Jim Beam whiskey, and flopped down in his easy chair. He was still shaking so much he could barely raise the glass to his lips.

Harley heard the explosion as it echoed around the mountains. He had seen the green pickup when it neared Woolsey Peak and watched as it made its way up the wash toward Site One. He smiled with satisfaction when he heard the blast. The big green truck didn't look like something the cops would drive, but it was driven by someone who clearly knew where his camp was. Then, he saw the truck come back out of the canyon a little later. So, he thought...the mine didn't get them all. But he figured it might discourage others from looking for him.

CHAPTER 30

The sheriff's air posse reported something suspicious near Woolsey Peak. One of the surveillance planes noticed a white pickup truck parked near the peak for several days. They also reported seeing a green pickup exiting the canyon they had been watching. The sheriff's office relayed it to the district office to investigate.

The district commander assigned Sean to check it out. The Jeep had been temporarily reserved for activity related to the search in the Woolsey Peak area. It was kept ready with a full fuel tank, five gallons each of water and extra gasoline, and a large first aid kit. The commander wanted it prepared for quick action whenever needed. Sean said, "Sir, if it's okay, I'd like to take Brad along. We never know what we'll find out there, and it's a good idea to have a patrol car as a backup in case there's a problem with the Jeep." The commander agreed, and the two men made preparations to leave early the following day.

They left before daylight the next day. It was Saturday, and Sean had his first date for dinner with Miss Preston that night. He wanted to be sure he was back on time. As usual, Brad followed the Jeep in his patrol car and parked it near the turn-off to Agua Caliente Road.

The report said the pickup truck was parked near the southeast base of the peak. They neared the area, and Sean spotted two sets of tracks that veered off the road toward that area. The Jeep bounced over the rocks and small washes as Sean dodged the prolific cactus that grew everywhere. The men were both surprised when they reached the truck—the glass in the back window was missing, and there was a bullet hole in the windshield. There were also several bullet holes in the body on the right rear side. It had a license plate from Mexico.

Brad said, "Do you think there was a gunfight here?"

Sean ran his hand over the bullet holes. "These weren't made today. You can see dirt in the holes." He opened the passenger door and looked inside. "There are a few broken pieces of glass around the floorboard and a few in the fold at the seat back. Since there's no glass in the back window, it would indicate they were shot out. This truck may have been involved in the shooting at Ruby's house." He stood quietly and studied the peak, then said, "You know, I think whoever left the truck here climbed the peak from this side. Maybe they went over to the canyon on the other side and dropped down into the canyon where Harley's camp is. They might have tried to sneak up on him like we did."

Brad nodded and said, "Look here. That other set of tracks ended right beside this truck."

"Yep. And I think I recognize those tracks. They look like the ones made by the oversized tires on Harley's truck. Let's head around the mountain to the canyon leading to Harley's camp and see what we can see. That other truck the air posse reported must have been up to something there. Maybe it's all related."

They backtracked to the road and continued to the wash leading up to what they now called Harley's Canyon. There were fresh tracks, and they could see where a vehicle had dodged around Harley's makeshift tire puncture traps. Brad whistled and said, "Damn. Looks like our boy expected trouble. Those nails would do serious damage to tires." They carefully followed the tracks around them. Then Brad said, "Look up there, Sean! Have you ever seen so many vultures circling one place?"

Sean shook his head and took off up the canyon as fast as he could, dodging the second tire shredder. They got close enough to see there was no vehicle at the camp and figured it was safe to approach it. They pulled up to the site and parked, scaring off a pack of coyotes working on several bodies on the ground. At least a dozen vultures were vying for space with the coyotes and quickly moved in when the coyotes retreated. The coyotes backed up a little way, sizing up these new intruders. Brad fired a shot from his pistol, and the coyotes took off, yelping down the canyon to a safe distance. The vultures flew off in a storm of flapping wings and joined others circling above. The coyotes sat and watched the men.

The bodies on the ground were disfigured, their arms and legs at odd angles to their bodies. Blood had oozed from their eyes, noses, and mouths. It looked like a nightmare scene from a horror movie. The putrid smell of decaying flesh was almost overpowering.

Sean whistled softly. "My god, Brad. This was some kind of massacre!"

Brad started to walk toward the nearest body, and Sean grabbed his arm to stop him. "Hold on, Brad. I've seen this kind of thing before in the war. See how the bodies were flung backward? And look at that steel door on the bunker. Those indentations were likely made by shrapnel from a land mine's mortar shell. These guys were killed by the blast from a land mine. It looks like they were probably all standing close together when someone triggered the mine's fuse. They have some shrapnel wounds, but it was the blast that killed them. There could be more hidden around here."

"A land mine? Where in hell would Harley get a land mine?"

"I've heard you can get almost anything through the black market right now. We need to back away and get a munitions crew from the National Guard to come up here and search this area. It's too dangerous for us to walk around here or try to examine these bodies."

Brad pointed up the canyon. "The vultures are working on something up there, too. Maybe we should check that out."

"Okay. But let's climb up the slope on the other side and try to avoid any obvious path up there."

They slowly worked their way up the canyon and found another body. The coyotes and vultures had worked it over pretty thoroughly. Sean said, "This body's in bad shape— it looks like this guy has been here longer than the others. He knelt beside the body. "I'd say he was shot, maybe hit twice. We'll need a coroner to find out for sure."

Brad picked up the man's wallet lying on the ground beside him. "This explains the Mexican license plate on the truck. This man had a Mexico driver's license. His name was Diego Alvarez. Why do you suppose he was after Harley?"

"Hard to say. But it looks like finding him was his last mistake. Harley's a damn dangerous man. Let's get back and get things started for a team to come out here and sort this out."

Sean called the district commander when they reached a payphone in Buckeye. "Sir, this thing is out of control. There are four more dead bodies at Harley's camp, and none of them are Harley. It appears he planted a land mine near the bunker, which killed three of them. Another man with a Mexican driver's license was shot nearby. We couldn't approach the three men killed by the blast—there could be more of the mines. We need a team of ordnance experts from the National Guard to sweep the area before the bodies can be moved."

He described the scene to the commander and said, "We need to move fast. Between the coyotes and vultures, there won't be much left of those bodies in another day or two."

The commander said he would make the necessary calls. Sean told him to advise the Guard they would need a vehicle with four-wheel drive to reach the site. When the deputies arrived at the district office, the commander said, "The National Guard has agreed to provide a team to help. They are also going to provide a helicopter to transport the bodies from the site to the coroner's ambulance. Tomorrow's Sunday, so they're doing a big favor by calling the men in. The county coroner's office will provide an ambulance and two men to examine the corpses and bring them in. It will probably take all day. I'm authorizing overtime for both of you men to lead the teams. I've arranged to have everyone meet you here at eight in the morning".

Sean said, "One more thing, commander. The truck the air patrol spotted likely belonged to the dead Mexican man at the site. The guy probably tried to sneak up on Harley by going over the peak, but that didn't work so well for him. I think that truck was probably involved in the shooting north of Buckeye a few days ago; it has some bullet holes in the body, and it's missing the back window. Maybe it has some connection to the Vegas bunch trying to find the bonds."

"We should have the crime scene crew check it out. I'll also see what I can do to get them out there tomorrow."

Harley had seen the Jeep with two men approach the Mexican's truck and then head up to his camp. That meant more cops, probably a lot of them, would be swarming over the area. He wasn't worried. They had no idea where he was, and it would be entertaining to watch them running around. He had a lunch of sardines and crackers, then spent the afternoon placing his remaining land mines in strategic locations on approaches to his camp. When that was done, he disassembled, cleaned, and oiled all his firearms. He was ready for whoever and whatever might come.

Sean barely had time to get home and clean up for his date with Miss Preston that night. He wore a freshly laundered, starched white shirt, grey slacks, and black lace-up oxfords. He had previously washed his Chevy pickup and cleaned the interior. He fed and watered Buddy, told him to take care of the house, and dashed out the door. He didn't want to be late.

The ten-mile drive to Liberty seemed like a blur—he was as nervous as a teenager going to his first prom. As he pulled into her driveway, the setting sun painted the sky with brilliant coppery light. She opened the door before he knocked and stood smiling at him. He was speechless for a few seconds, stunned by her beauty. Her red hair was done in a victory roll, with lustrous curls framing her face; her hair seemed to glow in the sunset's light. She had on a green summer dress that matched her eyes.

Sean thought she might be the most beautiful woman he'd ever seen.

He finally found his voice and said, "Good evening, Miss Preston. You are a sight for my sore eyes!"

She laughed. "Good evening, Sean. It's very nice to see you."

They exchanged a few pleasantries, and Sean helped her into his pickup. He was a little embarrassed to take such a beautiful woman to dinner in a pickup truck. But it was all he had, and she didn't seem to mind. It was a half-hour drive to the steak house in Phoenix to meet Ricky and his girlfriend.

"How was your day?" she asked.

Sean hesitated a little, unsure of what to tell her. "Well, it was a pretty unusual day. My friend Brad and I were assigned to investigate an abandoned pickup truck out by Woolsey Peak."

"I don't know where that is," she said.

"It's a big black mountain in the desert about twenty miles southwest of Buckeye. It's an old volcano in a very remote and rough piece of country, and difficult to get to. There was a plane crash there about a month ago."

"Oh…I do remember hearing about that. There were two men killed, as I remember."

"That's right. There's been a lot of activity out there since the crash, and we were investigating whether that pickup might have had anything to do with it. We found the truck and later found its owner dead, along with three other people. It was a pretty gruesome sight."

"Oh, my! What happened?"

"We don't know yet for sure. It appeared three of the men were killed by some explosion, possibly a military land mine. A fourth man had been shot. We're going back there in the morning with a team to find out exactly what happened and to bring the bodies out."

Sandra was silent for a minute, then said quietly, "Do you have to do that sort of thing often? It sounds very dangerous."

"Well, thankfully, it's not the kind of thing that happens frequently. This is a very unusual situation. Our job can be dangerous, but we're trained to be very careful with our investigations."

He changed the subject to avoid having to go deeper into the circumstances of the plane crash and its aftermath. They chatted about her time in college and teaching fourth graders until their arrival at the restaurant. "Here we are," he said. "It looks like our friends are already here."

He helped her out of his truck and escorted her into the steak house. Ricky waved to them from a table toward the back. The place was busy and noisy with a Saturday night crowd. Ricky stood, and Sean introduced Sandy to him and his date, Christiana. "Call me Sandy, please. I've almost broken Sean from calling me Miss Preston." They all laughed, and Sean said to Sandy, "Ricky is my oldest and best friend." Then he turned to Christiana and said, "When are you going to make an honest man out of this scoundrel, Christiana?" Everyone laughed again, and the two men exchanged a few playful barbs.

They ordered their dinners, and the two women made a trip to the powder room. Ricky said, "Wow, Sean! Where did you find that gorgeous woman?"

"I responded to a call about a suspicious man in Liberty, which turned out to be her call. I was head over heels as soon as I saw her."

"I can see why, amigo."

"I feel a little guilty going out with her so soon after losing Annaleigh, but I couldn't help myself."

"It's time, my friend. You shouldn't feel guilty about being attracted to another woman. It will all work out if she is right for you."

"Thanks, Ricky."

The women returned, and their T-bone steaks were served. The conversation mostly revolved around Sean and Ricky's escapades. The women laughed and teased them about being silly teenagers.

Sean said he had a very early morning the next day. He had to rehash the day's events, but he avoided any of the gory details. Ricky figured he would get the full story later.

The trip back to Sandy's house in Liberty ended far too soon for Sean. He wanted to spend more time with this woman. He walked her up to her door and waited while she unlocked it. She said, "Thank you for a lovely evening, Sean. I enjoyed meeting your friends. And I enjoyed being with you."

"I enjoyed being with you, too."

She raised a little on her toes and kissed him on the cheek. "I hope I can see you again soon," she said. Then she went inside and closed the door.

He stood there for a full minute, the feel of her lips tingling on his cheek and her faint perfume hanging in the air. Her kiss was like an electric jolt he felt all the way to his knees. He drove back to his home in Goodyear, lost in a blizzard of thoughts about what would come next—and whether Annaleigh would approve. Buddy met him at the door, Sean scratched him behind his ears, and the dog followed him to the bedroom. They were both instantly asleep.

CHAPTER 31

Sean awoke to Buddy barking and whining beside him. He sat upright and saw the dog with his front paws on the bed, watching him intently. It took him a few seconds to get his bearings. The first glow of the coming dawn lit the room. "Hey, Buddy, it's all right. It's okay, Buddy. You're a good dog." He stroked the dog's head and sat up on the edge of the bed.

Sean was soaked in sweat. He had been thrashing around on the bed and yelling—another dream. He thought the scene at Harley's camp must have touched it off. The dream was still vivid in his mind. He had been back in the little Normandy village on D-Day, trying to save his team leader, who lay wounded in the street. A grenade had gone off and knocked him onto the street. He looked up and saw a German soldier running toward him with his rifle's bayonet poised to stab him. The German was killed by one of his teammates shooting from behind the cover of an abandoned truck, but then two more took the German's place. They were shot, and four more took their place. Sean was frozen in place, unable to urge his muscles into movement. The scene repeated over and over. Then Buddy woke him up.

It was the first nightmare of the war in a couple of weeks. At least they had become less frequent.

His dog, Sarge, would wake him from a dream by licking his face. He thought he preferred Buddy's method. It was time to get up anyway. There was a long and busy day ahead of him. He made a pot of coffee, put food and water in Buddy's bowls, then sliced a banana into a big bowl of Wheaties and poured milk over it. He didn't have time to make anything more substantial. He had to get to the district office early to prepare for going back to Woolsey Peak.

He was the first one to the office. He fired up the Jeep, drove to a nearby Chevron station, and had the attendant check the tire pressure and fluids under the hood and top off the fuel tank. Then he went back to wait at the office. The district commander had arrived when he returned, and they waited for the various specialists to arrive.

Two National Guardsmen showed up at seven forty-five, followed by the crime scene team a few minutes later. The soldiers were driving a military version of a Dodge Truck, but the crime scene team was driving a Ford sedan. The coroner arrived in his county car, followed by an ambulance.

The men met in a huddle in the parking lot. The commander introduced himself, Sean, and Brad, then asked the others to introduce themselves. He said, "Thank you all for being here on a Sunday morning. We have an emergency on our hands— A man we are searching for has been on a killing spree. We need all the help we can get. I've asked Sean and Brad to brief you on the plan for the day. Sean…"

Sean said, "First, the area we are going into is remote and rugged and requires four-wheel drive to reach the camp where the bodies are. The cars and ambulance can travel part of the way, and then we'll have to park them and set up a staging area to transport you to the site. We'll have the helicopter bring the bodies out and drop them at the ambulance."

One of the guardsmen raised his hand, and Sean nodded to him. The man said, "We can use our truck to help transport the others to the site. Might make it easier. We have the helicopter pilot on standby. He will meet us around noon."

"Thanks," Sean replied. "That will make it a lot more efficient. We appreciate it." He waited to see if there were any more questions, then continued, "The tricky part of this will be clearing the scene. I've seen damage from land mines during the war, and it looks like that may be what killed three of the men. The suspect we are looking for has killed several people before this, and we think he might have hidden more mines. Doing anything around the area would be dangerous until our National Guard friends can clear it. Brad, tell them about the fourth body."

Brad described the Mexican man they had found with what appeared to be gunshot wounds a short way up the canyon from the camp. He said the man was killed sometime before the others, judging from decomposition and damage from vultures and coyotes.

"One more thing," Sean said. "You need to be prepared for a gruesome sight. The coyotes and vultures have been at the bodies for several days…it's awful."

There were several questions, and the deputies explained the details the best they could. One of the crime scene team asked if they were concerned their suspect might try to kill any of them. Sean replied, "It's unlikely, but we all need to be alert to any movement outside our work area. We believe the man has gone into deep hiding and is probably waiting for all the search activity to die down before he makes a run for Mexico. Also, the people he has killed so far were all associated with the plane crash on Woolsey Peak and a large amount of bearer bonds that went missing from it. We think he has those bonds."

They loaded their vehicles, headed out in a caravan on Highway 80 towards Buckeye, turned off the Agua Caliente dirt road, and traveled a few miles until Sean had them stop. He told the group: "This will be a four-wheel drive road only from here on. We need to leave the ambulance and sedans here." He looked at the coroner and the crime scene team and said, "I'd suggest you ride with the Guardsmen in their truck; it's much roomier than our Jeep. It's a rough ride in places, so hang on!" They pulled the cars off to the side, loaded up, and headed toward Woolsey Peak. The two ambulance medics stayed behind to handle the bodies when the helicopter ferried them out.

Sean had cautioned the driver of the guard's truck about Harley's nail shredders in the wash, and they proceeded slowly toward the campsite. They parked the vehicles well clear of where the three men had been killed in case there were other

213

mines nearby. The foul odor of death was inescapable; the men pulled handkerchiefs over their noses to try and reduce it.

The guardsmen unloaded two metal detectors and began sweeping the area. The flock of turkey vultures that covered the bodies flew off in a loud beating of wings and either sat on rocks nearby or rode the air currents above the canyon, making lazy circles over their feast below. The pack of coyotes had already moved off a safe distance when the vehicles arrived.

Clearing the area was a slow process; it was nearly noon when the guardsmen signaled that it was all clear. They didn't find any more mines. One of them said, "You were right about this, Sean. This was probably an Army M-2 mine. We found a lot of widely scattered shrapnel with our metal detectors. And the way the bodies were thrown outward is consistent with a mine detonation. Those things have a kill radius of about thirty feet. It would have likely killed them all even if they weren't standing close by when one of them triggered the fuse. It was placed directly in front of that bunker's door. It was a trap for anyone curious enough to get close."

Sean and Brad worked with the coroner to pull information from the three dead men's wallets. Brad said, "No big surprise here, I guess. These guys all had Las Vegas addresses."

"Yep," Sean replied. "I guess they didn't get the point when Harley killed the first guys they sent."

The bodies were severely mutilated from the coyote's and vulture's work. The coroner confirmed their cause of death as resulting from a proximity land mine detonation. Then, they put them into the body bags they had brought.

The deputies led the coroner up the canyon to the fourth body, again interrupting the vultures' feast. The birds raised their bald heads as the men approached. Their beaks were covered in blood, and Brad swore the birds were giving them the evil eye for disturbing them. The man's body was in even worse shape than the others, but it didn't take the coroner long to determine two gunshot wounds had killed him. He said he would have to wait and do an autopsy to give them more information and possibly find the slugs. Then, they placed El Puma in a body bag.

They could hear the helicopter beating the air long before they saw it. It circled over the area and landed on a flat spot a short way down the wash. The pilot walked up to the camp, and the guardsmen introduced him to the others. He said, "Hey, Sean and Brad. We ought to quit meeting like this." The comment elicited a weak chuckle. It was hard to find humor amid the carnage. The pilot looked around and said, "Damn! You boys sure pick some wicked locations for gathering up bodies. The last time I was here, they were up on the mountain. It's a little tight in this canyon, so be patient when I come down into it to get in position."

Sean watched him walk back to his helicopter. Then something caught his eye in the distance—it appeared to be a bright reflection. It was across the narrow valley between their position and the mountains to the north. Sean was puzzled for a minute; nothing in those mountains should reflect light like that. As he watched, it flashed again. Now it was clear—someone was watching them with binoculars. The bright sunlight was reflecting off of their lenses. Harley! It's got to be Harley, Sean thought. That's where his other camp is. Ruby had told them there was a second one somewhere around Signal Mountain. That shiny reflection gave it away.

He pulled Brad aside and said, "I know where Harley is." He explained about the reflection and how it fit with what Harley's girlfriend had told him. "Don't stare or anything," Sean cautioned, "just wait for it to catch your eye. If he's watching us, we don't want to tip him off that we can see where he is."

A couple of minutes later, Brad confirmed what Sean had seen. "Now that we know where he is, how are we gonna get to him? He would see anyone coming toward him from a long way off."

Sean replied, "I don't know yet. We need to study the location and come up with a plan. We sure as hell don't want to go charging toward him. There's no telling what kind of firepower

215

he might have up there, not to mention land mines and god knows what else."

The deputies were quiet for a few minutes, and Sean said, "How about this—let's see if we can go up with one of those air posse planes tomorrow, fly over the area, and get a better look. Maybe there's a way we could approach him without getting our asses shot off."

"Good idea, Sean. I want to keep my skin intact, too."

The pilot had to maneuver his copter slowly and carefully between the narrow canyon walls. The rotor's downdraft nearly knocked the men off their feet. It took a couple of hours to ferry the bodies out to the waiting ambulance. The men were preparing to leave, and one of the guardsmen said, "You know, we've got some C-3 explosives back at the base. You could put some of that around that door on the bunker and take it off its hinges. Let us know if you want us to help you with it. I've been itching to try it out."

"That's a great idea," Sean said. "When this is all over, we might take you up on it."

The last body was removed, and the men loaded their gear and left. It was getting late in the day by the time they returned to their vehicles and headed back to town. On their way back to the district office, Sean and Brad stopped at the pay phone beside the little Hassayampa River store. Sean called the commander, told him what they had seen, and asked if he could arrange for them to join one of the air posse flights tomorrow to better see where they thought Harley holed up. The commander said he'd set it up.

⚓

Harley watched the activity with great interest. It was obvious the land mine he planted served its purpose. He saw the helicopter carry four body bags out of the canyon. That meant there were three dead men besides the Mexican he had shot. They musta been more of that bunch from Vegas, he thought. Well, maybe now they'll quit chasing me. Damn fools oughta know by now that I'm no dummy and I ain't gonna hand over them bonds. "I found 'em," he said aloud, "and by god, I mean to keep 'em!"

He made a small campfire after all the activity died down. It was sheltered between some rocks, and Harley figured no one below could see it. He'd shot, cleaned, and skinned a fat cottontail rabbit that morning and put it on a spit over the fire for dinner. A can of pork and beans topped off his menu, and he put it in a small pan on the coals to heat. He ate his fill, sat back on his folding camp chair, and watched the shadows crawl across the valley as the setting sun bathed the mountains in a rosy glow.

CHAPTER 32

The next morning, Sean and Brad met the air posse pilot at Sky Harbor Airport in Phoenix. They each had a pair of binoculars, and Sean had a folded USGS topographic map of the area. Brad also brought along a Kodak camera. They explained what they wanted to do to the pilot and boarded the bright red Howard DGA-15. It had a single wing on top and could carry four passengers besides the pilot. The cabin featured three windows on each side in addition to the windshield, which curved slightly to each side. It had excellent visibility, perfect for what the deputies needed.

"Wow! This is some plane!" Brad said.

Rusty, the pilot, said, "Yep. She's my pride and joy. They don't call 'em DGA models for nothing."

He waited until Brad took the bait. "DGA?"

"Damn Good Airplane!" Rusty said with a laugh. "And they really are. These planes are the Cadillac of the airways. Lots of rich folks, even movie stars, have them. Wallace Beery flies one to his movie sets. You boys buckle up— the weather report says there may be turbulence today. Supposed to be some storms moving up from the Gulf of Mexico. If you get sick, there are barf bags in the seat pockets. Let's fire this baby up and go find your outlaw!"

He went through his pre-flight check and hit the starter. The huge Pratt and Whitney radial engine roared into life, and they taxied out of the hangar area. The control tower gave them clearance to taxi out to the runway and take off, and they were soon in the air over Phoenix. Rusty banked around, making a one-eighty turn, then lined up on the Salt River. They skirted the South Mountains in Phoenix, passed over the confluence of the Salt with the Gila River, and continued past the Estrella Mountains following the Gila. They passed south of Buckeye,

218

banked south, passed over the farming community of Arlington, and then banked to the west. Woolsey Peak loomed before them with Signal Mountain further west. The pilot throttled back to slow their passage as much as possible and skirted the mountains along the north side of the big Woolsey Wash.

Sean scanned the area carefully with his binoculars as they passed by the mountains on their right. He picked out what he thought was an anomaly among the black rocks on one of the lower hills, and then it was out of sight behind them. He told the pilot to swing back and make a pass along the Woolsey Peak area. He didn't want Harley to know they were focusing on his new hideout location.

Sean explained to Brad what he thought might be Harley's camp and told him to get some pictures when they made another pass. They swung around for another look. Sean had the pilot drop lower and fly as slowly as possible without stalling. He knew what to look for this time and picked out the spot that had caught his attention. "I'll be damned," he yelled over the engine's noise. "That's a camouflage tarp—probably over Harley's big truck. Get plenty of pictures, Brad!" He could also see some faint signs of a camp before they passed by the site. Then they swung around again and headed back toward Phoenix.

Sean and Brad were excited when they climbed out of the plane. They shook the pilot's hand and thanked him for his help. "You boys find what you were looking for?" he asked.

Sean replied, "We think so. You'll hear about it on the news in a few days if we did."

They dropped the Kodak off at a photo shop and put a rush on developing Brad's photographs, then returned to the district office to work on a plan. The commander saw them enter the office and asked what they had found.

"I think we've found him, sir," Sean began. "I'm ninety percent certain it's Harley's second camp, the one his girlfriend told me about when I interviewed her. I saw a camouflage tarp over a vehicle, most likely that big truck Harley has. And there were signs of activity around the site. I can't imagine anyone else being out there."

The commander nodded and said, "Well, let's go get him!"

Brad chimed in, "It won't be that easy, sir. We'd be sitting ducks if we approached him head-on. And there's no telling what kind of guns he has with him. If he got his hands on military land mines, I'm guessing he might have acquired some pretty high-powered firearms, too."

"What do you men propose?"

Sean replied, "We need a very careful plan, sir. Brad took a lot of photographs of the area, and we left them to be developed. They should be ready this afternoon. We can use those to map out an approach that hopefully keeps anyone else from being killed. Harley's turned into a lunatic and most likely won't stop at anything to keep from being captured."

"All right. See me as soon as you have a proposal. We have to get this guy. Everybody from the governor down is putting heat on the department to bring him in. The sheriff calls me at least twice a day for a report."

Harley had watched from deep shadow as the plane flew by that morning. He didn't think much of it; there had been frequent flights over Woolsey Wash. They all did the same thing—a couple of passes, and they went on to another area. This one had been no different, although its second pass was a little lower than usual. He figured they'd seen one of the big buck mule deer that were common in the area. He went on with his daily routine, secure in the secrecy of his hideout.

Brad picked up the developed photographs from the shop after work and met Sean at his house. They cracked open a couple of cans of Coors, then spread the photos out on the coffee table in front of the living room couch. They sipped their beers for a few minutes while they studied the images.

"Damn rough country, Sean."

"Yep. It's even rougher when you're on the ground. I used to hunt this area with my dad. He had a buddy who raised horses, and we'd go out there on horseback." He was thoughtful for a minute and continued, "That gives me an idea. You had any experience riding horses?"

"A little. What are you thinking?"

"Maybe the way to capture Harley is to come up on him from behind. We don't want to walk into the fire zone ambush he's laid out. But I doubt he gave any thought to anyone coming up on him from the mountains behind him. Look here," and he put his finger on one of the photos. "There's a gap in these lower hills to his east where we could work around him. There are game trails all over those hills we could use."

"He would hear the horses coming, and that would be the end of the surprise," Brad observed.

They were quiet for a few minutes, thinking about options. Finally, Sean said, "How about this? We can have someone go with us until we're fairly close, then leave the horses with him and walk in. I know a guy we can hire horses from, and I'm sure he'd help us go in there."

"I think that's a good plan, Sean. What are we going to do with Harley if we capture him? I don't want to try and walk that big gorilla out of there!"

Sean got them two more beers while they pondered the problem. Brad said, "Here's an idea. We could have some other deputies come in and wait for a signal, maybe a flare, then they could come and get him. We could send up a flare when we have him."

"I think the commander would buy that, Brad. Let's run it past him in the morning."

They spent another hour discussing the plan's logistics, what gear to take, and how to approach Harley when they found him.

CHAPTER 33

They went over their plan with the commander the next morning. He listened as they laid it all out, then said, "It's a good plan, men, but it's dangerous. You're betting your lives that he wouldn't be prepared for someone coming from behind."

Sean replied, "Yes, sir, there is that risk. But I doubt Harley thought it was likely enough to do anything about it. It's a long way around in extremely rough country to get into a position behind him. Everything he did at his other camp was oriented to a frontal approach. Brad and I went that way, and nothing indicated he had considered protecting himself from the rear."

"So did the Mexican man you found dead there," the commander wryly replied. "That maniac has killed too many people already. I don't want to add you men to the list."

"We don't want that either, sir," Sean replied. "But if we try the head-on approach, I can almost guarantee more men will die. He's been preparing for this a long time. He's got military explosives and maybe automatic weapons. I think it's sort of like the Alamo to him—he might die, but he'll take many others with him."

The commander said, "Maybe we can starve him out without risking any lives."

Sean said, "Yes, sir, that's a possibility. But we know he's prepared to be there a long time. His girlfriend told me he had a huge stockpile of food and supplies at both his camps—enough to last for months. And we'd have to have someone out there night and day to keep him from slipping away."

The men lit cigarettes and watched the smoke rise in lazy curling circles while they thought. Finally, the commander said, "All right. We'll try your plan. I'll authorize hiring horses and a wrangler. Work out a timeline for when we can put additional men in place to help bring him in. And don't get yourselves killed!"

Sean and Brad spent the morning working on the details of the plan. Sean called a man he knew with horses and explained what he needed. They agreed on a price, and the two deputies drove out to his place to meet the horses and make preparations.

"Hello, Sean. I haven't seen you since you got home from the war," the horse wrangler said as he shook Sean's hand. "Heard you're doin' good as a deputy."

The wrangler was a lanky, bowlegged cowboy. He was in his fifties and had several days' growth of grey whiskers. His craggy chin jutted out from a deeply tanned face gone leathery from years in the sun. He had on leather chaps over denim jeans, a denim work shirt, and a sweat-stained Stetson straw hat. He was a little under six feet tall, now slightly stooped from an old back injury in a rodeo.

He shook hands with Brad and said, "I'm Jim Cunningham. I've known Sean since he was a kid. His dad was a good friend."

He looked at Sean and said, "I'm awful sorry about your folks, Sean."

"Thanks, Mr. Cunningham." Sean's parents died from injuries in a car accident while he was in a hospital in England recovering from his wounds after D-Day.

"Call me Jim. I haven't seen you since you and your dad hunted deer with me. I think that was just before you went into the Army. In fact, we hunted some in the same area we're going into."

"Yes, sir, I remember. It was one of the last times I spent with my dad."

"So…you boys are goin' after Harley, eh? He's a tough one."

"Yes, sir. That he is," Sean replied. "We appreciate your help. Here's what we plan to do." He unfolded his USGS topo map and laid it on the hood of his patrol car. "This road is rough but passable, so long as it's dry," he said, tracing it with his finger.

223

"I know the place, Sean. It ain't gotten any smoother since I was last out there."

"We figure to get as close as possible to this point." He placed his finger beside the first of the lower hills east of Harley's camp. "Then we'll ride in to about here," he pointed, "then leave the horses with you and walk the rest of the way."

The wrangler studied the map for a minute and nodded his head. Then he leaned away from the car and spit a long brown stream of tobacco juice into the dirt. "Well, it looks like a damn fool plan, but if you boys think you can pull it off, I'm glad to help."

They went into his barn, and he showed them the horses they would use—a mare and a gelding. He held out a couple of apples to the men and said, "Feed 'em one of these apples, and they'll be your friend for life. Let 'em smell your breath, talk to 'em a little. Then scratch 'em behind their ears and rub their withers." They spent a few minutes with the horses and made arrangements to meet Cunningham with the horses at the Agua Caliente turnoff the following day.

Next, they met with two other deputies the commander had assigned to work with them. Sean explained the plan to them and laid out the photographs and the topographic map to show them how to reach their rendezvous point. Sean said, "You may hear some gunfire, but stay put until we send up our flare signal." He pointed at the map and said, "Don't come any closer than this point. It's possible Harley planted some landmines on the approaches to his camp. We'll walk him out if we can. And, in the meantime, the National Guard guys can clear the area of mines." The commander had arranged for the National Guard to send their team to clear the area of mines. Their truck would give them a second four-wheel drive vehicle along with the department's Jeep, and they could secure Harley in the truck's bed to transport him back to town. The two deputies would meet the Guard's vehicle at the Agua Caliente turn-off the next morning.

4

Sean and Brad met the wrangler at the turn-off early that morning. They left their patrol car there and rode with Cunningham in his truck the rest of the way. He pulled a trailer with their three horses and gear with a 1938 one-and-a-half-ton Ford truck. The truck had originally been forest green but was now badly faded from its years in the desert sun. The truck didn't have four-wheel drive, but it had good clearance and plenty of power to negotiate the rough desert road and a few minor washes.

They reached their drop-off point, brought the horses out of the trailer, and helped Cunningham saddle them and get them ready for their trek. He handed Sean and Brad a few sugar cubes to give their mounts before they saddled up and said, "The sugar is just to remind them that you're their friends. Give 'em a couple now and save a couple for later."

The deputies had two water canteens on their belts and small backpacks with beef jerky and first aid supplies. Brad had the flare pistol in his. Both men had .30-30 lever action carbine rifles slung over their shoulders, along with bandoliers carrying extra ammunition. Sean had his Colt.45 automatic in a side holster and two full clips of extra ammunition in side pockets of his military-style belt. Brad carried a regulation S&W .38 Police Special revolver in a belt holster with extra ammunition in holders on the belt.

The wrangler looked them over and said, "Damn. You boys look like you're goin' off to war. You figurin' to need all that ammo?"

Sean replied, "You know that old saying—better to have it and not need it than to need it and not have it."

Cunningham chuckled and said, "Yep. Guess you're right. You think it will come to a shootout with Harley?"

"I hope not," Sean replied, "We'll avoid it if we can, try to bring him in alive if possible. I guess how it will go will be up to him."

Brad said, "Yeah, I'd rather avoid a shootout, too. I have a wife and two kids at home, and I'd like to get out of here in one piece."

They set off into the hills about ten miles east of Harley's camp. They hadn't gone far when they spooked two fat doe mule deer. They went bounding off around the hill.

Cunningham said, "You can bet there's a big ol' buck close by around here. There are some bucks out here with record-sized racks. I make a little money once in a while bringing city folks out here to hunt 'em."

"I remember the one my dad got when we were out here," Sean said. "It wasn't a record, but the biggest one I'd ever seen."

"You know, Harley used to guide hunters out here once in a while, and I'm pretty sure he poached a deer once in a while for food. He poached bighorn sheep, too, even though it's been against the law forever. I heard there's big money for a big ram as a trophy."

Sean replied, "Sounds like something Harley would do."

"You boys gotta be careful with him. He knows this desert better'n me—better'n anybody, for that matter. You might never see him til he was right on top of you."

They followed a game trail higher up and worked around the first of several foothills below Signal Mountain. An occasional deer jumped out of cover and ran away from them. They saw one buck with a massive rack of antlers. "That big boy's a trophy if I ever saw one," Cunningham said.

They reached the spot where the deputies planned to leave the horses about noon. They gave their horses one last sugar cube and rubbed their manes. Cunningham said, "Well, I wish you boys luck. Stay safe, never let your guard down. I'll be lookin' to hear how all this turns out."

They shook hands, and Sean said, "Thanks, Jim. It was great to ride with you again. We appreciate your help."

"Just come back alive, both of you." Then he tied their two horses' reins together, tied them onto his saddle, climbed onto the back of his horse, and went back the way they had come.

The two deputies arranged their gear and checked each other to be sure nothing was loose that might rattle or make a noise. "You ready, Brad?"

"Ready as I'll ever be. Let's get this done."

They headed out, following another game trail that led around the hill in front of them. They were about a mile from Harley's camp.

❦

Harley was perched in the shade of a massive black boulder on a ridge below his camp. He spent most days there, keeping watch across the valley. Movement caught his eye in the distance, and he saw two vehicles moving toward him. He saw through his binoculars that one was a jeep; the other appeared to be another one of those military trucks they had used when they took the dead men out of his other camp. They stopped about two miles out. Then he could see some men standing around talking and pointing in his general direction. But then they didn't do anything. They all just stood around like they were waiting on something. Maybe they're waiting on reinforcements to come after me, he thought. Have they found my camp? Maybe that last plane he saw spotted something. Well, let 'em come. I'm ready. And they'll get a nice surprise if they come up here.

He settled himself into a comfortable position, munched on a big piece of venison jerky, and waited to see what would happen next.

❦

The deputies approached the top of the hill above Harley's camp. The hill was topped by a jagged ridge where the men took up a position. Sean had cautioned Brad about being quiet because sound carried in the silence of the desert, and they whispered back and forth about their approach. Sean whispered, "Be careful with the binoculars to avoid a flash from reflected sunlight; it

227

could be enough to get Harley's attention." Sean used his monocular, a tool he had kept after the war. They carefully studied the camp layout.

The site was near the base of the hill at the edge of a small wash. The slope of the hill flattened enough to make it a usable location, very similar to the setup at the other camp by Woolsey Peak. Harley's access from the valley floor was a wash, and its banks were shallow enough to drive his truck over. There appeared to be another bunker with a steel door like the first site. The door was open, and a cot and camp chair were set up near a small rock fire ring. There was barely enough room on the flat space for the Beast, which was under a large camouflage tarp. Harley seemed to be keeping signs of his activity there at a bare minimum. He had built two shooting hides that the deputies could see. They were built using stacked rocks in strategic locations below the campsite to give him clear shooting fields from cover. He could pick off anyone who approached.

The deputies studied the area for a few minutes, and Brad whispered, "Where is he? I haven't seen any movement."

"He's in some kind of cover, probably watching our men's approach down the valley," Sean answered. Then: "Look there! In the shadow of that big boulder a little below the bunker door. I saw him move!"

They focused on that spot, confirming Harley used it as his observation post. Sean said, "He'll probably stay there a while, watching the men approach below him, trying to figure out what they're up to."

They watched quietly for a few minutes. Harley didn't move from his position. Sean said, "How about this—let's split up and approach him from two sides. We would have him in a crossfire."

"We'll have to break cover to do it."

"I think we can do it if we're cautious. He's focused on the activity below, and I doubt he would see us unless we make noise. We'll have to watch every step to keep from kicking loose a rock. That's all it would take, and we'd be in a firefight with him. Do you think we can do it?"

"Let's try it, Sean. We can't sit here all day."

"Okay. I'll work my way to the left, and you move straight down from here. That should put us in a good position to cover him. I'll give you a hand signal when we are close enough. If the shooting starts, try to find a rock big enough to give you some cover. Have your rifle ready, and I'll call out to him to surrender when we're in position and have him in our sights."

They started moving slowly and carefully down the hill toward the camp. They were within fifty yards of Harley's position when Brad stepped on a rock that appeared flat but was rounded on the bottom and slightly embedded in the soil. When he put pressure on the rock to step off, it rolled out from under his foot and skittered down the slope, taking several more rocks with it. Brad lost his balance and landed on his side, then recovered into a crouch. Sean froze into position.

Harley reacted instantly to the commotion of noise above and behind him. He instinctively knew no game animal would make that much noise. He stood up and looked toward the noise up the slope behind him, saw the two deputies, and made a dash to his weapons beside the bunker. Sean got off a quick shot at him, but Harley was moving too fast, and the shot missed. Harley grabbed the Thompson submachine gun and then rolled into a firing position. He sprayed the area around Brad with .45 slugs from the weapon, and he went down on the ground clutching his leg. One of the bullets caught him in the leg below his knee and shattered his shin bone.

Sean had time to duck behind a rock that gave him a little cover before Harley turned the Thompson on him. The bullets ricocheted off rocks around him and kicked up clouds of dust. Sean leaned around the rock and fired a shot at Harley with his rifle. The bullet hit the submachine gun and knocked it out of Harley's hands. He hit the ground and tried to scrabble back to his weapon cache, but Sean's next shot nicked him on the left shoulder. He was able to get behind the partially open bunker door for cover. He grabbed his .357 magnum revolver he kept tucked into his belt, leaned around the door, and fired two quick shots at Sean. Then he yelled, "Is that you, Sean? You shouldn't have come after me!"

Sean yelled, "Come on out of there with your hands in the air, Harley. We don't want to hurt you."

Harley gave a mocking laugh and replied, "Sure. That's why you fired the first shot, right Sean?"

Sean glanced at Brad. He had removed his pants belt and used it for a tourniquet around his leg. He gave Sean a thumbs-up sign.

"It's over, Harley. There's no way out for you. More deputies are coming up below you. You're trapped, and there's no place for you to go now," Sean yelled. "Come out now, and I promise you won't get hurt!"

"You guys will never take me alive! Your buddies down below won't make it up here alive, and you ain't gonna get away either. So, how you wanna do this? You wanna do a quick draw like the Old West? See who has the fastest gun?" He laughed hysterically.

It sounded to Sean like the man was on the edge of sanity. Maybe he had gone over the edge. "No quick draw contest, Harley. But I will shoot you if you don't surrender."

"Aww, I don't think so, Sean. You were always a pushover. Like in high school when you always gave me a wide berth. Didn't have guts to duke it out with me."

"You know better than that, Harley. It was always you slinking away from trouble."

Harley gave another maniacal laugh and yelled, "What we got here is what they call a Mexican standoff. Neither one of us has anywhere we can go. And I'm bettin' your buddy up there is gonna bleed out if you keep yapping away about surrender. Why don't you help him and you two high tail down the valley and meet your friends? I won't shoot you if you do that, Sean." He waited a few seconds and yelled, "What you gonna do, Sean? You gonna let your buddy die on this hill?"

Brad flashed the OK sign when Sean looked at him. He knew Harley was lying about letting them go. He yelled, "My friend is okay, Harley. You don't need to worry about that." Harley gave another cackling laugh. Sean went on, "I remember how it was in high school. You always acted like a big, tough guy, but the only people I saw you push around were guys a lot smaller than you. I think you were afraid to take on someone your own size."

"You're full of shit, Sean, and you know it. So how bout you? Yer more my size. You were the big football star and all that, then you got shot up in the war, and everyone called you a hero. I think you're a pussy, Sean, and you always were. I think you were scared to take me on 'cause you knew I'd kick the crap out of you. Your old man was a cop, and you were hiding behind his badge."

"Not the way I remember it, Harley. Remember when you had Donna Miller backed into a corner by the gym at school? You were trying to kiss her and feel her up. Who was it tapped you on the shoulder then shoved you away from her? Do you remember Harley? You slunk away like a kicked dog. Everyone made fun of you after that. Do you remember? That's why no girls would have anything to do with you after that!"

"Damn you, Sean! Why don't you come on down here and show me what you're made of? You think you're a tough guy? Show me!" Harley's voice quivered with anger.

It was the opening Sean had hoped for. It might be a way out of this standoff if he could goad him into a fight. Brad called, "Don't do it, Sean! He's not worth it!"

Harley laughed and yelled, "See there, Sean? Even your buddy thinks yer a wimp."

"Here's the deal, Harley. Throw out your pistol and come out. I'll come down there, and we'll settle this mano y mano!

"How do I know you won't shoot me as soon as I step out?"

"You know me better than that, Harley. I've always been as good as my word, and I promise I won't shoot you. I'm giving you a way out without either of us getting killed. If you win, you walk away and take those bonds you stole with you. If I win, you come with me."

Sean knew Harley could never resist a fight. He had gained a reputation as a barroom brawler after high school. He was such a troublemaker that all the bars in Buckeye barred him from coming in. Sean also knew that the incident with the girl by the gym had eaten at him all these years, and he would relish the chance to get even. He was giving him that chance.

Sean was six feet tall and weighed about two hundred pounds. He was in excellent physical condition and continued his regular workouts after discharge from the Army. Hand-to-hand combat had been part of his commando training, and he was good at it. He figured he would need all his skills in a match with Harley.

Harley was three inches taller and outweighed Sean by a good forty pounds or more. He was strong as an ox and always had been. What he lacked in speed in a fight, he made up for in weight and brawn. It had always allowed him to gain the upper hand in a fight. He was sure a fight with Sean would end the same way. He wasn't impressed that Sean had fought in the war. He would leave him lying unconscious on this hillside and drive away in the Beast. Sean's ultimatum was irresistible, and he could see it was probably the only way he would get out of this alive. He yelled, "It's a deal, Sean. Come on down, slowly."

Sean walked down the hill into the camp. He had his rifle at the ready. "Toss out your pistol, Harley, and I'll put down my rifle and sidearm."

Harley looked around the edge of the bunker door, then tossed out the revolver. Sean laid his rifle on a rock, took out his pistol, and laid it beside the rifle. Then he faced Harley with his arms wide. "Let's do this!" he said.

Harley charged at him like a bull zeroing in on a matador in a bullfight, but Sean was ready. He sidestepped his charge and

232

struck him hard in his right ear with his fist. Harley was momentarily stunned but spun back and tried to grab Sean in a bear hug. Sean drove his fist into Harley's solar plexus, and the air came out of him with a big whoosh. But it didn't stop him. He grabbed Sean, pulled him in, and wrapped both arms around him. Sean felt like he was being crushed between a pair of timbers. He drove the heel of his boot into the top of Harley's right foot causing him to yelp with pain. His grip loosened slightly— enough that Sean could let his body go slack and drop out of the grip. Then he spun to the side and gave a practiced sideways kick to Harley's right knee. Sean heard a distinctive crunch and jumped to his feet. Another man would have fallen on the ground, but Harley just howled in pain and came stumbling at Sean again, swinging wildly. Sean ducked the first punch, but the second one caught him on the side of the head. I was like being hit with a sledgehammer. He was momentarily dazed, enough for Harley to hit him again, this time square in the face. Sean felt his nose break as a gusher of blood spewed from it. He backstepped from his opponent, trying to keep his balance. Harley thought he had him and lurched at him with fists swinging again. Sean ducked the first punch and hit Harley square in the throat with his fist. His eyes bulged out, and he gagged, trying to suck in a breath. Sean hit him again in the solar plexus, pushing the remaining air out of his lungs. Then he pistoned the palm of his hand upward into the big man's nose, and he staggered backward. His heel caught on a rock, and his momentum caused him to fall backward. His head hit the sharp edge of a rock with a sickening crunch. Then he lay still, his eyes rolled into the back of his head. He was not breathing, and Sean checked him for a pulse. It was the end of the road for Harley.

Sean's nose was bleeding freely, and the front of his shirt was soaked. He tilted his head back and put pressure on either side of his nose to slow the bleeding. Then he placed his palm against the side of it where it was pushed out of shape and gave a sharp shove to move it back in place. It hurt like hell, but the bleeding slowed to a trickle. He found a semi-clean rag inside the bunker and held it to his nose to catch the blood.

He went up the hill to Brad and said, "How you doin', buddy?"

"My damn leg is broken. I think the bullet shattered my shin bone. Most of the bleeding has stopped, but I'm pretty useless."

"I'll find something to make a splint. Then we'll get you out of here."

"Harley?"

"He's dead. Hit his head on a rock when he went down. Nothing I could do for him."

"That was a hell of a thing, Sean. I thought he'd crush you like a Cracker Jack box. They teach you to fight like that in the Army?"

"Yep. Had to get my ass handed to me a few times practicing the moves, but they've stuck with me. Hang on while I find something to make a splint."

"I'll get the flare gun out of my pack and signal the others. Hopefully, they'll have a good first aid kit."

Sean found a one-by-six board being used for a shelf inside the bunker. It would have to do. He found two rocks about the same size with relatively flat surfaces and placed them about three feet apart. Then he laid the board across them with its center between the stones. He took careful aim and smashed his foot down on the center of the board with all his force and weight. The board splintered in two. He used his Ka-Bar commando knife to remove most of the splintered wood, then cut several pieces from one of Harley's wool blankets. There was a length of rope in the bunker, and he cut off two pieces about two feet long.

He went back up the hill and said, "Here we go, Brad. Let me have a look at your leg before we put the splints on. He sliced his pant leg open above the knee. There was a nasty wound where the bullet hit his leg, and he could see fragments of bone sticking through the skin. There were a couple of gauze bandages and adhesive tape in the small first aid kit in Brad's pack. He opened a pack of sulfanilamide and sprinkled it into the wound, then

234

dressed it with the bandages. "That should keep the bleeding down until we can do something better," Sean said. Then he carefully straightened Brad's leg. He placed a couple of strips of the blanket on each flat board for padding, then tied them onto each side of the injured leg. "Let's see if we can get you down to that cot in Harley's camp. It'll be much more comfortable while we wait for the cavalry." He helped Brad off the ground and half-carried him down the hill as he hobbled along on his good leg.

It took the men waiting in the valley about thirty minutes to reach them. Sean flagged them down about two hundred yards away from the camp. He told the Guardsmen, "I wouldn't go any further without sweeping the wash for mines. We know he had some and no doubt placed some in the obvious approach to the camp." The two National Guardsmen got out their metal detectors and got ready to clear the wash. Sean asked before they started, "Do you guys have a first aid kit in your truck? I need better bandages for my friend. He was wounded in the leg." One of the men got it out from behind the truck seat. "Thanks," Sean said and headed up the hill. Robbie Fuller, one of the deputies in the Jeep, went with him.

They got to the camp, and Robbie said, "Hey, Brad. How you doin'?"

"I've been better, Robbie," came the strained reply.

"Yeah, you look a little worse for wear." Robbie looked at Harley and gave a low whistle. "Don't see any bullet holes in that big lug. What'd you guys do to him?"

"Sean explained the facts of life to him, and then he fell down and accidentally bumped his head. Didn't have much to say after that!" Brad said with a weak chuckle.

"Holy cow. He looks deader than my cat's mouse!" Then he noticed the pool of blood around the rock and gave another low whistle. "Must've been a pretty good bump! Let me have a look at your leg, Brad. I've had a lot of first aid training." He gently loosened the splint and unwrapped the gauze pads Sean had applied. "You've got a nasty-lookin' wound, Brad. I'm going to put a better bandage on it." He opened the large first aid kit from the Guard vehicle and went to work. "I'll give you something to help with the pain." He gave him a shot of morphine from the kit, and Brad's eyes fluttered a little, then he passed out. "That ought to hold him til we can get him to a hospital. You did damn good under the circumstances, Sean."

Sean said, "Thanks. I'm not much of a medic."

"He's gonna be okay. You don't look so good yourself. What happened?

"Harley busted my nose, but I fixed it. Looks a lot worse than it is."

"You're lucky that's all he broke."

"Yep."

They nosed around the camp and bunker while waiting for the National Guardsmen to finish sweeping for the mines. Robbie looked at the machine gun lying on the ground near Harley and said, "Damn! A Thompson! Did he use that on you guys?"

"Yeah, that's what he hit Brad with. One of those .45 slugs shattered his shin bone. He nearly got me with it, too, but I was able to get behind some rocks. Then I got off a lucky shot and knocked it out of his hands."

Robbie picked it up and looked it over. "Your shot broke the stock. That was a hell of a shot!"

Then they found the Browning automatic rifle, a box full of hand grenades, two land mines, a .30-06 hunting rifle with scope, a Remington shotgun, two .30-30 lever action rifles, and an assortment of handguns. Robbie said, "Wow. Looks like he was prepared for another world war! And look at all these supplies! He could have stayed here for months!"

"I think that was pretty much his plan," Sean agreed. "He figured he could stay here until we quit looking for him. Then, he could sneak away to Mexico with a million bucks in stolen bearer bonds. Could've worked if he hadn't made a rookie surveillance mistake."

"What'd he do?"

"When we were over there by Woolsey Peak taking out the dead bodies the other day, I noticed something shining on this hillside. I studied it for a while and figured Harley was watching us with binoculars. When the lenses caught the sun's light, it was like flashing a mirror. I got a good fix on his position, and then Brad and I came back with an Air Posse pilot the next day and confirmed it. His mistake was not shading his binoculars so they wouldn't flash in the sun.

"Hello, the camp!" one of the Guardsmen called.

Sean walked down into the wash to meet the National Guardsmen. "You were right, Sean. We found three of those nasty buggers along this wash. They were all M-2s. Lethal as hell. Dug 'em all up and defused 'em. My partner went back for the truck. We'll box these babies up and take 'em back to the shed."

Sean said, "Thanks. That's a big relief. We need some help getting a wounded deputy and a dead guy out of here."

"Sure. We can put them in our truck."

Sean and Robbie rigged up a stretcher from the canvas on the cot and carried Brad to the Guard's truck. Then, three of them carried Harley's body to the truck.

They loaded up all the firearms and the hand grenades, and Robbie said, "He musta been collecting all this stuff for years. It's a good thing nobody tried to take him from the front!"

Sean said, "We'll leave all this other stuff here for the crime scene guys to take care of later. But there's one more thing I need." He walked over to the bunker and found Harley's key chain on a hook. He compared the key in the padlock to one on the chain—it was the same manufacturer. "We'll need this key to open the door on that other bunker. Save us blowing up half the canyon!"

Murphy, the other deputy, brought the Jeep to the site when he got the all-clear. Sean rode in the cab with the National Guardsmen, and they followed the other two deputies out of the wash, down the valley, and back to the highway where Sean and

237

Brad had left their vehicle earlier. There was a pickup with a horse trailer behind it parked across the road. Jim Cunningham sat on the edge of the truck's bed, whittling on a stick. "Bout time you boys showed up," he said to Sean. "Where's your partner?"

"He's in the bed of the truck, wounded in the leg. We have to get him to a hospital."

"You're kinda bloodied up, too. At least you're both alive. Where's Harley?"

"He's in the truck, too. He didn't make it."

"Well, hell. Live by the gun, die by the gun, they say."

"He didn't die from a gunshot. He hit his head on a rock."

The old wrangler just shook his head.

They radioed ahead for an ambulance to meet them at the police station in Buckeye for Brad and for a coroner's ambulance to transport Harley's body. Sean heaved a sigh of relief when the medics loaded Brad on board and headed for a hospital. The coroner's people put Harley in a body bag before putting him in their ambulance. Sean called the office, explained what had happened to the commander, and asked him to call Brad's wife.

When he returned to the district office, Sean was too exhausted to work on reports. He gave the commander a brief report on what had happened, then left for home. He heard Buddy barking a greeting when he got out of his pickup in his driveway. He opened the door, and the dog went cavorting around the house, happy to see his master. Sean got down on a knee, gave the dog a rub, scratched his back and behind his ears, and told him what a good dog he was. Then he put food and water in his bowl and opened his refrigerator to see what he might have to eat. He ended up frying some bologna with melted cheese on top for sandwiches, added some sliced tomato, spread mayo on four pieces of bread, and sat down to eat. He washed it all down with a can of Coors.

After eating, he opened another beer and sat in his easy chair in the living room. He picked up his guitar and strummed a few idle chords. The mellow sound of the old Martin always relaxed him. He picked out Wildwood Flower and a couple of other tunes he knew.

Buddy lay at his feet, listening. The music seemed to relax him, too. It was still early, but he was exhausted and headed for bed. Buddy curled up on his bed on the floor beside him, and they were both snoring peacefully in a couple of minutes.

CHAPTER 34

Sean met with the commander early the following day to give him a detailed report on what happened with Harley. Brad was in St. Joseph's hospital awaiting surgery on his leg to remove bone splinters and set the break. When they finished, the commander said, "Great work, Sean. I'll see to it you and Brad both receive commendations. But Sean…What the hell were you thinking about going one-on-one with that maniac? This could have had a far different outcome."

"Yes, sir…but it was like this—Brad was wounded and a sitting duck. If we had continued the shooting, he would be dead now. Harley had that Thompson submachine gun he used to spray the hillside, and there wasn't much cover. I knew Harley pretty well; we were in high school together. I thought it would rile him up if I brought up some of his old high school grudges, enough to get him off his guard. He'd always disliked me and might jump at the chance to get even in a one-on-one match. I decided my commando training in the Army would give me an edge, and I took the chance."

The commander studied him for a minute. "You're just like your dad, Sean. He always met any situation head-on and looked out for his fellow deputies. I'm glad you looked out for Brad in this situation. He'll be out of commission for a while, but he will recover."

"The crime scene crew will be here shortly," Sean said. "I'll lead them to the scene and make sure they all come back."

"You won't be fighting for your life this time, so look around for where Harley might have stashed those bonds. It would be good to get them to the feds; otherwise, we'll have to put up with those guys nosing around for who knows how long. They may be using them for money laundering, but that's between them and the feds. That's not our problem, but we can't have a bunch of goons running around roughing up people. See what you can find."

"Yes, sir, I will. But I wouldn't hold your breath thinking they'll turn up. No doubt Harley hid them very well."

"Let me know what you find."

"There's one other thing, sir. This experience has taught us the value of four-wheel drive vehicles. We can only do so much with a Jeep. I recommend the department acquire a couple of those Dodge Trucks. They'll be available now that the war has ended."

"Good idea, Sean. I'll discuss it with the Sheriff."

"In the meantime, Harley's truck is still out there. Is it okay to use it to ferry the crime scene crew and their equipment to the scene? Their vehicle won't make it."

"If the crime scene crew can clear it, you could use it. We're going to have to get it back here for impoundment anyway."

The crime scene crew showed up, and Sean used the Jeep to lead them as far as their vehicle would go. He took two of them with him to the camp to start work. They looked the truck over and said it would be okay to use it. The truck roared into life as soon as he hit the starter, and he went back to get the remaining man and their gear.

The crew went about their work, and Sean wandered around the vicinity of the camp, looking for any clue as to where Harley might have stashed the bonds. Certainly not in one of the bunkers—that was too obvious. He didn't think he would have buried them in the ground. Someplace dry and inconspicuous would have been Harley's style; a cave or rock outcropping might work. There were plenty of those around. He'd have to check the other bunker if he didn't find them here.

Sean sat down on a large, flat rock, lit a Lucky Strike, and studied the landscape around him. Think like Harley, he told himself. What would he have done? He certainly would have kept them close, somewhere he could get at them quickly if needed. There were three or four places with jumbled rocks Sean thought he might have used. He began checking each one, looking for anything unusual or out of place. They all proved to be just what they appeared—piles of rocks. By then, it was time to start packing up and getting back.

The crime scene crew finished their work and loaded their gear into Harley's truck. They returned to their car; one of them would drive the truck to the county's impound lot in Phoenix. Sean led the little caravan back to the highway for the drive back to town.

🌵

It was quitting time when Sean returned to his office. He put off his report until the next morning. He went home, fed Buddy, showered, and put on clean clothes. Then he drove to St. Joseph's hospital. He found Brad's wife, Ann, in the room with him, sitting by his bed and holding his hand. Brad's right leg was suspended in a contraption with pullies and straps. "Hey, Sean. Come in," Brad said.

"Hello Brad, hi Ann." She stood up, hugged Sean, and said, "Thank you, Sean. Brad told me you saved his life. We'll always be grateful to you."

Sean was visibly embarrassed, red in the face, and unsure what to say. "I'm glad he's okay," was all he could get out. Ann left the room so the two men could talk.

"What have they done for you, Brad?"

His voice was a little weak and hoarse from the anesthetic and breathing tube they used in surgery. The pain drugs they gave him made him groggy. He said, "They put the bones in my leg back together with metal pins after they took out all the fragments. Said I'll be walking on it after it heals. The docs said it could have been much worse without the first aid you and Robbie gave me. Thanks for doing that."

"It was nothing, Brad. You would have done the same for me."

"So…did you go back out there today?"

"Yep. Took the crime scene crew out to the site, but I had to use Harley's truck to get all their stuff up to the campsite and back."

Brad chuckled at the image of that.

"So, it's over, Sean. It's finally over!"

"I couldn't have done it without you, Brad. We make a great team."

"Thanks, Sean." His speech was starting to slur, and his eyes were fluttering.

"I'll let you sleep, buddy. See you tomorrow."

"See ya…" and he was asleep.

He spent a few minutes in the hall with Ann, giving her the details of what had happened. He said, "It's pure luck we're both not in here, or worse. I'm so sorry it had to be Brad who was wounded."

"I know it comes with the job, Sean. But I was scared to death when I got the news. Thank you for being there for him when he needed you." She gave him another hug before he left.

He stopped at his favorite diner on Van Buren Street and had a big meal of comfort food: Meatloaf with mashed potatoes and gravy, corn, green beans, and a biscuit on the side, followed by a big piece of apple pie a la mode. It was the first decent meal he'd had in days. As soon as he got home, he called Sandy Preston and made a date for Saturday night. They spent an hour chatting about trivial things, learning more about each other.

They hung up, and Sean called Ricky Martinez. He answered and said, "Hola, amigo! Como estas? What you been up to?"

"More than I want to talk about on the phone, amigo. How bout meeting for a beer and burger tomorrow night, and we can catch up?"

"Sounds good. Same place, same time?"

"Yep. See you then."

Wrapping up the case with Harley was like having a huge weight lifted from his chest, and he got the best night's sleep he'd had in weeks. Buddy snored peacefully beside the bed.

The next morning, the commander called a meeting with Sean, the two detectives, and the leader of the crime scene team.

"Damn, Sean—you've been a busy boy!" Detective Johnson said. "Good to see you're still alive and well!"

The commander said, "We all are. I called you all here so we can hopefully tie a ribbon around this business with Harley Henderson. Let's start with the crime scene report."

James, the lead crime scene technician, said, "Most of it is pretty straightforward. There was no evidence of anyone but Henderson being at cither camp—except for the four dead guys at the first camp, of course." He chuckled at his wry humor. "As you know, three of them were connected with the casino operation in Las Vegas. They all died of concussion and shrapnel wounds from the land mine blast. The Mexican citizen was a dead end, so to speak." He chortled again at his attempt at humor. No one else was laughing. He continued, "His driver's license had a false address, and we haven't found anyone through the Mexican authorities who knew anything about him. We did find traces of human blood in the back of Henderson's pickup truck. That's all I have. Questions?"

There were no questions, and the commander turned to the two detectives. Johnson said, "We have contacted the FBI and the Treasury Department about the bonds. The Treasury Department will take the lead for money laundering charges. They would like to know when and if we find them. The FBI has a secondary interest in their organized crime activities. I told them we should get half the money for helping them out with their case. They were not amused." That brought a little laughter from everyone.

"Better be careful, Johnson, or they'll arrest you with the rest of them," the commander joked. There was more laughter around the table.

Sean asked, "Could you explain how money laundering works?"

Johnson said, "I'll let Detective Harper answer that. He knows more about it than I do." He looked at the other detective.

"Well," Harper began, " it can be complicated, but basically how it works is this: Financial instruments like bearer bonds are ripe targets because they have a certain level of anonymity, meaning there's no record of them being bought and sold. They are exactly what the name says—the bearer is entitled to whatever face amount or coupons the bond has. When a bearer bond is purchased, the money launderer will often deposit it into a brokerage account and use it to purchase other assets. They might turn around and sell them and then use a wire transfer to send the proceeds to another account. Organized crime and others are known to send the money to offshore accounts that can't be traced. That creates another layer of the scheme that makes it difficult to track. They are also often used to hide the identity of the owners of a shell company. The feds think the Lucky Joker Casino is part of a larger organized crime outfit that uses those bonds to avoid tax liability. It's difficult to prove because there are no records of where the bonds go once they are issued."

"Thank you, detective," Sean said.

Johnson continued, "The feds are also organizing a team to look for the bonds. I doubt they'll have more luck than we have. And there's still the loose end of who was shot at Harley's house that night. We figure it was two goombahs from the mob that Harley shot and then planted someplace far away in the desert." He asked if there were questions and looked around the table. Seeing none, he said, "That pretty much does it for us. We'll let you know how things work out with the feds."

The commander said, "Sean, do you have anything to add?"

"Yes, sir. I looked for where Harley might have stashed the bonds, but I didn't have any luck. They could be anywhere out there. If the feds find them, it will be by sheer luck. They'd have to kick over every rock on a bunch of hills. And there's an awful lot of them." He paused and went on, "One more thing. I visited Brad at the hospital yesterday evening, and he is doing well. They've patched up his leg, and the doctors say he'll be able to walk on it. He seemed to be in good spirits."

"Thank you, Sean," the commander said. "I want to thank all of you for your outstanding work on this case," the commander said.

"It's been the toughest one I've seen in my career. You should all be proud of bringing it to a close."

The meeting ended, and the men shook hands all around. Sean went back to writing the report for yesterday's actions.

✤

Sean met Ricky that evening at the Wishing Well Bar. It had been their favorite hangout since they came home from the war. They grabbed a corner booth and ordered cheeseburgers, fries, and cans of Coors beer.

The jukebox was playing "Stars and Stripes Over Iwo Jima" by the Sons of the Pioneers.

Ricky said, "Funny, that song started playing when we walked in. Iwo Jima. I didn't make it there after I was wounded, but all those Pacific islands were tough nuts to crack. Thank god that war's finally over."

They were thoughtful for a couple of minutes, sipping their beers, and each lost in his own memories of their war experiences.

"Amen to that, Ricky. Sometimes, it seemed like it might go on forever."

"Yeah. War is hell. I'm glad both of us survived. And I'm glad you called Sean. I've been wanting to talk to you."

"I've been crazy busy, Ricky. But we just wrapped up the case that's been taking all my time."

"You want to talk about it?"

"Do you remember when we were in high school, a big fight started in the bleachers at a Tolleson and Buckeye football game in Buckeye, and they had to call the police to break it up?"

"Oh, yeah. Some big guy got into it with some kids from Tolleson. Didn't he throw some of them off the bleachers?"

"Yeah. The kids were hurt, and they hauled the big guy off to jail. That big guy's name was Harley Henderson, and I've been chasing him ever since that plane crashed on Woolsey Peak a while back."

246

"I heard something about that. I think I even saw a wanted poster for him. Did you catch him?"

"Another deputy and I cornered him at his camp in the desert the day before yesterday. He put the other deputy in the hospital with a gunshot wound. I managed to avoid getting shot and badgered the guy into a grudge fight."

"Grudge fight?"

"Yeah, he hated my guts in high school. I was sort of everything he wasn't, and he resented it. I brought up that old stuff and goaded him into fighting me instead of having a shoot-out."

"Whoa! Are you nuts? That guy was big as a house!"

"It was nip and tuck, but I got the better of him. I knocked him down, and he hit a rock. Split his head open. Nothing I could do for him."

"You look a little worse for wear, amigo."

"My head is still sore where he connected a good shot with his fist. He broke my nose, too. My eyes are gonna be black for a while. He would have had me while I was dazed if he hadn't been so slow." He took a sip of beer and continued, "I'm gonna have to see the doc and find out if my nose is set properly. I just shoved it back in place, but I can't tell if there was damage to the bones."

"Damn. You are one lucky hombre. What happened to the other deputy?"

"He's recovering in the hospital from a gunshot wound in his leg. A .45 slug did a lot of damage to the bone beneath his knee."

Their food arrived, and they ate their cheeseburgers in silence for a few minutes. The jukebox changed to Jimmy Davis singing "There's A New Moon Over My Shoulder." A couple danced to the lively swing tune, stirring the fresh sawdust on the floor.

Sean said, "The hell of it is. I really wanted to bring him in alive. He needed to pay for the murders of at least eleven people we know of."

"Whew…eleven?"

"That we know of. He went off the deep end somewhere along the way. Even killed his girlfriend for talking to me. He stole a bunch of bonds worth a fortune from that plane crash. He was the first one there, even before me. I think the money made him crazy."

"I am glad you are okay, amigo. Sounds like you took a big risk."

"It was the only way I could save my wounded friend."

They were quiet while they finished eating. Then Ricky said, "Damn, man! I would've paid good money to see that fight!"

They laughed and ordered more beers. Then Ricky said, "Remember those scumbags that were shaking down my parents for protection money?"

"Yep."

"I heard through the Mexican grapevine that they were all killed in Juarez. The rumor was that their bosses were unhappy with their performance, and that was that."

"How do you feel about that, amigo?

"Well, they chose to be criminals. But the dumbasses didn't need to die for it. I'm guessing the next bunch the bosses in Mexico send to take their places won't be so easy to scare off."

"Let me know if you need any more help. We have to keep that kind of stuff out of here."

They toasted each other with their beers and talked about happier subjects. Sean told him he was going on his second date with Sandy the next night, and Ricky toasted him again.

❦

The commander gave Sean the day off on Saturday. He said he'd more than earned it for bringing the Henderson case to a close. He used the time to catch up on household chores he'd not had time for. Besides, staying busy kept his mind off his upcoming date that evening. When he thought about Sandy, he wandered into daydreams and forgot about his chores.

He spent extra time with Buddy, reviewing the commands his friend from the department had taught the dog. He was a quick learner and mastered sit, stay, here, heel, down, and come. They would teach him more the following weekend. His friend handled the department's police dogs, and Sean had asked him for help training Buddy as a guard dog and responding to more commands.

It felt to Sean that the clock must be slow as he waited for the time to pick up Sandy for their date. He fed Buddy an early dinner, then headed for Liberty to pick her up. He couldn't believe his eyes—she was even more beautiful than the last time he saw her. She was dazzling in a light blue bow tie-neck dress and pearl earrings. A matching blue ribbon complemented her red hair. Sean felt embarrassed again to help such a gorgeous woman into his pickup truck. She deserved a Cadillac limousine with a uniformed driver. But she didn't seem to mind and was right at home in his Chevy.

She had told him before that she enjoyed Italian food. He took her to Riazzi's Italian Restaurant on McDowell Road in Phoenix. He ordered lasagna, and she had spinach ravioli. They shared a bottle of Italian red wine and had a great time over dinner. Sean felt as if he'd known her all his life.

He took her downtown to the Fox Theatre after dinner. They were showing "The Bells of St. Mary's" with Bing Crosby and Ingrid Bergman. After the movie, she told him that Ingrid Bergman was her favorite actress and thanked him for bringing her to see the film. Then she leaned in and kissed him on the cheek again as they were walking to his pickup.

It was a long drive from downtown Phoenix back to Liberty, but it seemed to Sean the time flew by way too fast, and they were pulling into her driveway. She invited him in and said she'd make a pot of coffee. Sean sat on the couch while she was busy in the kitchen. He was nervous about being in her house, unsure of what would come next. She brought the coffee and a couple of homemade chocolate chip cookies, then sat close to him on the couch. He could feel the warmth of her hip where it touched his. They sipped the coffee and ate the cookies, lost in idle chatter about where they had grown up. Sean put his arm around her shoulders and pulled her closer, then she leaned in and kissed him on the mouth.

They let the kiss linger, and then she said, "I've never known anyone like you, Sean. Most men I've dated couldn't keep their hands off me. They never had more than one date. But you are a perfect gentleman. Then she kissed him again. They sat that way for a time, sharing an occasional kiss and discussing intimate details of their lives. Sean told her about Annaleigh and their wedding plans. Sandy cried when he told her how she had died when it should have been him. She said she'd never been in a serious relationship and only dated a few times while attending Arizona State College; she had been too busy for any meaningful relationships. She graduated and was offered the position to teach fourth grade at Liberty Elementary School the year before.

"I knew we had a connection as soon as I met you, Sean, and I couldn't wait to see you again."

"I felt the same way, Sandy. I guess we should thank the guy who broke into your house." They laughed, and Sean said, "I should probably go." They stood up, and Sean said, "When can I see you again?"

"How about tomorrow? I'll make you a home-cooked meal, and you can tell me more war stories. Is six o'clock okay?"

"More than okay." He took her in his arms for a goodnight kiss and floated back to his truck. He hardly remembered the drive back to his house.

🌵

Sean had a nagging feeling that he had missed something since the showdown with Harley. He had a picture in his mind of a rock formation he hadn't checked out. It didn't strike him as important at the time. But he couldn't escape the idea niggling at the back of his mind that he should go back and look.

Monday morning, he told the commander he wanted to have another look. The commander agreed, and Sean loaded up the Jeep and headed out. Rain clouds were building early; giant, fluffy thunderheads with angry-looking black bottoms were forming off to the southeast. He would have to work fast to avoid getting caught in a downpour and possibly be stuck until flood waters went down. He pushed the Jeep on the dirt road, bouncing over ruts and rocks to beat the threatening weather.

He parked at Harley's campsite and walked up the hill above it. He heard thunder rumbling in the distance and quickened his pace. He studied the outcrop for a few minutes. There was a jumble of loose rock below the jagged ridge. At first glance, there didn't appear to be anything out of the ordinary. On closer inspection, he noticed a couple of the smaller rocks had scratches in the black desert varnish that covered most rocks in the area; the scratches left lighter-colored lines on the surface. He bent down for a closer look and could see that the loose stones were piled in front of what seemed to be a wide crack in the rock face of the ledge; they were a little too neat, in Sean's opinion. His pulse pounded as he pulled the loose rocks away from the crack. And there it was…the attaché case was wrapped in oilcloth and jammed far back inside the opening.

Sean left the case where he found it so it could be properly documented. Then he went back to the jeep and got his Kodak camera. He carefully photographed the attaché case inside the crack before he extracted it, then took more shots of it lying on the ground in front of the opening in the rock where he had found it. He didn't open the case—he knew beyond doubt what was in it.

Lightning flashed nearby, and thunder echoed off the mountainsides. He caught movement out of the corner of his eye and looked up just as a large bighorn ram walked up in front of him. It was a beautiful animal and showed no fear of him. They stood there looking at each other for maybe two minutes, oblivious to the impending storm. Then, the ram bowed its head toward Sean, looked at him again, and calmly walked away. Sean stood in a daze, trying to understand what just happened. He had the distinct impression the sheep somehow was thanking him for what he had done. Sean wasn't prone to believe in such things, but he couldn't come up with any other explanation for this encounter. He finally decided to accept it for what it was. Perhaps it was the ram's way of thanking him for removing a danger to him and his kind. Sean would keep it to himself but always remember how the big ram looked at him.

The first raindrops were splattering on the dry rocks as he headed down the hill to the Jeep. He laid the case on the passenger's seat and covered it with a green tarp. He closed up the side covers on the Jeep and started back down the wash, moving as fast as was safe. Hail peppered the windshield and thumped on the vehicle's canvas canopy top. That was followed by a torrential downpour that overwhelmed the Jeep's windshield wiper. Sean was almost going by the feel of the ruts in the road to continue on. The ruts turned to muddy tracks, and then he reached the road that led to Agua Caliente and back to the highway. He heaved a sigh of relief that he had crossed the washes before the flood waters came. This kind of rainstorm caused them to run from bank to bank.

The storms settled in along the Gila River's drainage, and he was in intermittent heavy rain all the way back to his office. He picked up the oilcloth-covered attaché case, carried it into the office, and laid it on the commander's desk.

The commander gave it a quizzical look, and Sean said, "Here it is, commander. I found it! The case with the bonds!"

"I'll be damned. How did you find it?"

Sean told him how he had studied the area around the camp, trying to put himself in Harley's shoes. He said he'd had a nagging hunch about a particular rock outcrop that he hadn't checked, and there it was. "I just got lucky!"

"Did you open it?"

"No, sir. I didn't want to take a chance on anyone thinking I might have taken some of them."

"Good. I'll bring in the detectives, and we can open it together and count them out. That'll give us plenty of witnesses."

The detectives showed up and sat for a minute, just looking at the bonds. None of them had ever seen anything worth that kind of money. The commander asked Johnson to count them. They verified that there were bonds with a face value of nine hundred sixty thousand dollars in the case. "That tracks with what the deceased lawyer had said he cashed for Henderson," Johnson said.

The commander said, "All right. I'll get in touch with the Treasury and FBI agents. They can take custody of this and start reeling in the casino mobsters. I don't want to leave this sitting around in our office." Then he put evidence seal tape on the case's opening."

The agents were there within an hour. They thanked the commander and his staff for their outstanding work and left. The commander and his men heaved a sigh of relief to be done with the bonds and all the death and commotion they had caused.

CHAPTER 35

A month later, Sean invited Sandy, Brad, and his wife Ann to his house for a barbecue. They had two things to celebrate: First, Brad had healed well enough to get around on crutches. Second, Japan's Official Instrument of Surrender was signed in Tokyo Bay aboard the USS Missouri on Sunday, September 2, 1945. The war was finally and officially over.

Sandy arrived before the others with two apple pies warm from the oven. It was the first time she had been to Sean's house. Buddy pushed past Sean to greet her at the door; she scratched his ears and rubbed his back, and they became instant friends.

She looked around the kitchen and living room with interest. She noticed an unusual, long, black stick made of highly polished wood leaning in a corner of the living room. She picked it up and said, "What's this, Sean? A walking stick?" It was about four feet long with a well-worn knob on one end.

"It's called a shillelagh. My grandfather brought it over from Ireland. It's made of native Irish blackthorn; it could be used as a club or a walking stick.

"The wood is beautiful."

"I loved hearing my grandfather tell stories about using it in the old country."

Then, she noticed Sean's guitar leaning against the wall by the armchair. "I didn't know you played guitar."

"Well, I don't play very well. Just a few chords and tunes my father taught me. This old Martin was his guitar. He gave it to me before I went into the Army."

She ran her fingers across the strings and listened to the mellow tone of the strings. "I'd love to hear you play."

"Maybe after dinner."

She put it back and looked at several photographs on the wall. "These must be your parents' pictures on the wall."

"Yes. I miss them every day."

"Your mother was a beautiful woman…and you look a lot like your father. Handsome men…both of you." She smiled that disarming smile and his tongue tied itself in knots.

Buddy gave a short woof, and Sean said, "That'll be Brad and Ann. I can't wait for you to meet them." He went out to see if Brad needed any help, thankful for the reprieve from Sandy's critique.

Brad had managed to get out of their car and onto his crutches without aid. Ann lifted a big bowl of green salad out of the car for their lunch. Sean invited them in and introduced them to Sandy and Buddy. The dog gave the newcomers a polite sniff and went out to the backyard to investigate the barbecue grill.

Sean had burgers ready to go on the grill outside and got them started. He had also made a large bowl of potato salad using his mother's recipe. When all was ready, they sat down at the table.

The conversation drifted inevitably to the men's harrowing showdown with Harley.

Brad said, "I thought I was a goner when Harley's shot hit my leg. If he'd fired in my direction again, I would be dead. He went after Sean instead. I thought you were a goner when he sprayed that hillside with that Thompson, Sean."

"Yeah, I thought so, too. Lucky thing on my part… a couple of large rocks gave me cover, or we would have both been in the hospital…or worse."

"I'll be forever grateful to you for saving him, Sean," Ann said.

As usual, Sean turned bright red from the attention.

Brad asked, "Sean, remember that bighorn ram that we saw by the plane crash the first time we were there?"

Sean nodded, and Brad went on, "I've thought a lot about that. It almost seems like it was some kind of omen…like that sheep was willing us to save him and his kind from Harley. I know that sounds weird, but it was a strange encounter."

They explained to the women how the sheep had approached them at the crash site. Sean was quiet for a moment and said, "I haven't told anyone about this, and I'd prefer you all keep this to yourselves. But I was visited by another big ram the last time I was at Harley's camp. He walked right up to me after I found the bonds and removed them from their hiding place. We just stood there, looking at each other. And then, I swear the ram bowed his head to me. It wasn't like he was angry and preparing to charge. He just stood like that for maybe a full minute. I was dumbfounded. Then he looked at me again and walked calmly away. I stood and watched him until he disappeared around the hill."

Everyone was quiet for a minute. Then, Sandy asked, "What do you think it means, Sean?"

Sean was thoughtful for another long minute and said, "I don't know what to make of it. Harley was a bad man and had illegally killed who knows how many bighorn sheep in those mountains. Maybe, somehow, the sheep sensed that we had done them a service in saving them from him. The image of it bowing to me will haunt me for the rest of my life."

They discussed the possible meanings of the encounters and agreed there was some unspoken communication between the men and the animals. They all agreed to keep the experiences to themselves.

⚘

The commander brought in the detectives and all the deputies who had assisted in bringing the case with Harley Henderson to a close. The small conference room at the division office was packed and already hazy with cigarette smoke before the meeting began. There was a lot of speculation about the purpose of the meeting.

The commander stood and said, "Men, I've brought all of you together this morning because each of you had a hand in our investigation of the Henderson case. I have important news to share with you about the fallout from the case. I've asked Detective Johnson to brief you on what we know."

Johnson lit another Pall Mall and adjusted his belly on his lap before he began. "First, and most important, our contacts with the U.S. Treasury and the FBI have informed us that the bonds we recovered helped them make a case against the organized crime interests operating the Lucky Joker Casino in Las Vegas. The head of the casino's operation has been arrested along with several of his associates in New Jersey— they're awaiting trial for money laundering and tax evasion. The casino is now closed." That brought a round of applause from the men.

The group quieted, and Johnson continued, "Coordination with our counterparts in the Las Vegas Police Department and the FBI resulted in the arrest of a number of wanted criminals, including low-level mobsters in Las Vegas as well as several locations on the East Coast. We've confirmed that the man Sean shot and killed in his home, his two accomplices, and the two men killed by Henderson in an ambush at his house were part of that group of wanted men." Johnson lit another cigarette and continued, "The Las Vegas police were able to tie a murder case there to the man who stole the bonds from the casino and was subsequently killed in the plane crash on Woolsey Peak. That's all I have for now, commander."

The commander took over and said, "Thank you, detective. Unfortunately, we lost one of our own helping with the investigation on Woolsey Peak. Let's take a minute of silence to remember Deputy Steve Riggs."

Afterward, the commander continued, "Our department's work on this case had results far beyond anything we foresaw. You men all deserve a commendation for helping bring about those results. I have two special commendations from the Sheriff to present before we break up. The first is to Deputy Brad Jones in recognition of being wounded in the line of duty while pursuing a wanted fugitive. Stand up, Brad." He presented him with the framed commendation, and the men gave him a round of applause.

"The next commendation is for Deputy Sean O'Conner for his role above and beyond the call of duty in finding and subduing a dangerous wanted fugitive. Stand up, Sean." The men started applauding as he stood, and the commander handed him the framed commendation. He was embarrassed again by the attention.

The commander continued, "Sean and Brad will both be recognized by the Sheriff at a formal ceremony honoring them and other department personnel at headquarters later this week. You men all have my sincere gratitude for a job well done."

Sean endured all the handshaking and back-slapping from the men, and he had to retell the story of how he had subdued Harley. He made it as brief as possible, finally escaped to his patrol car, and went out on his normal rounds. He was glad to get back to his routine duties and hoped he would never again face an investigation like the one with the Ambush Artist.

###

Want to know more about Deputy Sean O'Conner? Use the link below to join my email list and get a free copy of bonus content:

https://bartambroseauthor.author-pages.com/landers/free-bonus-content-offer-the-weighmaster-a-wolf-among-sheep-the-deputy-sean-o-conner-s

Keep reading for the first chapter of The Revenge Squad, the next exciting novel in the Deputy Sean O'Conner series:

CHAPTER 1

ARIZONA, MARCH 1946

Joe Kobayashi parked his faded green John Deere tractor next to his farm shed. Its two-cylinder engine made a pop-pop-pop-pop sound that could be heard a mile away, earning it the nickname "Poppin' Johnny." It was the only usable tractor he had been able to find that he could afford when he had gotten out of the Japanese detention camp after the war ended.

Three men rushed around the corner from behind the shed as he climbed down from the tractor's platform. Two of them grabbed him, while the third stuffed a greasy rag in his mouth before he could call out for help. Then they slipped a sack over his head and tied his hands behind his back.

A fourth man brought a pickup truck from behind the shed and parked beside them. "Get him in the truck," a rough, deep voice said. The men marched him around the tractor, and Joe's world went black as something struck his head.

"Load up, and let's get the hell out of here," the gruff-voiced man said. The men lifted him into the bed of the pickup, then bound his legs together at the ankles. Then, three of them piled into the rusty Dodge step-side pickup's cab. The fourth man climbed into the truck bed with their prisoner. The driver slung dirt from the tires and raced past the little farmhouse and into the street.

Joe's wife, Mary, heard a noise and was startled to see the pickup race by as she looked out her kitchen window. The truck roared away on the dirt road in front of the farm and disappeared in a cloud of dust. She ran out on the porch and saw that Joe's tractor was parked by the shed, but he was nowhere in sight. She knew something terrible must have happened. Joe wouldn't have left without telling her, and he certainly wouldn't have missed dinner. She called the Sheriff's Department and reported the incident. They didn't seem too excited; the dispatcher told her they would be on the lookout, but he would probably turn up soon.

平和

Maricopa County Sheriff's Deputy Sean O'Conner's first assignment of the day was to investigate the theft of a pickup truck late the previous day. Sean met the owner at his home in the nearby town of Tolleson. He introduced himself as Ronald Hollister. "I always park the truck in the driveway when I get home from work around four in the afternoon," Hollister said. "I'm a damn fool for leavin' the keys in it. But hell. We never have a problem with that kinda thing around here."

Sean said, "I understand. Do you know when the truck was stolen?"

"Musta been right after I got home. I'd gone inside to clean up, and it was gone when I came out of the bathroom. My wife, Donna, got home a little before five, and it was gone. I figure whoever took it was waiting for me to get home and didn't waste any time grabbin' my truck."

Sean took down the truck's description and license number and told the man he'd put out an alert to be on the lookout for the vehicle. Before he left, an urgent call came over his radio to investigate a man hanging from a tree. The dispatcher said the reports were that the man was dead and provided directions to the scene. It wasn't far from his present location. That's a first, Sean thought. He turned on his lights and siren and raced to the scene on a busy road a few miles east of Tolleson.

Sean found several cars parked along the road and a half-dozen curious onlookers near the body. It appeared to be a Japanese man hanging from a limb on a huge cottonwood tree. He told the crowd to move back and approached the body. Grisly wartime scenes were common during his service in World War II, but he'd never seen anything like this. The man was completely naked; his body was streaked with blood, front and back, as it slowly twisted in the breeze. The blood had come from letters crudely carved on his chest, stomach, and back.

The letters on his front spelled out a gruesome message:

J A PS

G ET

OU T

The message on his back said:

B A CK WH E R

U

C OME F RO M

Sean saw that the man had been severely beaten before being hanged; his face was bruised and swollen, and there were purple bruises on his sides and legs. He stood silently for a minute, trying to absorb what he saw.

Someone yelled, "Ain't 'cha gonna cut him down?"

Sean turned to the group of bystanders and said loudly, "I have to call for help to process this scene before he can be taken down. I want all of you to keep back at least fifty feet so our investigators can work here."

"Aw, hell. Just cut the poor bastard down," the same man yelled.

Sean looked the man in the eye and said, "Have a little respect, sir. Please do as I said and move back."

Another bystander loudly said, "Didn't ya read what was carved on him? Prob'ly deserved it!"

Sean started walking toward him, and the man shuffled back, mumbling, "Ain't nothin' but a damn Jap, anyways."

Sean didn't have time to mess with the man; he needed help. He got on his car radio and requested additional deputies, crime scene analysts, and investigators. As he was doing that, another deputy arrived.

"Hey, Sean! What the hell?"

"I don't know, Robbie, but I'm glad you're here."

Robbie Sanders and Sean had been friends since working together in an intense shootout with bank robbers the previous year.

"We need to keep these folks away from the scene," Sean said. "I've called for the cavalry—hopefully, they'll get here soon! I see more cars coming, and it's gonna be hard to keep people away." Both deputies continued to push the gathering crowd back from the crime scene.

An old Ford sedan pulled up behind the deputies' cruisers. Four Japanese people, two men and two women, emerged and stared at the body. One of the women fell to the ground in hysterics, crying out in Japanese and screaming at the deputies.

Sean tried to talk to the woman, but her grief overcame her. He asked one of the men who had arrived with her if they knew who the dead man was.

"It's Joe," one of them said. "He's Joe Kobayashi, my brother. He went missing last night. We just heard this on the radio news. They said a Japanese man was found hanging from a tree. . ." Then the man broke down in tearful sobbing.

The other Japanese man and woman tried to help the hysterical woman. The man said, "She is his wife. Please cut him down from that tree. It's too horrible for her to look at!"

Sean said, "Sir, I am very sorry for her loss, but we have to wait for our investigators to arrive before we can move him. They need to do their jobs so we can find out who did this. Please try to keep her in your car until they arrive."

The men helped the hysterical woman to her feet and got her to sit in their car.

"Damn Nips! They're everywhere," someone in the crowd yelled

平和

Two more deputies arrived, followed by the sheriff's department district commander, Allen Burroughs. Robbie waved the new deputies over to help control the onlookers.

The commander approached Sean and said, "What happened here, Sean?"

"Sir, all I know is this man was beaten really bad, probably before the hanging. Some anti-Japanese stuff was carved on his front and back. It's pretty gruesome. There were several people here when I arrived; they were close to the body, so the scene is

263

likely messed up. Robbie and I've been keeping them back. The man's name is Joe Kobayashi." He motioned to the Kobayashi's Ford and said, "That's his wife and brother in that car."

"The crime scene crew and coroner are on the way," the commander said, "and I've called for detectives to investigate. They should be here soon." He walked over to the Kobayashi's car, offered his condolences, and promised the Sheriff's department would do everything possible to find those responsible and bring them to justice.

The victim's brother said, "Sir, this is not the first time we've had problems." Many people still blame us for the war, and several of us have received death threats. We are just trying to live our lives in peace."

"I understand," the commander replied. "I have not heard any reports of death threats."

"We are afraid to report them. We don't want to cause trouble or make things worse than they are. But—now this. I fear things are going to get worse. Someone has been posting hunting licenses for Japanese on some of our homes and properties."

"Hunting licenses!" The commander was incredulous. "I've not heard of them since the war ended. They were around for a while after the attack on Pearl Harbor."

"It is very troubling for all of us," the man said. Then he pointed at the man hanging in front of them and said, "And now this horrible thing. Please find whoever did this!"

"We will do everything we can to find who is responsible and bring them to justice," the commander said. He handed the man his card and said, "Please contact my office if you receive any more threats. Pass the word in your community to do the same. I assure you, we will investigate any threats."

The detectives arrived and examined the scene. The crime scene crew showed up a few minutes later, followed by the coroner and the ambulance. The commander left to confer with them.

"I wonder if his promises are good for Japanese people," the victim's brother muttered as he watched him walk away.

The crowd of onlookers continued to grow, trying to push closer for a better look as the crime scene workers went about their task. The four deputies held them back and fended off a babble of questions as best they could: Who did they think did it? When will they cut him down? It's only a Jap—why all the fuss? Then, a reporter from the Phoenix newspaper arrived and attempted to get closer for a photograph.

Sean put his hand on the reporter's chest and said, "Stay back with the others!"

"I'm press, and I am entitled to document this crime. I need a close-up photo of the victim," the man whined.

"Come any closer, and I'll arrest you for intruding on a crime scene. Now get back!"

"This is not right! You'll hear from my publisher," the man growled and grudgingly walked back to the crowd.

The detectives examined the scene and gave the okay to get the man down when the crime scene crew was done. They spent an hour gathering evidence and photographing the horrific incident. The ambulance was brought near the body, and the attendants removed the gurney. The victim was only a couple of feet off the ground, and two men held the body while another cut the rope with a knife. They lowered him gently down onto the gurney, placed him in a body bag, and put him in the ambulance for transport to the county coroner's office.

The crowd was leaving as the reporter cornered the district commander, peppering him with questions. The commander held up his hand and said, "We don't have any information about this crime as yet, other than what you have observed for yourself. You can be sure we'll update the press when we have something to report. Now, please excuse me; I have work to do." He left the reporter standing in the shade of the cottonwood where a dead man had recently hung.

As the sheriff's department group prepared to leave, the district dispatcher called about a car on fire near the Agua Fria riverbed near Avondale. The commander sent Sean and Robbie to investigate.

The fire turned out to be a Dodge step-side pickup truck. It had been burning for a while, but a few flames still flickered around the engine compartment. It had obviously been soaked with gasoline or kerosene from one end to the other, even inside the cab and the truck's bed. The interior was charred, and the seat's springs stuck up through the ashes. The exterior paint was black and curled. Acrid smoke burned the deputies' eyes as they examined the vehicle.

Sean said, "I investigated a stolen truck in Tolleson this morning before we got the call about the hanging. I'm guessing this truck is the same one—it fits the description." The license plates were barely legible, and Sean copied down the numbers. He consulted his notes from earlier and said, "The license matches; I'm sure this is the same truck. We'll confirm it when it cools off so we can get to the vehicle identification numbers."

"I wonder if this had something to do with the man's hanging, Sean," Robbie said. "Seems like a suspicious chain of events."

"I'm thinking the same thing, Robbie. We need to talk to Mrs. Kobayashi and find out if she saw anything when her husband was taken. One of us needs to stick around here to keep any curious folks away, just in case we need the crime scene crew here to check for evidence. I see a lot of tracks besides ours, and they could be significant.

"I'll do that, Sean. You met the widow at the murder scene, so it might be best for you to talk to her."

"I expect the detectives have done that or will soon. I'll see what I can find out and let you know if she saw anything." He got on his car radio, and the dispatcher told him the detectives were still at the Kobayashi farm.

平和

266

When Sean arrived, the detectives were standing outside the Kobayashi's home. "Hey, Sean. Sounds like you've got yourself involved in another hot potato here," Detective Johnson said with a little chuckle. Sean had worked closely with Johnson and his partner, Detective Harper, on a difficult case the previous year. Harper shook Sean's hand and said, "Good to see you, Sean. I look forward to working with you again."

"Might be a hot one, all right, detectives. That hanging will be all over the news before the day is done. I need to find out if this could be tied to a stolen vehicle I investigated this morning. We found a burned-out Dodge pickup that might be involved."

"Think it was used to kidnap the victim, Sean?

"Sure seems possible," he replied. "I hope to speak to Mrs. Kobayashi and see if she might have seen the truck."

"We're waiting to speak to her, too. A doctor gave her a sedative after she saw her husband, poor thing. What a shock for her."

The men stood in silence for a minute. Detective Harper said, "The doctor said she should be able to talk soon."

"There's some tracks back here, Sean. Have a look." The three men walked back toward the shed.

They stopped a few feet from the old John Deere tractor. Johnson said, "It looks like the guy was grabbed as he got off this rig. There are a lot of footprints beside it and signs of a struggle. We think there were at least two, maybe three men involved." They moved around the tractor, and the detective continued, "Kobayashi was probably loaded into a vehicle here. The tracks fit a pattern around the outline of a vehicle. There are also some clear tire tracks before they hit the gas and dug out of here. The tires kicked up a lot of loose dirt."

They followed the footprints and tire tracks around the shed, careful not to disturb them. "We've called the crime scene crew to come out and make some casts of the footprints," Johnson said. "The tire tracks continue toward the road in front, but have been muddled up by other vehicles since the kidnapping."

267

Sean said, "We should be able to get some casts from the tracks around the burned-out truck, too. I'll alert Robbie to be careful of tracks. He's waiting by the truck to keep curious folks away."

"Good thinking, Sean. Hopefully, we can link the kidnapping to the stolen truck."

The doctor came out of the house while Sean was on the radio talking to Robbie about what they had found. The detectives motioned him to follow them into the house.

Mrs. Kobayashi was waiting for them in the living room, seated in a chair facing a couch. She was a small woman with light skin and delicate features, dressed in Japanese-style monpe work pants with baggy legs and a plain white blouse. The room was spotless but sparsely furnished with well-worn furniture. She motioned to the threadbare couch and said, "Apologies for the condition of the furniture. It was all we could afford after our release from the camp. Please sit, gentlemen. Thank you for coming."

Sean was impressed by her crisp English. There was no trace of a Japanese accent; she had obviously been in the country for a long time, maybe even born in the States. She was poised and gracious even in the face of her loss and grief.

Detective Johnson said, "Thank you for seeing us, ma'am. We know this is difficult for you." He introduced his partner, nodded to Sean, and said, "I believe you met Deputy O'Conner earlier."

"Yes, we spoke with him when we arrived, where…where…" She trailed off, and her eyes welled up with tears.

The men waited for her to regain her composure, and Johnson said, "Ma'am, we need to know anything you saw when your husband was taken. Anything that might help us catch those responsible."

She said, "I had worked all day harvesting broccoli. It's our peak harvest time. I was in the kitchen preparing dinner when I heard my husband arrive on the tractor. Then I heard a lot of noise outside, like a car motor. I looked out my kitchen window and saw a pickup truck go by very fast, then slide around the corner onto the road out front. They stirred up a lot of dust."

"Could you see who was in the truck?"

"I think there were three men in the front. Do you think one of them was my husband?"

"We don't know, ma'am. We are trying to piece together what happened," Johnson answered.

Sean asked, "Mrs. Kobayashi, can you describe the truck? Its color or anything you noticed about it?"

She thought a moment. "Well, it was a dark color, maybe blue. And it looked kind of old." She paused in thought and continued, "It was the kind of truck with a place to step on the side. I think it was maybe a Dodge, like one my cousin has."

"Thank you, ma'am. That's very helpful," Sean said.

Johnson asked, "Is there anything else you can think of that might be helpful?"

The woman shook her head. "No, nothing. It all happened so fast."

"Did your daughters see anything?"

"No, they were setting the dining table in the other room and getting ready for dinner."

"Thank you for taking the time with us, ma'am. You've been very helpful. There will be men here shortly to take some impressions of footprints and tire tracks around the tractor and shed. Please avoid disturbing the tracks."

She nodded, and he continued, "Our deepest condolences to you and your family, Mrs. Kobayashi. We will do everything possible to bring your husband's murderers to justice." He handed her his card and said to call him if she thought of anything else that might be helpful.

Author's Note: 平和, used as section dividers in this story, is the Japanese symbol for peace.

The Vengeance Squad is available here:

https://www.amazon.com/VENGEANCE-SQUAD-Their-DEPUTY-OCONNER/dp/B0FBS1PYX6

AUTHOR'S NOTES

This is a work of historical fiction. All characters are fictional, with the exception of Maricopa County Sheriff Ernie "Goldie" Roach. The towns and general settings in Maricopa County, Arizona, are generally as they were in 1945.

Items of interest:

-The town of Buckeye plays a significant role in this story. The town's name came from two men from Ohio who developed an irrigation canal in the area. They adopted their home state's nickname for the canal. The town became generally known as Buckeye. Its population at the time of this story was around 1,300. It was 91,502 in the 2020 census. Today, it is one of the fastest-growing urban areas in the United States.

-Agua Caliente is Spanish for "hot water". It's on the far western fringe of Maricopa County. Natural warm springs there were first used by native Americans. It became a prominent health resort around 1873. The hot springs dried up due to groundwater pumping for agricultural use in the area.

-Liberty, Arizona, was formed as a small farming community. It is still a modest village on SR 85, about 30 miles west of Phoenix. Liberty School, built in 1910, is the oldest school in Arizona still in use.

-Woolsey Peak and the surrounding area are much the same today as described in this story. It is part of a Bureau of Land Management wilderness area. Today, as in 1945, it isn't easy to get to, requiring four-wheel drive.

- Bighorn sheep, or desert bighorn sheep, are still found in the mountains described in this story and many other locations. The Arizona legislature protected them from hunting from 1893 until 1953, when limited hunting was authorized. The current desert population is estimated at around 20,000 animals.

February 2024, Tucson, Arizona

Thank you for reading! A short review of the Ambush Artist would be greatly appreciated. This code takes you directly to the Amazon review page:

https://www.amazon.com/AMBUSH-ARTIST-VENGEANCE-KNOWS-LIMITS/dp/B0D12BSZ73

Visit the author's page for more books at:

https://www.amazon.com/author/bart-ambrose